LAST ORDERS

Dedicated to everyone who has ever joined me for a drink, whether in a pub, at a football stadium, on a work event, under the stars or over the skies.

hegeten 23/02/23

Chapter 1

MJ grabbed her Kanken rucksack and sprinted down the three flights of carpeted stairs, slamming the outside door behind her. She winced and looked back, half expecting to see the house shaking. Instead, she saw two bouncy boys frantically waving at her from the Juliet balcony on the first floor.

MJ occupied the compact top floor of an impressive five-storey terraced property in Pimlico, which was owned by her sister's brother-in-law, Niklas. In exchange for a few hours of babysitting a week, MJ received a heavily discounted rent agreement; a deal which suited her down to the ground, especially as the property was located within walking distance of the pub where she worked.

With a light covering of sweat above her top lip, MJ stood in front of the departures board at the station, scanning it for her platform. Seeing that she still had time, she bought a pasty to quieten her growling stomach. Once safely on the train, MJ removed an A5 envelope from her rucksack and unfolded the quiz she finished preparing the previous evening. Although not the official hen party organiser, she had been asked by the chief bridesmaid, Freya, to put together a fun quiz about her sister for the limo ride into London. She was more than happy to do so, she knew her sister better than anyone, and possessed a huge collection of embarrassing baby photos and stories on childhood crushes to use. She also wrote the weekly quiz for the pub where she worked and was getting quite good at it, even if she did say so herself. Looking at the childhood photos always evoked emotion, which she would put aside today. She and her sister, Kate, were both trying to get over the past and, largely due to their efforts and support from their dad, it was a battle they seemed to be winning.

It was a long walk from the station to her sister's house, so MJ treated herself to a taxi. As it pulled up at her destination, she took in the picture-perfect house façade, plant pots in order, grass all the same length, bushes impeccably trimmed and not a speck of dirt on any of the windows. Rather her than me, thought MJ kicking a couple of stones from the driveway on to the barren path.

The sisters spent the first part of that February afternoon lazing on the corner sofa: MJ sat on the end with her feet tucked up whilst Kate sat back with her legs outstretched on the corner chair. For a while, it was just like old times. They watched *Dirty Dancing*, a favourite for them to watch with their mum, which held happy memories, so they both stayed upbeat and shared smiles rather than tears. As the film finished, Kate checked the time on her phone, clapped her hands and told a sleepy MJ that it was time to open a bottle. The hens would be with them soon, so they needed to liven up and get going.

The doorbell rang not long after, and the pre-empted giggling voices could be heard on the drive. Kate took a deep breath and opened the front door, as her five friends let off party poppers and thrust an open bottle of champagne into her hands.

"Is it OK if the limo stays in your drive until we go?" asked Freya.

"Of course, although if he's in uniform and looks hot, you can bring him inside," Kate said with a wide grin.

Freya gave the driver the thumbs up before dancing herself into the house and organising drinks for everyone.

The limo ride into London was raucous, with MJ's quiz going down well, partly because it involved shots as forfeits for incorrect answers. By the time the driver dropped them off near the Embankment, the hen and her guests were completely sloshed and in desperate need of the toilet. While MJ was shown to their reserved booth by the hostess, the others made a mad dash downstairs. Arriving at the venue before 7pm meant free entry, a reserved corner booth and discount on a buffet. When Kate returned, MJ told her that Sarah and Niklas paid for a cash bar of £200.

"Wow!" said Kate, steadying herself on the back of the booth, "that's so kind of them, it's a shame that Sarah felt off-colour and couldn't join us."

MJ looked at Kate's friends stumbling back to the booth and rolled her eyes. It's not often she found herself being the responsible one, but it looked like tonight she may have to be. MJ went to the bar and returned with two jugs of water and seven plastic glasses, a vain attempt to make the party last until at least 9pm. Luckily, the water and stodgy buffet food seemed to stem the flow of bubbles somewhat and prevented the evening going into complete freefall. However, by the time the DJ played Ricky Martin, Kate and her friends couldn't resist getting things moving again, so they each downed a Jaeger bomb and hit the dancefloor, undoing all of MJ's good work.

The club was filling up with an older clientele, one of the main reasons it was chosen as the venue; "less annoying and more eligible bachelors," as Freya put it, who was already scanning the dance floor for tasty bait. She found some suitors and grabbed her friends' arms, encouraging them nearer to the shoal of males she'd identified. The guys didn't need much encouragement and were soon watching as the hens pouted and stuck their chests out whilst singing along to Lady Gaga.

5

Kate was drunk, but not so much she didn't clock the admiring glances from the youngest looking in the group and moved her hand to her chest, letting her fingers linger along her cleavage. He moved to her and they danced together to "American Pie", which he sang along to from beginning to end. With an increase in tempo, their dancing became more energetic and flirtatious. Kate's face started to redden, prompting her to fan it with her hand. Glancing over to Freya, she wiped her forehead and pointed towards the door. Freya responded with a raised thumb before proceeding to put her rear into the crotch of a cute blonde guy.

As Kate pushed past the hostess and first set of doormen, she stumbled but was steadied by a sturdy arm, the arm of the man she danced with just moments before. He handed her a bottle of water, which she opened and gulped down.

"Fancy walking down to the river?" he asked.

Kate nodded, but let out a visible shiver to which he responded by removing his jacket and putting it over her shoulders. They walked through the tube station and across the road, dodging some late-night cyclists, until they came to the wall overlooking the Thames. Still in silence, Kate stood by the wall and looked out to the river and brightly lit boats. She pressed herself back, allowing the man's hands to make their way across her waist, and moved her head back as he kissed her neck. But as she shivered again, he suggested he make her a coffee at his nearby office.

Five minutes later, they were in a small compact lift going up to the 5th floor. The doors opened, advising them to mind the gap. With one hand, he slid his key into the door and reached around the corner to put on one of the lights, the other held Kate's hand and led her into the office. Her body was evidently a second behind her brain as she tripped over her own feet and narrowly missed out on headbutting the photocopier. He laughed and encouraged her up onto one of the desks, stroking her hair and kissing her strongly, his tongue playing with hers. Not breaking eye contact, Kate started to unbutton his shirt from top to bottom and then ran her hand over his smooth chest. With her breathing growing faster and more audible, the alluring stranger began to lift Kate's top. He leaned in and nuzzled her ear and then let his mouth explore her neck. He removed her bra and continued to caress her body. Whilst his tongue was at work, his hand ran down her stomach and lifted her skirt.

Chapter 2

Back at the club, MJ stood in a musty-smelling toilet cubicle holding up the hair of one of Kate's friends, averting her gaze as an endless torrent of vomit was emitted into the toilet bowl. After what seemed like an eternity, the vomiting eventually stopped, and colour returned to the face of the hen party guest. MJ left her in the toilets to get cleaned up and went back upstairs in search of her sister, who she hadn't seen in ages. It didn't take long before MJ clocked Kate.

"Where the hell have you been?" said MJ, watching as Kate shuffled back a couple of steps.

"I went out for some air; I don't need your permission." Same old Kate thought MJ to herself, total disregard for everyone. "Yeah well, while you've been off God knows where, I've been looking after your friends as they throw up in the toilets."

Kate looked blankly at MJ before looking over to Freya. "Where did those guys go?"

Freya shrugged her shoulders. "Some other club I think; I wouldn't have had them down for coppers, would you?" MJ waved a dismissive hand and decided to leave. Kate ignored the gesture and clapped her hands.

"Right ladies, I don't know about you, but I could do with another drink."

MJ snatched her coat from the pile on the booth and began heading to the door, but a little voice inside told her to turn back and at least give her sister a hug, which she did and felt better for doing so. Outside, she ordered an Uber to take her to the Eagle, her place of work and second home.

As MJ entered the pub, Steve, the landlord, was changing the channel on the TV from *Sky Sports News* to *Match of the Day*. He noticed MJ walking around the bar to the hatch where the locals congregated. "To what do we owe the pleasure?" said Steve taking a glass and placing it under the Smirnoff optic.

MJ nodded and sat down on a bar stool. "There's only so much of my sisters' friends I can cope with, especially when I'm the one holding their hair back when they throw their guts up."

Alex, the chef, walked by and put his hands onto MJ's shoulders and started massaging them. "Aw, did you miss us babe?"

MJ looked around and let out a loud, contented sigh. She then did a double take as Graham, another of the locals, came in and took his place at the bar. "What are you doing here?"

Graham shook his head. "That's not a very nice way to talk to your favourite customer, is it?"

Steve gave MJ one of his don't ask looks before disappearing down to the cellar, his default safe haven when he wanted to avoid conversation.

"Actually, as a member of the female species, you may be able to help," Graham said, his eyes widening.

MJ moved her stool round next to Graham. She revelled in this aspect of pub life - the gossip, the revelations, the relationship talk, the juicier, the better in her opinion.

Talking a lot with his hands and not looking MJ in the eye, he told her about his wife Georgia and how she seemed to be acting strangely recently.

"She's started to stay up in London a lot, saying she has breakfast meetings or dinners scheduled with clients. I mean, she's in recruitment, how many meetings and events outside working hours are there?"

"You'd be surprised," said Alex.

"Yeah, but they don't all finish in the early hours do they? Why can't she just get the last train back? It's not like Tunbridge is hundreds of miles away."

"That's a matter of opinion," said Alex, just loud enough to be heard.

"Yeah, maybe to you Alex, but not to most people."

By now, the few people left in the pub were tuned in to Graham's story. MJ asked if he'd noticed any other changes in Georgia, for example taking extra care over her appearance or using her phone more often or perhaps she was less receptive to affection from him. Graham pursed his lips and nodded. MJ thought she could literally hear clogs turning in his head. She shuddered thinking about Graham being affectionate, but knew she shouldn't judge, everyone is different, and love is love after all.

"Well, if I'm totally blunt, she hasn't gone down on me for ages, but she doesn't complain when I'm giving it to her." MJ shut her eyes and shook her head, trying to dismiss the image from her mind.

"Have you taken her out recently, you know, wined and dined her?" said Steve who had returned from the cellar.

"What, you mean bring her in here for one of your all-day breakfast specials and a pint of Stella?"

"Why not mate? Hey MJ, you love a good sausage, don't you?"

The conversation went downhill from there and reverted back to football, and who topped their league of current female Sky Sports presenters. Time to leave, MJ thought, and she left them to it. She gave the pub dog, Roxy, a Doberman Pinscher, a couple of treats, and walked the short distance home, pondering about Graham's situation with his wife.

10

Chapter 3

Andy arrived at a chilly Paddington Station early, too early, but after being seen running along a platform trying to stop the train last February, he couldn't face further embarrassment this year. Attempting to make smoke rings with his breath, he looked around the station trying to seek out a familiar face, before deciding to go and get warm – and some much-needed caffeine – in Café Nero.

Case in one hand and full to the brim cappuccino in the other, Andy rushed to the last remaining stool and put the drink down on the table without a drop being spilt. With his case wedged between the wall and table leg, he reached in his jacket pocket for his phone and audibly muttered fucking battery, when he noticed it needed a charge. The guy next to him raised a furry eyebrow before returning to his collection of Apple devices. Luckily, Andy had put the charger at the top of his case and reached down to extract it. As he brought it out of the bag, his head clipped the edge of the round table and sent the cappuccino slopping out of the cup, over the saucer and onto the table.

"Fuckity, fuck fuck!" Andy said, much louder than he'd muttered before. A few more eyebrows were raised this time and were joined by some wary frowns. Ignoring the liquid lolloping around the table, Andy plugged in his iPhone and saw he had two new messages. The first from his flatmate Phil asking if he fancied joining him and some of his police mates again on Saturday night. Count me in. He would welcome a repeat of last weekend when he managed to screw a bride-to-be on her hen night, a first even for him. The second message was from his manager, Anne-Marie, saying that she couldn't make it to the event and for him to call her when he could. That's a bugger, he

11

thought, he'd miss her and her loose tongue. She was always good value in a debate that involved a Q&A and could be relied on to ask some provocative questions - the industry knew Anne-Marie only too well, so her hand would be the last one the microphone would gravitate towards. Andy respected Anne-Marie and thought they worked well together, his yin to her yang. They both worked for the national tourist board and were responsible for the digital campaigns used overseas to promote the country. This ranged from website promotions and billboards to short films and advertising videos. Anne-Marie did take getting used to, her volume and bluntness alone were not everyone's cup of tea, but nobody disagreed that she did a great job professionally, often directing many of the promotional films herself, a skill that she excelled in.

Andy dialled Anne-Marie's number. As he waited for her to answer, he glanced up and noticed a small gathering of other delegates milling around under the departures board; he'd go and join them after the call, he thought, looking at the unappealing cup of coffee.

"I know, I'm fuckin gutted too, but my mother needs me," said Anne-Marie in a strong Scottish accent.

"I'm sure I'll cope."

"Aye, of course you bloody will. Listen, do me a favour will you? Make sure Leah gets asked some tough questions. Perhaps find out what she knows about real tour operators as opposed to online ones."

"You really don't like her, do you?"

"10 out of 10 for observation."

"OK, I'll see what I can do. Take care of your mum and I'll let you know how it goes." He had just finished saying goodbye when Robin gave him a firm pat on the back.

"Ready for another fun-filled conference?"

"I should be asking you the same question."

They chatted for a while about work before the conversation moved to rugby and football. Noticing the time, Andy bent down and unplugged his charger. Forgetting about the table above him again and banging his head for the second time as he stood up.

"Fucking table!"

"She's rubbing off on you, isn't she?"

"Who?"

"Anne-Marie, who else?" said Robin failing miserably at mimicking a Scottish accent.

"I wouldn't be too rude about her, because she's definitely Camp Robin; in fact, she's asked me to probe Leah about her knowledge of traditional tour ops."

"Has she now," said Robin, his eyes narrowing.

The 09:05 departure to Cardiff Central is on time and will be boarding from Platform 4, please have your tickets and passes ready to be inspected at the barrier.

"Shall we?" asked Robin.

Like ants picking up on the scent of a crumb, groups of people started scuttling towards platform 4, hurrying to get on to the train. Robin boarded the first-class carriage, and Andy continued to walk down the platform alongside the grubby train until he reached carriage B, where most of the conference-goers had congregated, if the commotion was anything to go by.

A few cheers rang out congratulating Andy on making the train this year: he grinned, coyly holding up his hands and taking in the applause. The din in the carriage didn't die down throughout the journey. Most of the conversation revolved around the impending election of Chief Tourism Director, now just under two months away. It was an important position. With numerous different trade groups and associations representing the UK tourism industry,

13

the decision was made to appoint a person to be the spokesperson for the media, in addition to being the key point of contact between the industry and Government. The election process started during World Travel Market, the major tourism event in London last November, with around fifteen candidates being put forward, well above the number anticipated. They were now down to the final two candidates and, much like Marmite, the industry found themselves either in Camp Robin or Camp Leah. Much excitement surrounded the impending penultimate debate.

***

Robin spent the first part of the journey with his usual broadsheet paper sprawled out in front of him, crackling the pages with every turn, much to the annoyance of the passenger behind him, who took out her AirPods early into the journey and stuffed them in her ears. Robin, however, was oblivious to her actions and stared out of the window. Refocussing, he folded away his paper and took out his notebook, underlining the words traditional tour operators and writing several exclamation marks next to them. He made some more notes before turning his attention to a photo of his wife in his wallet.

The clatter of the trolley being pushed along the aisle woke him from his thoughts, and he watched a lanky boy with clumsy hands, pour a coffee and take a KitKat from the wire rack. Robin watched transfixed as a pair of long slender legs emerged from the seat. As the woman reached up, her baggy woollen jumper lifted, displaying a toned and smooth midriff. The well-manicured hands took the bag and placed it on the opposite seat. In the process, Leah turned round to look up the carriage and gave a wave. Robin paused momentarily, before rubbing his hands on his legs and returning the wave; he then produced a considerable sigh and licked his lips.

Chapter 4

Colin, the CEO of Great Britain Travel (GBT), tapped his finger several times on the microphone. "Sssh Sssh, I know you're all discussing those delicious desserts, but let's get the afternoon started."

The modern hotel conference room went pitch black, and the audience gasped. The sound of a heart beating began playing through the speakers and became louder with each pulsating thump. A clap of thunder vibrated around the auditorium, accompanied by sharp blasts of lightning piercing through the air. Silence fell before the lights slowly raised to reveal a lavish stage and plush seating: the audience, slightly stunned, clapped with enthusiasm.

"This year is going to be a remarkable one for our industry as it signifies a new beginning and the introduction of a Chief Tourism Director. As with political elections, the next few weeks will be crucial as each candidate will address the industry and tell us why they should have your vote. Today marks the first of two live debates between the final two candidates."

The lighting engineers began playing with their new toys again and shone a humongous spotlight on Robin, who squinted for a few seconds before he gathered his composure. With the brightness lowered, Robin pulled his jacket around his protruding stomach and stroked his bald head with a handkerchief; put a white beard and red hat on him and you'd have yourself Father Christmas. The spotlight then whizzed around the stage before homing in on Leah, a woman in her early 40s who exerted an air of confidence and elegance.

Andy messaged Anne-Marie as Robin was introduced.

"To my left, please welcome Robin Franklin, editor of Tourism Today."

It didn't surprise Andy to learn that Robin went to a top public school in Surrey and became editor of the school magazine. Alongside which, he also worked for the local newspaper before going on to university to study journalism. By the early 90s, Robin was researching and writing the highly acclaimed travel section of a leading Sunday newspaper. He then transferred his skills into the events and exhibition industry where he transformed Platinum Exhibitions into the major force it was today.

Colin continued as Robin sat nearby with his head lowered. "After a spell working for the travel publication FVV in Germany, Robin ventured out on his own and set up the publication, Tourism Today, which I think you'd all agree we wouldn't be without. Put your hands together for Robin Franklin."

Andy joined in with the clapping whilst thinking that Robin didn't have any actual experience of working for a tour operator either, the one thing Anne-Marie picked out about Leah. Interesting, he thought, maybe a relevant question should be asked to both of them? He began scribbling down on his pad.

"Thank you. And to my right, we have Leah Pope, Director and Co-founder of Global Tickets. Leah graduated from the University of Manchester with a degree in Computer Science, which led her straight to California where she spent most of her early career working and developing programmes for Apple."

Andy considered an apple-based joke and started to doodle various pieces of fruit, all of which featured smiling worms coming out of them.

"She put this experience into practice when she worked for the major US outbound travel company, Holidayz, transforming their B2C platform into a robust B2B system enabling huge expansion into the travel agency segment. Leah returned to the UK with a wealth of knowledge of the latest technology and set up Global Tickets, undoubtedly the leading European ticket distribution platform."

The next hour flew by and the audience contributed well to the fast-paced debate. Andy raised his hand and waited for the roving mic to arrive. He asked Anne-Marie's question directly at Leah. "Do you think that developing a ticketing system qualifies you to represent the tourism industry and, in particular, traditional tour operators?"

"Thank you, Andrew, the answer, in a nutshell, is yes. I built the system as a B2B platform and now around two-thirds of our business comes from tour operators and OTAs, both of which I hold with equal regard. I have a team whose sole purpose is to understand and work with tour operators both in the UK and overseas. They keep me up to date on the evolving nature of this sector so that we can keep one step ahead and make sure our offering is not only relevant but also is what the partner and end consumer wants."

Well answered, thought Andy. Perhaps it would've been more fun to ask a question on apples after all.

***

After answering a few more questions, the debate drew to a close with another round of intelligent lighting. Leah was pleased with how it had gone and headed straight to the lifts in the lobby and pressed the call button. She moved aside as the doors opened, and a couple of smart businesswomen, deep in conversation, walked out with no sign of a thank you. Typical, muttered Leah as she swiped her room key and pressed floor 9. Walking into her room, she cursed the temperature and opened the window before taking off her jacket and undoing a couple of buttons on her shirt. Holding her phone, she hopped up onto the giant bed and sent a text to Georgia *I'm free so call me when you can x*

Leah gave out a sigh and lay back on the mountain of pillows. She checked an email from Helena, Head of HR, asking for her opinion on a potential new Sales Manager. She was more than happy to be part of the recruitment process and would often sit in on interviews and ask questions where she thought appropriate. Helena had become used to Leah's habits over the last couple of years and welcomed her off the cuff and unique way of questioning interviewees.

Leah's thoughts then wandered across with fondness to the meeting she and Helena had with their new account manager, Georgia, from the recruitment agent a couple of weeks before Christmas. Throughout the meeting, Leah recalled that Georgia had been fiddling with her wedding ring, pulling it on and off with relative ease. When Helena popped outside to take a call, Leah went to the bar and concluded that Georgia was either recently married or in an unhappy marriage. She was going to casually ask the question, but as she returned with a carafe of wine, she sensed Georgia's eyes tracking her every move and decided against it. She walked behind Georgia's chair and put the wine down. As she leant over, she inhaled the sweet perfume and felt her body shudder. By the time she'd sat down and glanced across the table, she noticed that not only was Georgia looking at her differently, but also the wedding ring had completely disappeared. And now, here she was a couple of months later in a full-on relationship with her new account manager. She looked at the phone and Georgia's name flashed on the screen.

"Hey you."

"How did it go? Think you have an advantage over Robin Hood?" said Georgia.

Leah gave her a potted version of the debate and then became side-tracked as she noticed from the event guide next to her that the final debate would take place in Berlin.

"Fancy a trip to Germany next month? I'm keen to mix business with pleasure." Before Georgia could answer, there was a knock at the door. "Sorry, back in a mo." Leah dropped the phone on the bed and went towards the door, not bothering to look through the peephole.

"Robin! What can I do for you?"

He quickly moved his eyes up from her chest. "I wondered whether you would like to join me for a drink in the bar before the coaches arrive; it may be good to display a united front?"

Keen to get back to her phone call, Leah agreed to meet him at the bar at 6:30. "I'm back, I was just being asked out."

"Really?"

"Just by Robin, don't worry."

"OK, as long as you're not going to turn into his Maid Marian."

"As if."

Chapter 5

MJ woke up feeling spritely, a rare occurrence after going out with her sister. Last night had been a very civilised affair, dinner with no alcohol. MJ presumed that with the wedding fast approaching, Kate was watching her weight; either that or she was embarrassed by the amount of booze she'd got through on her hen night. MJ wasn't complaining though, it felt good to have a clear head, especially as she was due to look after Oskar and Jakob for most of the day.

She put a load of washing on, gave the floors a quick hoover and then sat down on the sofa to call her dad for a catch up. He seemed upbeat and enjoyed talking about Kate's wedding plans. As the time neared 10am, MJ said goodbye to him and headed downstairs.

The boys were as excitable as ever, acting like they hadn't seen MJ in a year. Once their mum, Sarah, had kissed them both and left the house, they began to calm down.

"What do you fancy doing today?" asked MJ.

"Playground and ice-cream."

"Ice-cream in this weather?" said MJ emitting a brrrr, "is the playground OK for you too, Oskar?"

"Only if Marshall comes?" said a defiant little voice squeezing the Paw Patrol teddy tightly to his chest.

By now, MJ was well versed in Paw Patrol and knew the characters inside out. "Absolutely, we need him with us in case we have to put out any fires."

After a few hours of playing on the swings, kicking the ball, eating sandwiches, and unintentionally terrorising an old lady's chihuahua, the boys still exhibited bundles of energy and wanted to move on to the next activity. MJ suggested hide and seek but then came to her senses and remembered that it wasn't the '90s and she wasn't in a park in rural Berkshire, the safe leafy suburbs where she grew up.

"Oh, but why can't we play Versteckspiel?"

"Because it's dangerous, and it's more fun if we play together."

"Why dangerous?"

Why do children always answer a question with a question, said MJ in her head, thinking that the word why must be the most commonly used word in a 3-year-old's vocabulary. "Because there are some bad people in the world who want to do bad things."

"We live in London not World."

"London is part of the World."

"Why?"

"Is that man bad?" asked Jakob pointing to a stocky figure who appeared to be shouting at a woman a few metres in front of him.

MJ couldn't be sure, but the man looked decidedly like Graham from the pub. The woman he ranted at continued to walk a few steps ahead but didn't appear in danger as such. MJ was tempted to follow them but, realising she had responsibility for two children, she watched on from a safe distance.

"How about we go back home and make some biscuits for mummy and daddy?"

That did the trick and moved the subject away from bad men. As the three of them traipsed out of the park, MJ spotted the ice-cream van but kept the boys distracted with talk of how they were going to decorate the biscuits. She thought she'd managed to divert their attention, but the van began playing its music, sending every nearby child into a frenzy and every adult reaching into their pockets, waiting for the imminent cry of Can I have an ice cream pleeeeeease? Jakob and Oskar were no different, and the instant they heard the music, they looked up at MJ with sheer delight and excitement on their faces. "Ok then I …" and before she could finish the sentence, they'd bolted over to the ice-cream van, which by now had turned the music off and had an impressive queue in front of it. MJ imagined what pub life would be like if a mystic tune existed, which magically enticed people to the pub. Maybe Steve should invest in a Pied Piper style outfit and flute.

By the time they'd got off the bus, both boys were covered in sticky vanilla, chocolate and raspberry gloop, so MJ decided to take a slight detour to the Eagle and have a handwashing session before they went to the shop for their baking ingredients.

"Any objection to using the facilities to get these two cleaned up?"

Steve looked around to see MJ holding up a couple of pairs of hands, which were stuck to hers like glue. He smiled and, with screwdriver and hammer in hand, waved them on.

A few minutes later, three pairs of ice-cream free hands emerged from the toilets. Steve held up two bottles of coke and bags of crisps, encouraging the boys to take them, but MJ's facial expression said it all and the offer was quickly retracted.

She looked at her phone and saw a message from Sarah checking everything was OK with the boys. She decided against saying they were in the pub drinking coke and eating crisps, and instead responded with all good thanks and a smiley face. As soon as she'd put the phone back in her pocket, it beeped again. Kids suit you, want me 2 give u 1 of ur own? MJ looked up trying not to laugh and shook her head at Steve whilst holding his gaze. He put his mobile back in his pocket and reached for the screwdriver and hammer again.

"There, on the roof, there's no chimney," said Jakob. Opposite the bar, the boys were ensconced in the flashing lights of the quiz machine. Jakob sat on his own stool and took control of the screen, whilst Oskar sat on Polly's lap. They were enjoying a game of Spot the Difference and were doing surprisingly well.

Polly started working at the Eagle just after MJ, and the two of them soon became good friends. Steve referred to them as his dream team as, not only did they bounce off each other with banter, which the punters liked, but they were also exceptionally efficient. Some of the regulars, Graham, in particular, was sceptical and rude about Polly though due to her looks and non-committal gender identity. He'd sarcastically ask whether Polly or Paul would be pulling his pint and then have a chortle to himself. MJ accepted everyone as they were, but always liked to delve a little further into people's feelings and lives. Polly's background was fairly straightforward; she grew up being described as a tomboy and just carried that on into her adult life, sometimes she felt like a boy and other times a girl.

"Right, come on you two, those biscuits aren't going to bake themselves, are they?"

Reluctantly, Jakob jumped down from his stool and Polly placed Oskar down from her lap.

"Say goodbye and thank you to Polly," said MJ.

Oskar ran back to Polly and gave her a squeeze in a similar style as he gave to Marshall. As they were leaving, Steve passed them with a collection of glasses from the front.

"And say goodbye to Steve."

Jakob looked at MJ and asked if he was a nice man.

24

"Yes, a very nice man." MJ looked over at Steve, who gave her a wink.

The day was mild for February, but a couple of big black clouds were looming and looked menacing. MJ hoped that they wouldn't burst until they arrived back but didn't want to take any chances especially as she didn't have the boys' waterproof coats or an umbrella, so she made sure they walked quickly; well, as quickly as the three of them could. You can always tell real mothers, thought MJ, because they always leave the house prepared for any eventuality, carrying everything from antiseptic wipes and spare pants to toys and healthy snacks.

MJ enjoyed baking, with and without the boys, so she easily rattled off in her head the ingredients required. She expected that Sarah and Niklas would have most things but didn't want to risk using the last of the eggs or finishing off the butter, so thought it safer to buy all the ingredients from the local shop. Managing to find all the biscuit elements with ease, the boys packed the large shopping bag and took a handle each before walking out of the shop. Jakob's jaw fell and he dropped his side of the bag, shouting, "There's the bad man!"

MJ headed quickly to the door and looked up the road. It was Graham.

Chapter 6

Guests began to filter through security at the British Embassy, disposing of their coats and umbrellas at the cloakroom. Whilst the weekend had been crisp and sunny, the weather had turned grey, windy with a steady flow of drizzle, which felt like it could turn to sleet or snow at any minute. A keen member of staff frantically chased the wet footprints with a mop the second they appeared in a desperate attempt to avoid any slips on the immaculately polished floor. Spotlights in the wall followed the stairs up into a vast modern space with striking architecture. At the top of the stairs, trays of champagne, beer and orange juice were offered to guests.

After nearly an hour of networking and drinking, the crowd of chatty tourism professionals were ushered through into a side room that was set up theatre style facing a large pull-down screen. In the left-hand corner was a small, raised area with a lectern and microphone, next to which Robin and Leah stood chatting together with the British Ambassador.

Following an amusing introduction from the Ambassador and an update on the German market, Leah was invited to the podium to give her speech, followed fifteen minutes later by Robin. Both were adept at public speaking and came across well, their arguments well-constructed and backed up with concrete evidence and statistics.

A handful of questions were taken from the audience before the Ambassador thanked both candidates and announced that drinks and canapés would be served shortly. Like a couple of famous actors, a number of guests waited eagerly to congratulate and talk to Leah and Robin. After the interest died down, the pair breathed a sigh of relief and went in search of champagne, hoping that the alcoholics that are the travel industry hadn't managed to drink the Embassy dry of bubbles.

Anne-Marie called over loudly. "Hey Leah, have you got a second, please?"

Leah made her apologies to Robin and said she'd be back with him shortly. "Hello Anne-Marie, nice to see you. How can I help?"

The pair hadn't spoken for a long time and there was an awkwardness. Anne-Marie, as always, was straight to the point, though. "My cousin Noah, from here, Berlin, will be in London in a few weeks and he's looking for some work experience. As he's studying IT and enjoys the theatre, is there any chance he could work at Global Tickets for a few months?"

Leah nodded. "Absolutely, our current intern is leaving on Friday, so it would be perfect timing. What's his English like?"

"Better than mine," said Anne-Marie, "do you want to meet him whilst you're here?"

Leah suggested they meet the following morning in the foyer of the Westin Hotel. Anne-Marie nodded in agreement and took out her cracked phone to message her cousin straight away.

"Sorry about that," said Leah returning to Robin, "she wants her German cousin to do work experience with me, so I've agreed to meet him tomorrow."

"You're very kind," said Robin, his eyes scanning every inch of her body.

"I'm always on the look-out for young talent."

Robin cleared his throat, "Leah, would you care to join me for dinner tonight?"

"I'm sorry, but I'm rather shattered so was just planning on having an early night."

Robin looked disappointed and gave a reluctant nod.

Leah put down her half-full glass on the table and headed over to say goodbye to her sales team before walking back down the shiny staircase. She collected her long coat and scarf from the cloakroom and left through security giving a courteous smile to the two stern-looking guards. Outside, a biting wind swirled around, and the drizzle had turned to snowy raindrops. Leah took out her phone to order an Uber. She frowned when she saw there was a 7-minute wait and, as if a mind reader, one of the security guards suggested she wait inside. Heading back in, she sent a message to Georgia. *Just waiting for an Uber, run the bath and I'll bring the champagne x*

***

Less than a mile away at the Westin Hotel, Georgia felt a few flutters go through her body as she read the message. She could definitely get used to travelling with Leah, it was a completely different life to what she was used to, in so many ways. The hotel was amazing, and, thanks to Leah's contacts, they were given an upgrade to a suite and not just any old suite, a spa suite. Georgia had had her eyes on the jacuzzi bath since they arrived on Saturday afternoon, but to her disappointment, Leah had a full weekend of sightseeing planned, including visits to some top restaurants and bars. Tonight, however, would be the night to experience bubbles, champagne and get her claws into her beautiful woman.

As she removed her clothes and put on the fluffy dressing gown, her phone beeped again and she half expected a suggestive photo from Leah, but much to her disappointment, it was from Graham. Having recently moved into her mother's saying she needed space, he

28

didn't know of her whereabouts. A good job, really, as she spent most of the time with Leah instead of where he thought she was. *Can I call, need to talk?* Shit, not now, thought Georgia and texted back *Sorry can't talk now, am in Berlin on work trip, will call when I'm back.*

She continued to look at Graham's text and suddenly felt all over the place. Opening the door to the minibar under the TV, she removed a miniature Beefeater gin and poured it into a glass along with a can of tonic water. After taking a couple of large gulps, Georgia felt more rational and gave herself a couple of objectives, which she would assign dates to. After all, she thought, remembering a quote from her university lecturer, an objective without a date is simply a dream. Right, number one, within a month tell Graham that our marriage is over and number two, tell Leah about my marriage to Graham. Hmm let's also put a one-month deadline on that too.

She stood up straight and took another mouthful of gin and tonic. Until she met Leah at the end of last year, she found herself becoming dependent on alcohol; it was the only way she could deal with her husband's outbursts of rage and anger. She dreaded going home after work and opening the front door. Opening a bottle became a source of comfort, which she'd get shouted at for doing. Ironic, as she knew he went straight to the pub every day after work before getting the train home and probably sank half a dozen pints. Before moving out, she became an expert in anticipating when he'd start to get physical and begin his indoor bowling practice, taking anything of a certain size and hurling it at a nearby wall. Whilst he never hit her as such or raised a hand, she sometimes wished he would as then she would have a reason to get out of the relationship. Occasionally, he'd be nice and cook a meal for her or take her out and she'd think maybe he was going through a tough time at work or something, but it never lasted more than a couple of days before returning to his usual dark ways. Even recently, on a winter's walk around London, he'd turned on her and started shouting. She used to joke with herself that life would be so much easier if she went out with a woman but deep down, she knew that wasn't the solution. But since meeting Leah, she believed she might have actually found somebody that finally treated her with respect and as an equal. Her thoughts were interrupted by the arrival of another message from Graham. *Want to come to the pub quiz on Thursday evening?* Not really, she thought, but at least it would be a good opportunity to see the pub, where he seemed to spend half his life. She sent a text back saying simply *OK* but then wondered if she'd made the right choice.

***

With the arrival time of the Uber getting later by the minute, Leah decided to walk back after all. As she turned up the collar of her coat and put on her black leather gloves, ready to brave the elements, Robin approached and offered to walk her back to the hotel. Without time to think, she agreed, and they walked together along Unter den Linden, leaving the impressive Brandenburg Gate lit up behind them.

"I'm staying at the Maritim Hotel, which is just a couple of minutes past yours I believe," said Robin, as he opened the umbrella and like a gent, held it over Leah.

They shared some chit chat about Berlin, but there was no mention of either dinner or work, which suited Leah down to the ground. As they approached the shiny gold overhang of the Westin, with a queue of yellow taxis under it, Leah turned to say goodnight to Robin, but he said he needed to visit the little boys' room, so they walked into the luxurious foyer together before saying their goodbyes. Leah headed across to the bar and talked to the mature-looking barman, who took the request for a bottle of champagne for room service like a regular occurrence. She smiled, signed the receipt and headed across to the lifts.

Having the lift to herself, Leah took the opportunity to touch up her lipstick and apply a generous amount of body spray. Smiling to herself, she undid all her shirt buttons before fastening her coat back up. The lift arrived at floor 6 with a brief jolt before the gleaming silver doors opened. She strutted along the plush carpeted corridor before knocking on the door and waiting with anticipation. The door opened to reveal Georgia had her own surprise, wearing her dressing gown very loosely, and showing a considerable amount of flesh, her shiny brown hair flicked to one side, and her tongue licked her lips. She moved towards Leah and gently pushed her against the wall, closing the door with a forceful kick of the foot.

***

Robin waited until the lift doors had closed before strolling over to the bar and propping himself up on one of the sturdy orange stools. The bar looked immaculate with the brightly coloured spirit bottles glistening after a recent polish. He ordered a whisky and struck up a conversation with the head barman, who was impressed by his German.

Finishing his drink in one, Robin shook hands with the barman before making his way to the lift. He waited with an elderly American couple; they entered together, and the couple pressed 2 and asked which floor he wanted. "6 please," replied Robin.

The couple exited on floor 2 and said goodnight to Robin; the doors closed, and the lift continued to floor 6. He turned left and proceeded along the hallway until he came to Spa Suite 1. He hesitated for a moment and checked the corridor – all quiet. He crept towards the door and took out a small device from his pocket, which he raised to the peephole in the door. After a few seconds, he lowered the device and stared at the door, his eyes unable to blink. He lifted his chin and walked back along the corridor, his fists clenched and knuckles ready to rip through his skin.

Chapter 7

Despite his head pounding, Andy was up, showered and dressed in his suit by 7am. He then returned to being horizontal, urging the Nurofen to start taking effect, as he thought back to the previous evening. The event at the Embassy went well, Andy wouldn't admit it aloud, especially not to Anne-Marie, but he thought Leah had an edge over Robin on the debate front. The snippets of humour she added certainly made a difference but overall, it was just the way she engaged with the audience, that seemed to have people captivated.

After the event, he and Anne-Marie stopped off for some schnitzel and chips before going to a weird little bar for a drink. Maybe it was the alcohol, but Anne-Marie opened up about her mum being ill and inferred that she may need to take a break from work as and when the time came. It was a more tender side to her than she usually showed. As if realising, she changed subjects and caught Andy off guard asking about his family. He told Anne-Marie that he only saw his mum occasionally and didn't have anything to do with his dad or older brothers anymore. Whether it was the cosy, homelike interior of the bar, the drink or Anne-Marie being motherly, but Andy remembered talking about his teenage years being weird. He admitted that he still didn't know the identity of his real dad, just that he's Spanish and someone his mum had a one-night fling with whilst on holiday with her friends. He confessed that he didn't like dealing with his emotions, which probably explained why he'd never managed to hold down a proper relationship with anyone. Anne-Marie made some comment about him not holding back from sleeping with lasses though, to which he explained it was just physical and didn't mean anything. He assumed those he went with felt the same as they never said anything to the contrary; either that or he was totally crap in bed and nobody fancied coming back for a second helping. After a wave of self-consciousness, he recalled it was his turn to change the subject and asked Anne-Marie if she had anyone special in her life. She pointed to her head and told Andy how she was fucked up, and how her mouth didn't listen to her brain before it opened. Not knowing what to say, another example of how he couldn't deal with other people's emotions, let alone his own, he suggested going back to the hotel for a nightcap.

The second alarm went off signalling that it was time to haul himself off the bed and head down to breakfast. Andy walked a few metres along the corridor and knocked on Anne-Marie's door. She was dressed and looked spritely, although behind the heavy make-up, Andy expected there was a dehydrated and tired face. He was amazed by how much beer she could put away, not to mention the bottle of red wine, which she referred to as a nightcap.

"How are you feeling?" said Andy.

"On top of the fucking world ..."

Andy and Anne-Marie enjoyed a hearty breakfast before heading out of the hotel towards the main station and along to the U-Bahn.

"Isn't that Robin over there with his case?" said Anne-Marie.

Odd, thought Andy, the trade show was only starting today. He watched as Anne-Marie trudged over to him and plodded back a few minutes later, looking a little out of breath. "Well, what's he up to?"

"Off to Hamburg apparently."

After three stops on the U-Bahn and one change, they walked into the Westin Hotel.

"You know it would've been quicker to walk, don't you?"

"Aye, but I didn't want to walk; there he is." Anne-Marie walked over to her cousin and gave him one of her special bear hugs. She introduced Andy to Noah and sat at the sofas to wait for Leah.

Before long, the lift doors opened and two women walked across the lobby; one was Leah and they didn't recognise the other one. The two shared a brief kiss before separating; Leah walked towards them looking professional in her trouser suit and heeled boots.

As Leah approached, Anne-Marie muttered something under her breath and put on a completely over the top cheesy grin. Andy wondered what she was up to, as, he expected did Leah, despite her facial expression not changing in the slightest. Noah stood up and waited patiently to be introduced to the person he hoped to be working for in a few weeks' time. He addressed Leah formally as 'Miss Pope' and shook her hand firmly. Maintaining eye contact, he waited until Leah had sat down and then took his seat seconds after. Andy looked on, impressed by his natural politeness and manners, worlds away from his foul-mouthed older cousin.

With Anne-Marie and Andy on the periphery of the conversation, Leah and Noah seemed to be getting on well and after fifteen minutes, Leah announced that she would be delighted to welcome Noah to the Global Tickets family. They discussed start dates and Leah made a few notes on her phone.

"Thank you, Miss Pope for your time. I'm genuinely excited to work with you."

"Please, call me Leah."

They shared another firm handshake and Leah said her goodbyes before disappearing swiftly back across the lobby.

Anne-Marie looked towards the lifts indignantly and shook her head. "Damn, I was hoping she'd order a taxi that we could've shared. Guess we'll have to get back on the train now."

"We can get a taxi if you want?" said Andy.

"On our expenses? I don't think so."

***

Returning to her hotel room, Leah made a mental note to ask her PA to get the paperwork sent out to Noah as soon as possible. He seemed very personable and had a grasp of the key system requirements, which meant one of her team wouldn't need to start the training from scratch, so better to get him signed up before he changed his mind. Deep down, she took some pleasure in the fact that Anne-Marie was starting to talk and be reasonable with her again, albeit taking a couple of decades to do so.

In the suite, Georgia sat at the end of the vast bed and looked in a world of her own.

"Earth to Georgia," said Leah.

"Sorry, just thinking how I'd like to stay here a bit longer." Leah walked over to the bed and gently pushed Georgia's shoulders back on to the crumpled duvet. She bent down, lifted up Georgia's top and gave her stomach a lingering kiss, which sent a shiver down her spine. "If you like hotels, then you've met the right woman." She continued to move her mouth along Georgia's bare skin, thinking she wouldn't mind staying there a bit longer either. Leah lifted her head to see her girlfriend's eyes closing in pleasure; but just then, the phone rang. "Shit, that's the taxi, c'mon let's get out of here."

Once in the taxi, with Georgia still in a thoughtful mood, Leah managed to write a few emails. As they approached the exhibition grounds, traffic became a little heavier; Leah put her phone away and reached for her girlfriend's melancholy face. "Hey, what is it?"

"I've had such a good time; I don't want to leave you."

The two shared an intimate hug before realising the taxi had stopped outside the hall and the driver watched them through the rear-view mirror. Leah handed Georgia some euros before shutting the door and blowing a kiss at the window. She'd miss her too, she thought, annoyed she'd fallen for her so quickly.

***

After two trains, and what seemed like hundreds of steps and a ridiculously long walk between the train station and the exhibition ground, Anne-Marie looked like death warmed up. Midway through using her scarf to wipe the sweat from her face, she clocked Leah getting out of a yellow taxi. "What the fuck is that about?"

"I'm not with you," said Andy as he looked around.

"Over there, looks like the bitch got a taxi after all."

Andy wondered if her hangover was beginning to kick in or whether it was the time of the month, as her level of crankiness had just reached a new high. "If she's such a bitch, why do you want Noah to work there?"

"No comment."

Chapter 8

After a productive day at the exhibition, Andy and Anne-Marie joined the rest of the contingent at the Hard Rock Café for a supplier party, which continued into the early hours. Thankful that they didn't have to endure further days at the show, they agreed to meet in the hotel reception at 11am, giving them both a needed lie-in.

The TXL airport bus finally arrived, but the initial relief was short-lived as there was only room for a couple of envelope sized people carrying luggage the size of a stamp. Andy looked at his watch and then at Anne-Marie guessing she was on the same wavelength … they were going to miss the flight. As they were flying EasyJet, the likelihood of being offered the next flight without an additional fee was virtually zero, so getting their scheduled flight was a must.

"Shall we take a taxi?" said Andy.

Before Anne-Marie could answer, an agitated looking German man piped up. "That is not the answer, there are problems going to the airport, all traffic has a problem and look at the wait for a taxi. This never used to happen in Germany twenty years ago. I don't know what's happening to my country."

Two more crowded buses arrived, and then like a mirage appearing in the desert, a completely empty double bendy-bus arrived. Regardless of the capacity, a considerable amount of pushing and shoving still took place. A couple tried to push their way into the queue right at the front, defiantly shouting that they had a flight to catch. The action proved too much for Anne-Marie, who shouted in her broad Scottish accent. "We're all trying to get a fucking flight, so I suggest you get to the back of the fucking queue and wait like everyone else."

Once they left the main station, the bus travelled at a snail's pace, stopping and starting for the next five miles. Andy spent the journey with his face wedged up next to the condensation covered window and Anne-Marie wore her Rottweiler face, snarling at anyone who looked remotely like they wanted her seat. "I need a drink!"

"Don't we all?" said Andy, "we can get one at the airport or on the plane from the Easykiosk or whatever they call their trolley."

"Aye, or both?"

Their names were being called for final boarding as they walked through the Gate. Passports were checked, luggage scanned and in they went to the holding pen.

"What is this excuse of an airport?" said Anne-Marie.

She's seriously in a bad mood, thought Andy, looking around for somewhere to buy her a drink. People were already queuing to go down to the plane, meaning virtually no space for anyone to pass. He squeezed through a gap, narrowly avoiding falling flat on his face after a passenger decided to wheel out their case, just as Andy walked by. To his right, he noticed a small Duty-Free area … which displayed a Geschlossen / Closed A-frame in front of it. At the back of the hall though, he clocked a café-bar.

Glancing back at Anne-Marie, who stood in the queue, or more aptly described crowd, he strode over to the counter and asked for a couple of beers. He was greeted with a shake of the head and an apology that the beer had all gone. Not bothering to find something else alcoholic with which to nullify his boss, Andy returned to Anne-Marie with his head held low. She didn't bother asking and just swore quietly under her breath.

The journey back continued in much the same vein, namely queues, delays and no beer. By the time the despondent pair arrived at Victoria Station just after 9pm, they were on a mission to go to a pub and get beer. As they didn't want to be around tourists at the pubs directly at the station, they quickly googled good pubs near Victoria and decided upon the Eagle, which had 4.1 stars and 282 reviews.

***

At the Eagle, MJ was sat at the bar looking through the quiz questions. Steve walked past and stopped next to her.

"Just a heads up that Graham is bringing Georgia in for the quiz tonight."

"Blimey, that's brave," said MJ, "has she been in before?"

"Nope."

MJ formed a picture of Georgia in her mind and looked forward to seeing how close the resemblance was; she wondered whether she was the same person she saw Graham shouting at the other week.

Steve took the final version of the quiz questions from MJ and started reading through them to check he could pronounce all the words. "Bloody hell, they're a bit difficult this week."

"Do you think so?"

"They are for me," said Steve with a chuckle.

The pub had become increasingly busy on Thursday evenings, partly down to the quiz, which had only been introduced at the beginning of the year. It took a while to get the format right, as it wasn't easy to please the different types of people who went to the pub, but now structured with two different sections, it meant that it suited both office workers, who tended to leave after Part One and tourists, who typically wouldn't arrive until Part Two. The regulars, though, would usually be there for the duration. As the prizes always consisted of both cash and drinks vouchers, the locals worked out that if they befriended the intelligent tourists, they were in with a good chance of inheriting drinks vouchers as many of the tourists would be leaving London the following day.

MJ loved working a Thursday evening as the quiz always proved good fun, with lots of banter between the regulars and random punters. Polly worked the shift with her too, and every few weeks, they'd agree on a challenge, which would either be a certain word to include in conversations or a particular drink that they would compete against each other to serve the most of. The previous week's task was one of the best yet with a challenge of how many shots of Baileys, Kahlua and cream aka Blow Jobs they could serve. Polly and MJ between them served just over two hundred, which at £3.00 a shot made Steve a very happy landlord.

"Any ideas for tonight?" said Polly.

"Well, after last week's success, how about another drinks task?"

"How about a Quick Fuck?" said Steve.

In a flash, Polly bent over and wiggled her bum. MJ thought Steve was going to give it a slap but instead he brought up a shot glass from the shelf and then reached to the back bar and took down the Kahlua, Midori and Baileys. He proceeded to layer each liqueur in order into the tall shot glass.

"And that, my friends, is a QF," said Steve, "if you put another £500 plus in my tills tonight, I'll give you each £50 back in cash."

Polly and MJ both nodded enthusiastically and looked around for someone to serve.

The door opened and in walked an attractive brunette with dark brown hair loosely tied back; she smiled as she approached the bar. MJ made eye contact and smiled back but decided against asking if she wanted a Quick Fuck. Instead, she took her request and started to pour a large glass of Sauvignon. A few minutes later, Graham walked in. Polly pushed in front of MJ to serve him.

"Evening Graham, can I offer you a Quick Fuck this evening, after you seemed to enjoy my Blow Job so much last week?"

Georgia looked up in surprise from her wine glass to see Graham ignore Polly and move along the bar to order from MJ. Although it was hard to picture Georgia and Graham together, the penny dropped between the barmaids, with Polly swiftly walking out embarrassed from the bar and starting to clear some tables.

"Usual Graham?" asked MJ.

By the time Part One of the quiz had started, the pub was packed full, and everyone was high-spirited. Polly recovered from her earlier embarrassment and was back in full sales mode, punting shots to the office workers. She couldn't look at Graham or Georgia, though.

MJ had subtly been watching Georgia since she arrived and could sense definite tension with Graham. Georgia didn't want to be with him one little bit, but she seemed to be enjoying the quiz itself. Every few minutes, however, she'd check her phone, which didn't go unnoticed by Graham.

With only a couple of rounds in Part One to go, MJ clocked Georgia going to the ladies, so she made her way out from the bar and across to the toilets. One cubicle door was open, the other closed, presumably with Georgia inside. A fact confirmed when MJ heard Georgia on the phone, "yeah definitely … just finishing off here … half an hour or so … dinner sounds amazing, I'm starving, but I'm also hungry for you … well you can do that later for sure … Ok, will do, love you." and with that, the flush clunked and the door opened. MJ, already washing her hands, smiled at Georgia as she came out thinking that she needed to make small talk and fast before awkwardness set in.

"How are you doing in the quiz? The landlord reckons the questions are difficult this week."

Georgia looked pleased for the distraction. "They're not easy for sure, but general knowledge isn't my strong point."

MJ studied her bouncy hair and soft features, thinking that she didn't look like Graham's type, or maybe Graham wasn't her type. After eavesdropping her conversation, she deduced that Georgia was having an affair … maybe with a woman. She couldn't be 100 per cent sure and wouldn't be sharing her opinion, well perhaps just with Steve, but if working in a pub taught her anything, it was how to be a good judge of character.

Georgia left the toilets and went back to Graham. She tapped him on the shoulder and the two of them took their drinks out to the front; neither came back.

Chapter 9

Anne-Marie struggled with her case now that it only possessed three wheels, the fourth probably becoming victim to an overzealous luggage handler at Gatwick. Andy thought she might just throw a giant tantrum and sit down in the middle of the pavement, so he grabbed the case and carried it for her all the way to the pub. She threw open the door and, with a huge sigh of relief, launched herself at the bar like she'd been walking up a mountain for the last twenty-four hours.

"Two pints of your finest Peroni please," said Anne-Marie, "and don't tell me that you're out of beer or I will literally kill you."

"Ignore my friend," said Andy, "it's been a testing day."

"OK," said MJ looking at Andy, "but how about you, would you like a Quick Fuck for £3.00?"

Andy opened his mouth, about to answer, but Anne-Marie butted in. "We'll both have a Quick Fuck, but I need a Peroni first."

MJ liked the Scotswoman's humour and sensed a fun evening in store. She served the drinks and then took them over a clipboard with a quiz sheet and couple of pens, just in time for Part Two.

"In what year did the first Now That's What I Call Music! album come out? A bonus point if you can name the month."

MJ didn't stop for the rest of the evening; it was a consistent busy which made for an enjoyable evening with time flying by. She made small talk with the office workers, shared jokes with the locals and spent time chatting to the Scottish woman, who introduced herself as Anne-Marie and her colleague, Andy. They had just returned from a work trip to Berlin and, on getting back to Victoria, sought out a pub to go to, which led them to the 4.1-star Eagle. MJ was pleased that the pub had a good rating, especially as she thought Andy, with his cute young face and striking eyes, made good eye candy.

"Please can we have somebody from Team Mint and somebody from the Blade Gunners to the top of the bar, it's time for the final showdown."

Steve loved doing the final Play Your Cards Right showdown, even more so now that he had somebody called Polly working, which meant the gag about Dolly do your dealing could be easily changed to Polly, do your dealing; it made him smile every time. Steve set the homemade wooden Play Your Cards Right frame against the bar and Polly held the giant playing cards. The game show's jingle came over the speakers.

"OK, Team Mint you have the most points, so you get to cut the cards and have a go at the board first. Just to remind you and everyone else, the idea of the game is to work your way across the board by predicting whether each card will be higher or lower than the preceding one. If you get all the way down to the last card accurately predicting higher or lower, then you get to take home the jackpot, which today is … oh it's a good one this week, £75 in cash and £50 in drinks vouchers. If you get a prediction wrong, then the Blade Gunners will have their chance to win the jackpot. If neither team wins, the money will roll on to next week's prize fund. Is everything clear?"

Some of the tourists were watching on with great bewilderment but seemed to be enjoying their evening.

"Right Polly, do your dealing."

MJ went and stood with Anne-Marie and Andy to watch the final as the bar always closed for ten minutes for Steve to do his impression of Bruce Forsyth.

"Hesh funckin hillyariosh."

MJ turned to Andy for a translation.

"I think she's trying to say that she finds the landlord funny. I better stick her in an Uber, before she invites herself for a lock-in and then you'll be stuck with her all night."

Although MJ fancied getting to know Andy some more, she didn't think she'd be able to get away with asking him to stay without his friend, but worth a try.

"Why don't you put her in a cab and then come back yourself for a lock-in?"

"Thanks, I really should get going as well, but can I take you up on the offer another time?"

"Sure, I'm here most Thursdays." Although disappointed that Andy couldn't stay, she decided to look on it as a positive as at least she could sit at the bar and discuss Georgia's brief visit and swifter exit.

Chapter 10

The decision had been made, and the appointment of the Chief Tourism Director circulated around the media channels, like a dose of morphine hitting the bloodstream and flowing to all the vital organs. In the office, Andy saw the news and waited for the imminent Scottish outburst.

"What the fuck!" said Anne-Marie in disbelief, "c'mon lad, get your things."

"Why? Has Leah invited us to her celebratory drinks reception?"

"Fuck off, we're going to the pub."

"It's 3pm!"

"Yes, it's not the fucking '80s anymore; pubs can open all day, you know."

"Yes ma'am," he muttered to himself as he shut down his PC and grabbed his denim jacket from the back of his chair.

"What was that, Andrew?"

"Just coming," he said with a sarcastic smile.

Since stumbling across the Eagle after their trip to Berlin the previous month, Anne-Marie and Andy had gone back there on numerous occasions. They enjoyed having somewhere to go that was nearby but at the same time, a little out of the way, so it was no surprise that's where Anne-Marie wanted to go.

***

The pub was reasonably quiet, just a few individuals contemplating life and a group of chatty tourists who appeared settled in for the afternoon. Steve sat in his usual position, perched on a barstool by the hatch reading the paper with an untouched pint of lime and soda, his staple drink, next to him. In his own pub, he always followed the same rule about drinking – never touch alcohol before 7pm. Steve looked at his phone just as a message from Graham popped onto his screen. *She's asked to meet me, so if you see me later, it's bad news.* From what MJ told him about Georgia's conversation she overheard in the toilet the other week, he expected to see Graham sooner rather than later. As it was MJ's night off, he sent her a quick message. *Georgia asked 2 c Graham, whats ur guess?* He could see MJ was online and that she was typing back.

Nothing's changed – she's having an affair … with a woman

Tenner says ur wrong

Add it to my wages

The group of tourists came to the bar and started discussing what to have next, or so Steve thought, as their eyes were going along the shelves and flicking between optics and pumps. He couldn't work out the language, but due to one of the group wearing a Bayer Leverkusen football shirt, he assumed they were German.

"Can I help you guys?" asked Steve.

"Yes, we would like something like a schnapps but something that the locals drink, what do you recommend?"

Steve continued the recent theme and asked if they all wanted a QF or Blow Job, and much to his delight, they ordered one of each for everyone followed by a round of pints. The icing on the cake was the £5 tip they handed over. As Steve poured the Guinness, Andy and Anne-Marie came through the door. "Afternoon," said Steve, "did the teacher let you out early today?"

"Need a drink before my head explodes," said Anne-Marie.

"Fair enough, shall I bring them over to you?"

"Aye, Aye, usual please."

48

Steve made a captain's hand movement from his head. Meant to be a joke, as Anne-Marie always said Aye, but it went over her head (and everyone else's) every time. Steve found it funny though and chuckled to himself. He'd seen a lot of Anne-Marie over the last few weeks and once he'd got used to her heavy accent and constant swearing, he began to like her, as did his tills. On an average night, she'd have six pints of Peroni along with a couple of shots, not to mention pork scratchings, which together equated to around £50. She had quickly become a favourite customer.

***

Georgia sat in Starbucks nursing a skinny latte, waiting anxiously for her phone to vibrate. The message came in. *I got the role!!!!*
Brilliant, I knew you would, you're amazing
My team have organised drinks later in the office, why don't you join us?
Georgia was excited but slightly apprehensive at the same time. Happy that Leah wanted to share her big moment, but nervous that their relationship would now be out in the open for all and sundry. She knew this day would eventually come, though, which is why she booked it off work. She made a pact with herself that she would meet Graham today, so regardless of whether Leah got the role or not, it would signify a new chapter in her life.
Georgia arranged to meet Graham in the Coal Hole, a pub on the Strand, loud enough so others couldn't eavesdrop, but not so loud that you couldn't hear yourself speak. When she arrived, she saw Graham already there sat at a small table with an empty pint glass in front of him. His hair looked greasy, and his face displayed dirty stubble; he looked like a slob. He motioned for her to sit down whilst he went to the bar and ordered the drinks without

49

asking what she wanted, one of his many traits she despised.

"So, let's get this over and done with," said Graham.

He's not beating about the bush, she thought, but two can play at that game. "OK, well, as you've probably gathered, I don't love you anymore and I don't want to be with you."

"Is there someone else?"

"Yes"

"Who is he?"

"She!"

"A SHE?" said Graham banging down his pint glass and drawing attention to himself.

"Yes, SHE is a very successful businesswoman, a director of her own ticketing company and loves me for who I am ..."

"Which is what, a cheating bitch?"

Georgia put her head down and picked at her nails.

"Is that why you don't suck my cock anymore?"

With more pairs of eyes on the couple, Georgia's face began to redden. "It's got nothing to do with women as such."

Graham stood up and banged his pint glass down for a second time, prompting more raised eyebrows. "You're a cheating bitch, that's what you are." He started to walk away but then turned back and pointed at her with an accusing finger. "You're going to regret this, do you hear me, and so will she; just watch your backs."

The pub manager had kept an eye on the exchange and moved to the door, "I suggest you leave now please, sir."

"Don't worry, this place stinks of dirty carpet munchers anyway."

Georgia waited long enough for Graham to have gone before she gulped down the rest of her drink and left the pub, shaking. The manager, who remained by the door, turned to her as she walked out.

"For what it's worth, love, I think you're better off without him."

She left the pub and went down the steps, past the side of the Savoy Theatre and into Victoria Embankment Gardens. Finding an empty bench, Georgia sat down and burst into tears.

Chapter 11

Andy clocked Robin walking into the pub. "Ah, shit there's Robin, how does he know about this place?"

"Because I told him about it."

Andy rolled his eyes, "We can't ignore him then?"

"Don't be silly," said Anne-Marie as she walked towards the bar holding out her arms inviting Robin for a hug, which he accepted willingly.

Andy looked at Robin and said, "drink?"

"Thanks Andrew, London Pride, please." Robin dragged a stool across from a poseur table to the bar, making an excruciating screeching sound as he did so. Steve gave a sideways glance and watched Andy and Anne-Marie do the same, thankfully minus the sound effects.

"Do you mind if we join you?" asked Anne-Marie.

"Be my guest."

"Not that it makes a difference, but we both voted for you." said Anne-Marie, "In fact, I don't know anyone who did vote for the fucking cow."

Robin raised an eyebrow. "My, Andy was right, you're really not her number one fan, are you?"

Andy held his hands up in denial and Anne-Marie gave him one of her death stares.

"I just don't know how she's going to benefit our industry when she knows more about APIs and XML than DMOs and TOMs."

Steve listened in on the conversation, but the talk of three-letter acronyms lost him, and he tuned back out.

"Very true, well the proof will be in the pudding as they say. Global Tickets is her pride and joy, so let's see if she even has time for this additional role. Who knows what challenges she's going to be faced with over the coming months. UK tourism could get tough at the drop of a hat, we've seen it all too often – terrorist attacks, foot and mouth, computer bugs, volcanic ash. Let's see how she manages should things become challenging."

"Aye … good … fucking … point Robin."

***

After a good sob and a pep talk by a lovely elderly lady who'd stopped to comfort her, Georgia felt more positive. As the lady pointed out, she'd told Graham what had been pent up inside her for months, and she was in love, so she had a lot to be optimistic about. Georgia took out her mirror and shook her head, thinking that she looked like death warmed up. Looking around, she decided she needed to sort herself out before she saw Leah and met her colleagues. Going past Embankment Station, she remembered the cocktail bar at the Corinthia Hotel, which she'd been to before with Leah, and headed there. In the lavish bathroom, Georgia took out her travel-sized makeup bag and put it on the marbled sink. After ten minutes, she looked in the mirror admiring her handiwork; mission accomplished. She checked the clock on her phone and saw a message from Leah. *Come over when you're ready, the bubbles are flowing.* Georgia put her makeup bag away, gave her hair a brush and quick puff of hairspray, and took a deep breath; you can do this, she said to herself, you can do this.

After a relatively short but packed tube ride, Georgia walked a couple of minutes along Tottenham Court Road until she reached the home of Global Tickets, the top floor of a 4-storey Edwardian property occupying a corner position. Georgia clocked Helena, the Head of HR outside having a smoke. They had met on a couple of previous occasions, including the memorable time when she'd first crossed paths with Leah, but most of their dealings were usually via phone or email.

53

"Hi, good to see you again. Sorry, I don't usually smoke at the office, I blame it on the champagne, which Anders cracked open for Leah over an hour ago." Helena stubbed out her cigarette on the floor and gave Georgia a heartfelt hug. "C'mon, let me take you upstairs."

They took the lift to the 4th floor, walked through the open-plan office, up a few stairs and out to the roof terrace, which had been converted into an amazing staff chill-out area, complete with bar, comfy seating and flowers. It looked quite Scandi, which Georgia put down to Anders' (Leah's business partner) input as Leah mentioned he was a bit of an expert on interior design. There were around thirty people on the terrace, all seemingly in good spirits, laughing and joking. She followed Helena to the bar and took one of the freshly poured glasses of champagne.

"That's Tomas; he's Anders' eldest son who works in the IT team, although by the ease he's working the bar, you'd think he's a professional bartender."

"Pleased to meet you," said Tomas, shaking Georgia's hand over the bar.

"Ah, there she is." Georgia heard Leah call from a distance.

OK, stay calm, Georgia told herself, she's coming towards you and is going to kiss you right in front of everyone, you can do this. Leah approached and took Georgia in her arms, giving her an enormous, lingering kiss. Georgia savoured the taste of Leah's lips and then remembered where she was. "Well done Leah, I'm so proud of you."

"Hey boss, does this mean that we're going to be seeing less of you around here?" asked a nerdy-looking guy with glasses.

"Maybe at first Josh, but you won't get rid of me that easily."

"I hope not," said Josh blushing, "you're a great boss; an inspiration."

Hakim joined in, "did you pay him to say those things?"

"Bribery, Hakim, goes a long way in business. Listen, you two, let me introduce you to my partner. Georgia, this is Hakim, he's a computer whizz who makes the best cup of tea, and I love him to bits. And this is Josh who crunches data and looks after all of my money."

"Great to meet you both," said Georgia, being put at ease by how normal and friendly everyone was. Another shorter guy walked over to join Hakim and Josh. Georgia only took over the Global Tickets account around seven months ago, so there weren't too many familiar faces. This guy she thought she recognised, though.

"This is Noah, he started as an intern with us on Monday and, from what I've been told, has settled in well both workwise and socially." Georgia shook his hand, trying to make a mental note of everyone's name and job title. Anders, Leah's co-director, came out onto the terrace and clapped his hands loudly, signalling to his son behind the bar to mute the music. "Thank you, thank you, thank you everyone. I'll keep this short and sweet. There's someone very special that we need to congratulate officially today. Leah Pope, my co-director and dear friend. We met back in California over fifteen years ago and started working at Apple on the very same day. I knew back then that she was a gifted woman who would go places in life. As well as being stunningly good looking, she is super talented, extremely funny and a true friend. Anyway, today she was announced as Chief Tourism Director. Ladies and gentlemen, please put your hands together for Leah."

Leah came forward and embraced Anders to rapturous applause. It was obvious to Georgia that her team, or family, as she referred to them, really did respect her both workwise and as a person.

"Thank you, I'm flattered. My, I really am lost for words."

"That makes a change," came a heckle from the back.

"Thank you, Helena. OK, firstly, thank you Anders, for those very kind words. The feeling is mutual, there's no way I would've been able to survive those first few months in the States if it hadn't been for you. You were my rock, and I'm so glad we decided to put our heads together and create Global Tickets. We now have the most wonderfully talented family for which I will be eternally grateful. Thank you, everyone; let's raise a toast to the Global Tickets family."

Anders rounded everyone up and looked in the direction of Hakim, Noah and Josh and made a please take a photo gesture. Leah and Helena took the reluctant Georgia by the hands to make sure she featured in the photo too. Afterwards, Anders was shown a few photos and asked for them to be emailed to him. Never one to hang about, he would have a photo printed, framed and hanging in Leah's office by the following morning.

Chapter 12

As a few of the tourist group picked up their cigarettes and lighters and headed for the door, a figure came crashing through, nearly colliding with them.

"Fuckin watch yourself, assholes."

Everyone in the pub looked up as Graham announced his arrival.

"What the fuck are you looking at?"

Steve called over to him. "Hey mate, stop shouting at my customers and come round here."

"Who's that?" asked Robin.

"Just one of the regulars, I've seen him in here before, looks at war with the world." said Andy, "the landlord will sort him out, he seems to know how to handle these situations."

"Maybe he should work for the UN if he's that good," said Anne-Marie sarcastically.

Andy shook his head and finished his pint, before saying his goodbyes. He couldn't take Anne-Marie when she was in this mood.

***

Graham sat in his usual spot at the bar with a full pint in front of him. Steve knew he had to ask the question before Graham became too drunk to think logically. "So, what happened?"

"She's left me, that's what happened."

"Shit, I'm sorry Gra."

"Yeah, not as sorry as I am, and guess who she's left me for?"

Steve wanted to say something funny but thought better of it. "Tell me?"

Graham looked up and drove his fist down onto the bar. "A fucking woman." Another bang. "A fuckin mother's dick of a woman."

Conversations in the pub stopped abruptly as the outburst continued. "My wife is a carpet munching whore bag."

"Ok mate, we get the message," said Steve, turning the music up a few notches to dull Graham's rant. He then messaged MJ. *£10 added to your wages.*

Robin turned to Anne-Marie who looked on with admiration at Graham's expletives. "There's too many of them around for my liking,"

"Who, drunks or lesbians?" asked Anne-Marie.

"The latter obviously."

"And you know who else bats for the other side don't you?" said Anne-Marie, looking like the cat that got the cream.

"Enlighten me."

"The newly appointed Chief Tourism Director."

Robin didn't respond. He finished his pint in a couple of large swigs and put it back on the bar in much the same manner as Graham did with his fist. Steve went behind the bar and asked Robin if everything was OK.

"Yes, another Pride please and a drink for my friend here."

"Sure, no problem," said Steve.

Robin and Anne-Marie waited for their drinks to be served before continuing with their conversation.

"Aye, has been for years, I was at Uni in Manchester with her. She didn't like to broadcast it then and still doesn't now."

"I saw her… with someone."

"Really?" asked Anne-Marie, eager to hear more.

Oblivious to whoever else might be listening, Robin continued, "The other week in Berlin, Leah's face was ... er ... pinned between the thighs of a pretty dark-haired woman."

"Berlin you say? My whore bag of a wife was there recently too," said Graham as he walked by.

"I'm sorry, are you talking to us?" said Robin.

"Yeah, you're talking about bitches with bitches, aren't you? My bitch went to Berlin about a month ago too, I assume with her lesbian lover." Graham spat, continuing to mutter obscenities under his breath.

Anne-Marie staggered off to the toilets, and Steve wandered along the bar to where Robin sat and started putting away some of the freshly washed glasses onto the shelves under the bar.

"Everything OK fella?" asked Steve casually for the second time that evening; he could sense volatility in the air.

"Yes and no," said Robin, "I've just lost out on a big job role and found out the woman I've had my eye on for a while is actually gay." Flicking on his phone, Robin loaded a photo and showed it to Steve. "That's her, the one in the middle holding the champagne bottle."

Steve zoomed in on the photo and could see why Robin wanted to get into her knickers. Neat body, good features and a kissable mouth. He noticed that the woman next to her was Georgia, no disputing that, her deep brown eyes gazing up in awe at the woman next to her. "Women eh mate, can't live with them, can't live without them."

As Steve rang the bell for last orders, there were only a handful of customers left – the German tourists (now only comprising four people) and, sat together at the bar, Robin, Anne-Marie and Graham. Mr Leverkusen brought back the empty glasses to the bar and beckoned Steve over.

"You have a great pub, I'm very happy but I'm very drunk. Is it OK if I make a photo of us?"

Steve held both hands up as if it was an everyday request. He walked around and stood with Mr Leverkusen, both with their backs to the bar and both giving a thumbs up.

"OK people, I better get the last train back to my empty house," said Graham, whose bags under his eyes looked twice as heavy as they usually did.

"Aye, take care matey, you'll get over her, you know that don't you?" said Anne-Marie.

Robin gave Graham's hand a firm shake. "Just out of curiosity, do you have a photo of your wife?"

"Why do you want to see the bitch, she wouldn't be interested in you."

"Just show me a photo," said Robin aggressively, but the tone went unnoticed by Graham.

Steve stood at the front door giving Roxy a fuss whilst keeping one ear tuned into the conversation. It was becoming all too clear why he sensed a storm brewing. He couldn't wait to tell MJ about his evening.

Graham took out his phone and squinted as he entered the passcode. After a couple of failed attempts, he managed to focus enough to click on photos. "There's the mother's dick of a bitch."

"That's her! She's the one whose thighs I saw Leah Pope's head between in Berlin," said Robin.

"You should make her pay, Graham," said Anne-Marie egging him on.

"Both of them need to be taught a lesson, once and for all," said Robin.

"I'm gunna fuckin' kill 'em both!"

"C'mon guys, have you not got homes to go to?" said Steve stepping in, immediately regretting it and hoping Graham wouldn't flare up.

"We're going, we're going," they all said in unison as they staggered out of the pub.

As soon as the door was closed, Steve messaged MJ. *R u awake? I have news 4u*

In an instant, Steve's phone rang. "Oooh, is it about Graham and Georgia, who's she seeing, do we know her?"

"It's been an interesting night for sure, so in short, you know the Scottish woman who's been coming in recently, swears a lot and drinks pints of Peroni like they're going out of fashion?"

"Surely not her, why would Georgia have an affair with someone who swears even more than her husband?"

"No no no, let me finish; she came in with that guy Andy, who I know you've been eyeing up recently ..."

"Brown hair, boy-next-door looks, nice eyes, funny...?"

"Yeah yeah, OK, I get the picture, that's the one. So, those two are in here and then an older guy comes in who they go and sit with at the bar, I think he may have been in here before but can't be sure. From what I can make out, he, the older guy, had gone for a job but didn't get it. Instead, this woman got it who the Scot really doesn't like. The older guy thought he had a chance with the woman (not the Scottish one) but turns out she's gay and ... wait for it ... she's the one that Graham's wife Georgia is with."

"Bloody hell, why do I miss all the good nights? So does Graham know now who Georgia is with?"

"Not sure; the older guy said that it was definitely Georgia's legs, that Leah's head was between in Berlin, but I'm not sure if Graham put two and two together."

"Didn't break it to him gently then?"

"Lol, no. They were all boozed up though, so not sure how much of the conversation Graham in particular will remember in the morning. Anyway, I'd better finish

61

closing up, so I'll let you get your beauty sleep. Good night."

***

After drinking champagne for a few hours, Leah and Georgia arrived back in West London feeling tired after the thirty-minute Uber ride.

"Shall we go straight upstairs?" asked Leah.

Georgia winked.

With every step taken, the less tired both women became, anticipating what awaited them. By the time they were together in the bedroom, their tiredness had completely evaporated. As Leah's hand lifted Georgia's top and began caressing her silky skin, Georgia's heart started to beat faster. Nobody had ever made her feel like this before, her body utterly at Leah's mercy. In slow motion their faces moved closer, and their lips met. Like a match being lit, their bodies were ignited and in no time at all they were one, glistening with sweat and love, fingers moving, exploring, muscles contracting, gasps of satisfaction being exhaled. Georgia had forgotten all about the threats Graham made earlier.

Chapter 13

MJ agreed to cover the bar for an hour as Polly was running late. An hour max though, as she had a wedding to get to.

"Hey MJ, fancy doing Sunday Dare Day again?" asked Alex, the pub chef.

Remembering how Steve worked a shift earlier in the year, wearing just his boxer shorts, MJ reluctantly agreed. The locals loved a good laugh and were always ready to put their hands in their pockets and donate for a good cause.

"OK, so I want you to ask the next person through the door out on a date. If successful, the guys in the bar will donate £20 each to our charity, so that's £160, do you accept the challenge?"

"Challenge accepted … but only if I can do a Jaeger beforehand?"

"Deal." Alex drummed his hands on the table, pretending to be in a circus … "Ladies and Gentlemen, this fine lady here has accepted the Eagle Challenge, so whoever is next to walk through the front door, she will endeavour to get them to go on a date with her; male or female, young or old, stunner or minger … if it's a group, then she gets to choose her victim. Give the woman a Jaeger bomb and let the challenge commence."

Steve burst through the bar, looking red-faced and stressed.

"What's up?" asked MJ.

"Bloody TV has gone again; it's the last game of the season, and I can't get a bloody signal." Steve faced the concerned punters who looked like they were going to choke on their beer. "Chill, the TV people are coming round shortly."

63

MJ helped herself to a second Jaeger, her eyes fixed on the front door, which soon swung open. Everyone forgot about the TV issues for a moment as they waited in anticipation to see who MJ would be flirting with.

"Blimey, you're quick," said Steve, nearly dropping his phone.

"Steve? I'm Naz and this is my little cuz Hakim; we were literally just around the corner, so you were in luck," said a lean man with an impressive scar on his neck.

With that, the group of locals cheered and clapped. Naz smiled and looked quizzically at the group. "Don't worry fellas, the football will be back on shortly."

MJ took a deep breath, smiled and asked if she could get them a drink. Five minutes later, she put down two coffees and flashed them an inviting smile. The older looking of the two men went upstairs with Steve, whilst the younger one stayed downstairs next to the TV behind the bar, holding his phone and awaited instructions from upstairs. MJ went over and sat on a stool next to him. "So, are you into your football?"

"Yeah, I'm a big Liverpool fan," said Hakim with a weird London accent.

"Don't tell the landlord, he's Chelsea and hates Liverpool."

"Thanks for the warning. Well, hopefully we'll be able to get this fixed, so I can get back and watch the game myself, we've got Brighton today."

"What do you do when the season is finished?"

"Normal stuff really, go to the gym, walk, visit new places around London. How about you?"

"You mean when the football season is over?"

Hakim laughed. "Yeah, or when it's still on?"

MJ noticed his boyish smile with a dimple on either cheek and put him in his early 20s, much younger than her usual type. "Same as you."

"Sweet," he said, answering his phone and following instructions on the TV remote.

A round of applause went up as the dodgy live football channel appeared on the TVs.

"Nice one, Naz," said Hakim aloud to himself.

MJ needed to ask him now before he and Naz left the pub. "So, when the football season is over, do you maybe want to do some walking around London with me?"

Hakim looked surprised at the suggestion but judging by his smile, was flattered. "Hey, yeah, that would be nice, what's your name?"

"You can call me MJ."

Naz and Steve came through the door shaking hands.

"Good work fella, shall I take your direct number, save me going through the company next time, could work in both our favours?"

"Sure," said Naz as he scribbled his name and number down on the back of a beer mat.

MJ did the same thing but handed her beer mat to Hakim.

"Hopefully see you soon then MJ," said Hakim, his eyes dancing as he held the door open for Naz.

The door closed and there was a burst of wolf whistles and claps.

"Cough up guys, £20 each please into the pot for the pub charity," said MJ swaggering around the group offering a pint pot, "In you go, a bet's a bet and I do believe I just won fair and square."

"Won what?" asked Steve, reappearing still clasping one of the TV remotes.

"Your favourite barmaid has a date with an Asian prince," said Alex.

"It was a bet," said MJ.

"Whatever," said Steve going down into the cellar. MJ followed him down the stone stairs and instinctively started checking barrels.

"Just be careful, there are some dodgy people out there; you know nothing about this guy."

"Yes, I do, he's a Liverpool fan."

"As I said, there are some dodgy people out there. Listen, just make sure you meet him somewhere public, alright? And get a taxi home!"

"I will, I promise."

"Good, you know I care about you, don't you?"

"I know," said MJ walking over for a hug.

"Now, don't you have a wedding to get to?"

Chapter 14

In the back seat of the BMW estate, excitement levels threatened to boil over, and MJ tried her best to contain Oskar and Jakob's hyper behaviour. They knew they were going to be page boys for over a year and, although they didn't quite understand exactly what that meant, it was still the day of the wedding, which meant time to get excited. Within half an hour though, they were sound asleep, both using MJ as a pillow and each sucking on their right-hand thumb.

From the front seat, Sarah looked back. "I know it's your sister's wedding, but I wanted to tell you beforehand in order not to steal her sunshine, but we're expecting again. It's going to be so good being pregnant with Kate, although we're due a couple of months before her."

"Yeah, you can gossip even more and eat gallons of ice-cream together," said Niklas.

It took a while for MJ to realise what Sarah had said. "Oh my god, what do you mean? My sister's pregnant?" MJ could see Niklas glaring across at Sarah.

"I'm so sorry, I thought she would've told you ..."

"It's fine, I'm sure she will when she's ready," said MJ through gritted teeth. Deep down she was gutted that Kate hadn't told her she was pregnant and instead chose to confide in her sister-in-law first. Maybe the closeness that had developed with Kate over the last couple of months was only a one-way feeling. Oh well, one step forward and two steps back.

The rest of the car journey went by without much talking, until the boys woke up, and then normal conversation resumed, albeit with no mention of pregnancy or babies.

"Wow, this is stunning," said Sarah as the car drove along the huge driveway.

The wedding venue was a beautiful stately home set in fifty acres of spectacular gardens. The Orangerie would host the ceremony, with guests moving to the vast barn for the evening reception. With 40-plus rooms, many of the guests were staying at the hotel, including MJ.

The wedding was originally due to take place on the Saturday, but when Kate and Jochen found out they would save nearly £3,000 by moving it to the Sunday, they agreed to swap the date. Not that they were short of money, but Jochen, very much a man of principles, decided that it was worth the saving. After all, it didn't really matter what day of the week he married the woman of his dreams, and the extra money could be put towards the honeymoon or, more importantly, buying things for the baby. To say he was happy about the news was an understatement, and he hadn't stopped smiling since Kate told him one lazy Sunday morning.

Growing up, he'd spent countless family holidays and days out with his dad, which usually involved either travelling on a plane, walking around a plane or watching planes. It was no surprise that after all the aviation exposure, he ended up working at the major air traffic control centre at Heathrow. As many dads dream about taking a child to their first football match or music concert, Jochen's dream involved holding his child's hand as they climbed aboard for their first flight.

The door to the bridal suite was open, so MJ walked in on a stressed looking Kate. Freya stood behind her with a brush in one hand and heated tongs in the other.

"Er, since when did you become a hair expert?" said MJ.

"Since the hairdresser went AWOL," said Freya.

Oh dear, that explained the stressed look on her sister's face. There was a knock on the door and Sarah walked in, much to the relief of everyone. Despite only being in her mid-30s, both Kate and MJ looked partially to Sarah as a mother figure. Thinking about it, that was probably why Kate confided in her about the baby before telling her own sister. MJ still felt peeved, though. If anyone was born to be a mum and bring up children, it was Sarah. MJ considered her the calmest, kindest, most practical person she'd ever met. She could tell when a storm was brewing, pre-empt a fight and diffuse a confrontational situation before it even began. She was, however, briefly nudged off her pedestal in the car when she let Kate's baby news slip.

"MJ," said Sarah taking the hairbrush from Freya, "the boys have asked for you to do their hair as you're good with the gel apparently, so why don't you get yourself ready and then head over to our room. Niklas will head down to the bar when you arrive as he's been summoned by Axel, the elusive younger brother."

MJ gave her sister a squeeze on the shoulders and told her that their mum would be proud. That seemed to set Kate off, but as if by magic, Sarah appeared with a tissue to prevent any makeup smudges.

When MJ entered the room, she saw the boys were nowhere near ready and Niklas looked agitated, the lines on his forehead more pronounced than usual. Oskar sat in his hat whilst Jakob used his elasticated bow tie as a catapult. Sensing intervention was required, MJ waved Niklas out of the room and grabbed the Paw Patrol teddies from the sofa bed and shouted ATTENTION. Both boys, who hadn't even noticed her come in, stopped dead in their tracks. She continued to act out a scene she'd watched the previous week, which involved a secret mission that needed to be carried out in record time. Staying in character didn't come easy, but she managed to keep it up and within twenty minutes, she walked downstairs with a couple of extremely well-dressed boys feeling pleased with herself. She'd overdone their hair gel, admittedly, but they looked smart, nonetheless.

At the bar, the boys spotted their dad and gingerly approached him as they didn't recognise the long-haired man next to him. MJ bent down and whispered to them that she thought it was their Uncle Axel, which prompted them to run over to him without any inhibitions. She watched as Uncle Axel put his hand through his shoulder-length hair and flicked it away from his face, which featured a neat layer of stubble. Hmmm nice, thought MJ admiring his tight black jeans, loose white shirt and cowboy boots. Axel was apparently an accident, who'd come along fifteen years after Niklas, the eldest son, was born, causing tremendous upheaval and change of lifestyle for the family. A sweet and unassuming child until his teens when the rebellion took hold in a major way, which came as a complete shock to his parents, especially as his brothers breezed through their adolescence. Frequently in trouble with the school and local authority, he got into sex, drugs and music. Luckily by his early 20s it was the music that took over his life, with the list of misdemeanours on the decline. He could definitely hold a room, she thought, half expecting him to bring out his guitar and start strumming.

"Komm, sag Onkel Axel guten Tag."

MJ thought it remarkable how bi-lingual kids could simply swap from one language to another. She offered her hand to Axel, but instead of a handshake, he gently took MJ's hand and kissed it.

"Do you think he's a nice man?" asked Jakob.

MJ counted to five and wondered whether she would be asked the same question every time she talked to a man from now on.

Chapter 15

The ceremony was truly beautiful; Kate looked amazing, glowing some would say. Jochen didn't move from his wife's side and acted like the perfect gentleman. MJ knew they'd make good parents and turned to her dad to say just that, before remembering in the nick of time that it wasn't common knowledge, the last thing she wanted was for his feelings to be hurt.

Jakob and Oskar looked at MJ expectantly, and she gave them the thumbs up. They eagerly rushed over to get the little boxes and stood either side of the aisle, ready to shower the bride and groom with a flood of confetti.

The photographers were snapping away and called the family members over to the idyllic Japanese bridge. MJ took her place next to Jochen, and then next to her were positioned Niklas and Sarah with the two boys, still looking cute, in front. As the camera clicked rapidly, MJ smelt a strong woodsy aroma; she glanced around and saw Axel just behind giving her a friendly smile, a gesture she was only too happy to reciprocate.

With just over an hour before the evening reception was due to begin, MJ joined her dad on a walk around the picture-perfect gardens. With her arm looped through his, she felt his loneliness which made her sad. He put on a brave face, but she could tell that he really missed his wife. "I miss her too dad, but I can feel her today, can't you?"

"I miss her every second, but even more when I'm with you and Kate, it's like I can see her in you both; does that make sense?"

"Sure, it's only natural."

"I promised myself I'd stay strong today, so let's change the subject … how's your love life, anyone special you're keeping secret from me?"

Their conversation was interrupted by the sound of Jakob and Oskar, who were burning off some energy. Sarah lagged behind and eyed up the spare place on the bench with intent. As she sat down, she removed her heels and began rubbing her toes.

"Here you both are, you managed to slip away quietly. The boys wondered where you had got to."

"We were just talking about MJ's love life."

"Ah-ha, the boys did mention something about a nice man."

MJ rolled her eyes, "That was Steve, the landlord from the pub." She sensed Sarah about to ask if her sons had been in a pub, so MJ quickly moved the conversation on.

"Actually, I am going on a date this week."

"Ooooh," said Sarah mocking a schoolgirl's voice, "but not with your boss though?"

Before they could continue, a shout could be heard from the fountain nearby. "Mum, look at me."

The three of them rushed over to see Jakob standing, completely naked in the fountain.

* * *

The wedding reception took place in the lavishly decorated barn, the word barn not doing it justice. The exposed vaulted beams were wrapped in twinkling fairy lights, a theme that continued along the walls and beams across the ceiling. Although it looked stunning, MJ could imagine it would be even more striking on a frosty winter's day, especially as it boasted an open fire. MJ was seated at the top table next to her dad, who, after a couple of whiskies, seemed more relaxed. He was getting a lot of attention from one of the German Aunties, who had the look of an Oktoberfest waitress, which he was enjoying.

In keeping with the 5-star venue, the food delivery and service could not be faulted; they'd even provided the children with special games and toys, which went down a treat with other guests as well as the kids.

After the trio of desserts had been served, Jochen stood up and welcomed the guests. He gushed over how beautiful Kate looked, and then gave a special mention to absent friends. Not wanting Kate to get upset, he quickly moved on to some funny anecdotes about Germans and made a few jokes about himself, which put most of the guests in complete hysterics. When the laughter had died down, he looked at Kate who nodded at him.

"There's one person we haven't mentioned yet, in fact it's someone that even we haven't met."

Kate stood up, blushing slightly and rubbed her tummy.

"Say hello everybody to baby Hoffman."

A collection of oohs and ahhs rang out around the barn. MJ was glad that she didn't mention it earlier, she realised now they wanted to announce it to everyone at the reception. She turned to her dad, who had welled up and looked fit to burst. Tears formed in his eyes and his cheeks turned pillar box red. MJ knew that her mum dreamed of becoming a grandmother, so she completely understood why her dad looked a wreck. She took his hand and encouraged him to stay strong, which to her amazement, he managed to do, partly due to the large whisky she ordered from the barman for him.

***

A night out with the Hoffmans wouldn't be complete without a touch of karaoke, and the wedding was no exception. MJ didn't have the world's best singing voice, but she could sing in tune and held a repertoire of lyrics in her head meaning she didn't need to rely on the bouncing ball moving under the words on the screen.

Rather than the bride and groom having the first dance, the happy couple each took a microphone for the first song. Kate stepped forward and, to everyone's surprise, started to sing "99 Red Balloons" in German. Jochen joined in and looked impressed by his wife's new language skills. They received a standing ovation. Kate smiled and informed her guests that the lyrics formed the extent of her German.

MJ's rendition of "Knockin' on Heaven's Door" didn't get quite as much applause, but she enjoyed it nonetheless. The spotlights made her hot and sweaty, so she headed outside to the wisteria-covered Japanese bridge to cool down. As she took in the tranquillity, MJ felt a moment of déjà vu as the woodsy smell returned, as did Axel's smile. They made small talk on the bridge, but all the while she could sense him moving closer to her. Whether it was the moonlit sky or the amount of champagne she'd consumed, she took no objection to him leaning in for a kiss. They were interrupted by MJ's ringing phone.

"Hey, where are you? Jakob and Oskar are heading to bed soon and they wanted you to sing their Paw Patrol song with them."

MJ reluctantly peeled away Axel's fingers from her waist and apologised. A few moments later, she found herself on stage with two over-tired boys singing about Marshall, Rubble, Chase, Rocky, Zuma and Skye. She kissed the boys goodnight and wished Sarah good luck in getting them to sleep, and then went and sat down with Kate, who sighed with contentment. They both clapped as their dad took to the stage with the Oktoberfest waitress, and began singing to "American Pie". MJ turned to look at Kate, who had gone completely pale and stared into space.

"Kate... Kate?" said MJ.

Kate took her arm but still looked blankly ahead. "I need the bathroom."

"Kate, are you OK? Shall I get Jochen?"

"No, no I'm fine. I just need to get some air."

Chapter 16

Georgia made short work of her third round of toast with Marmite, licking the remnants from her fingers. "Are you out at meetings today or in the office?"

"You've got an appetite on you this morning, haven't you?" said Leah.

"It's your fault for waking me up early."

"Morning exercise is good for your mental well-being," Leah said, massaging her girlfriend's shoulders. "And in answer to your question, I have my first CTD meeting today."

"Ah-ha, that explains why you're looking so fit then."

"Compliments will get you everywhere."

Georgia turned and attempted to kiss Leah, who moved swiftly away when her nose realised the mouth approaching her contained Marmite.

Leah checked the calendar on her phone and acknowledged a meeting scheduled for 11:30, odd she thought, convinced that the original request was for 10:30. Oh well, that would give her more time in the office to catch up with her emails.

* * *

MJ spent most of the morning cleaning her flat from top to bottom, or in her case, from side to side. The routine remained the same: bathroom, kitchen, bedroom and living area. By the time the wiping and mopping were complete in the first two rooms, the music would be cranked up and MJ would finish off the hoovering and dusting singing along to a classic album, which today was "Abba Gold". After putting the cleaning things back in the cupboard under the sink, MJ realised that her face and neck were covered in sweat. Remembering that she still wore her pyjamas, which needed a wash anyway, she pulled the t-shirt away from her stomach and used it to wipe away the sweat like a footballer. Still feeling hot, she opened the skylight in the kitchen a little further. She loved her top floor attic conversion, but it became unbearably hot in the summer. Seeing her phone flash on the living room coffee table, she grabbed a juice from the fridge and went over to the sofa.

Hope ur still OK 4 later?

Definitely, are we still meeting at 6 in the Eagle?

Yes, this is OK, see you later. Hakim

Although the date came about because of a bet, over the last few days, they'd been messaging each other, and he'd began to grow on her. He displayed manners, showed a genuine interest in her and made her laugh; she felt quite excited about seeing him later.

They'd arranged to walk from Victoria to the View from the Shard, where Hakim had booked entrance tickets for 8:30pm, which he guessed would be around sunset. They discussed eating beforehand and agreed that they'd just pick up some street food along the South Bank. The walk would be quite long, probably over an hour, but it would take them past a whole host of iconic sites, which meant they shouldn't be short of things to talk about. Her phone beeped again. Steve.

Fancy coming in 4 a drink before u meet lover-boy?

Yep, think I'll need one, it's been a while since I've been on a date.

It's a bet, not a date, remember.

It's a date, albeit one that started out as a bet.

Although she'd go to the pub for a drink, she'd make sure she left as soon as Hakim arrived; she couldn't risk him finding out about the bet.

Chapter 17

Not wanting to risk being late, Leah left the office just after 10:30am, which gave her ample time to get to the meeting. She'd already checked her appearance in the toilets before she left and ensured she had everything she needed. It was the first meeting, so it was vital that she came across well, after all, a whole industry depended on her to represent them and she didn't want to let them down. Since being appointed Chief Tourism Director, she made sure she had either met with or called the key influencers in the industry and, from these conversations, had drawn up a manifest of fundamental issues which needed to be raised.

Leah arrived and informed the po-faced receptionist of the meeting she was due to attend, apologising for her early arrival. Without the expression changing on her face, the receptionist seemed to take pleasure in telling Leah that the meeting started at 10:30. Shit, she should've double-checked the actual invitation. This wasn't the start she'd hoped for. As she walked towards the lifts at the end of the reception area, she encouraged her brain to give her a justifiable reason for her lateness. Whilst, in her personal life, she rarely arrived anywhere on time, she regarded accurate timekeeping as imperative in her professional life. She approached the door, gave a brief knock and entered the darkened board room. Her brain didn't want to play ball, so she just moved to one of the empty chairs, sat down and took out her Surface Pro. To her relief, before they could move on to the next point on the agenda, another person arrived and in a loud voice apologised as he scraped a chair around and clumsily knocked the table. Leah gave a wry smile and her guilt diminished, especially as the late imposter belonged to the MET police. Once settled in the chair next to her, she flashed him a pair of disapproving eyes, laced with a hint of playfulness.

The meeting continued, and Leah managed to gain the approval of the other participants as her arguments and points of view were put forward in a manner that appealed to the different sectors, including, most importantly, the representative from the Mayor of London's office.

***

For the rest of the afternoon, MJ chilled out on the sofa watching TV, appreciating her clean apartment and messaging her sister, who was loving Barbados although gutted that she couldn't drink now she was pregnant.

At 4pm, MJ headed up to the Eagle. Graham was outside having a smoke with someone she didn't recognise.

Inside, the pub seemed quieter than usual, a sign that days were becoming warmer and lighter meaning that many punters preferred beer gardens and terraces, where they could feel the warmth of the sun.

At the bar, MJ looked around and asked Steve what he'd done with everyone.

"As much as I like the nicer weather, my cash tills definitely don't."

MJ took out her phone and looked at the pub's Instagram account to check whether the photos made the place look unappealing in the good weather. "Hey, nice photo of you and some dude in a sports shirt."

"What's that?"

"Looks like you served them a shed load of shots. They reckon the Eagle is the best pub in London. Nice one. See, you need more people like that who don't care about being outside in the nice weather."

"Let's have a look;" said Steve as he enlarged the picture, "yes, I remember, a nice bunch, they were in a few weeks ago. See, it's not just you and Polly who can sell shots!"

MJ took the phone back and looked at the photo again. "It must've been that night you called me with the gossip about Graham, if you look in the bar you can see their reflections. They look as though they're cooking up a potion."

"Bloody hell, yes they do, don't they!" said Steve hurrying off to answer the ringing phone.

Graham walked back into the bar, and MJ thought it would be a good opportunity to find out whether he remembered anything from the night the photo was taken. He'd said very little about Georgia in recent days, which hopefully meant that the hatred had somewhat subdued.

"Hey, have a look at this photo – can you see yourself in the background?"

Graham took MJ's phone and enlarged the photo. "Yup, I remember it very well, that's the night I found out who my wife had been fucking."

"You know who she is?"

"Of course, the bitch is called Leah Jasmine Pope, she lives at 33 Vernon Close, Chiswick, date of birth 02-10-77, went to Manchester University, started out working for Apple in California, now owns a big ticketing company and recently became Tourism Advisor for the Government. Anything else you'd like to know?"

"Bloody hell!" said MJ, nearly knocking over a stack of glasses.

Graham looked smug but evil at the same time.

"Your date is here," said Steve.

"He's early," said MJ rushing out of the door.

"Hello, it's good to see you again," said Hakim smiling and leaning over to give her a kiss on the cheek.

"You too," said MJ, looking back to see Steve at the window mimicking a lewd act.

Inquisitive by nature, MJ couldn't wait to find out more about the handsome stranger. She debated what she should ask about first … home life, childhood, work, family? Hopefully, by the end of the evening she should have enough information to formulate an accurate character analysis. Going over what she knew already, i.e. he liked football, supported Liverpool and had a cousin who fixed TVs, she decided to get the football talk out of the way first. MJ had very little interest in football but since working in the pub, she'd come to realise that having a good grasp of the nation's favourite sport would endear her to more customers, in particular the locals, not to mention her boss. So, without making it obvious, she started to flick through the back pages of the newspapers at the weekend to absorb the comments and main points of discussion when matches were on. With Steve being a Chelsea fan, she paid extra attention to who The Blues were playing, their results and any subsequent gossip. Since finding out that Hakim supported Liverpool, she took note of their four nil win over Brighton on the last day of the season, which gave them 4th place in the league and qualification into the Champions League … ahead of Chelsea, a fact that she'd heard Steve cursing about on Monday in the pub.

"Are you happy about the Champions League?" she asked.

"Yes, of course, I think we can win it next year."

She decided to start moving the conversation subtly away from football as she didn't want him getting the wrong idea and thinking she was a fan. "Does your cousin support Liverpool too?" That question did the trick and MJ soon had Hakim talking about his family, although he managed to avoid certain questions and simply answered as if he'd been asked something completely different. By the time they'd reached the London Eye, she'd ascertained that Hakim was born in Turkey and had spent most of his life in Germany before moving to London with his cousin a couple of years ago. She knew very little about the rest of his family, though.

As they paused by the river, Hakim changed the subject and started asking questions about MJ, enquiring if she had always lived in London. Whilst she didn't mind talking about herself, she often felt embarrassed that, at 28 years old, she hadn't worked out who she was or what she wanted out of life, her opinions could change from week to week as could her likes and dislikes. Over the years, she used indecision as an excuse to never get anything finished or see things through to the end, including her love life. That's why she had no career as such nor been in a long-term relationship. Maybe this would be the year, she thought, standing close enough to Hakim to breathe in his fresh scent, that she would find someone special. With personal introductions over with, they both relaxed and chit chat became more natural about the iconic buildings they passed.

"This is one of my favourite buildings," said Hakim as they approached Shakespeare's Globe Theatre, "have you been inside?"

"No, you?"

"Yes, it's amazing, I watched a performance here last summer … in the rain though as it's open air."

As they continued, MJ couldn't believe how many places Hakim had been to and how enthusiastic and knowledgeable he was about them. He continued talking about his love for London as they sat together on a bench and ate their Mexican street food.

"Around every corner, there is something special in London, so much history as well as cool modern things, not to mention food and drink – have you been to Borough Market?"

MJ looked at him just as warm salsa from her burrito oozed down her chin. To her relief, Hakim carried on talking whilst she rushed to take out a serviette and clean herself up. Why didn't she choose something less sloppy?

"Just along here is the Golden Hind and … wait … as you like pubs, let me show you The Anchor, it's one of the oldest pubs in the City and it's said that Shakespeare himself went there for a drink."

When they reached the viewing platform at the Shard and were admiring the view, MJ turned to Hakim and asked him how he knew so much about the sites and attractions in London.

"Through work; we get lots of opportunities to see places and experience things."

"Who do you work for?"

"For a ticketing company that sells theatre tickets, attraction passes, pub vouchers and so on. I'm only in IT but it's company policy that we all get the same opportunities, so I often get invited to events and get given tickets for shows and things."

"Sounds great," said MJ thinking she couldn't remember the last time she went to the theatre. "You enjoy your job then?"

"Yes, very much so, the work is interesting, and the company very good. My boss, she is very understanding and kind of inspiring: you know what I mean? We're all part of the Global Tickets family and she treats us well. I also have good friends there."

83

Hakim and MJ walked back over the Millennium Bridge and then, as neither fancied the hour walk back, took the District line from Monument to Victoria, where Hakim said he'd continue to Finsbury Park. Both were hesitant when they said their goodbyes as to whether they should hug, kiss or shake hands. In the end, Hakim took decisive action and kissed her on both cheeks. She breathed him in and felt her body tense.

"Perhaps I invite you to the theatre next time?"

"I'd like that," said MJ.

"Goodbye, thank you for tonight."

She stood and watched as he turned and walked towards the Victoria line. He was long gone when MJ came out of her daydream, forgetting for a moment where she was. Walking up the steps and out of the station, MJ took out her phone to check the time, 22:27. Time for a drink she thought and headed to the Eagle.

"I win," said Steve as MJ entered the pub, "you owe me a score."

Graham took out his wallet and slapped down a £20 note on the bar and then left the pub saying something about not being able to get a kebab. MJ knew the bet involved her and whether she'd go back to the pub or invite Hakim back to hers, so didn't bother asking. Steve held up the £20 note and asked if she wanted a drink.

"Yes please."

"So, good night?"

"Yeah, we had fun."

"What does the little prince do for a living then, I can't see him running around watching his cousin fix TVs?"

"He's in IT, works for some ticketing company and gets all sorts of perks, he also waxed lyrical about his boss."

"I hope you were saying the same?"

"Of course, I get free booze and have the nicest, kindest, most wonderful boss in the whole wide world." As soon as MJ said aloud where he worked, her mind did a flashback to the conversation she had with Graham earlier that day. Didn't he say that Leah owned a big ticketing company? How many ticketing companies were there in London?

Chapter 18

Leah put her arms above her head, pointed her toes and stretched out giving out a loud groan as she exhaled. She glanced at the alarm clock, surprised that it was so early. She felt refreshed so she didn't dare to snooze and risk falling into a deep sleep. Instead, she looked to her left hoping the loud groan she'd emitted had woken Georgia, as she knew very well how she wanted to spend the time before the alarm went off. To her disappointment, Georgia remained curled up and continued to produce a rhythmic snore, so Leah decided to get ready and go into the office early.

She headed out of the terraced house and walked along the cul-de-sac to the main road, towards the tube station on Turnham Green Terrace. As she placed her Oyster card wallet on the yellow sign, her phone rang. It was Julia, her PA.

"Hi, sorry to bother you, but I thought you should know that there seems to be a big problem with the API feeds, we haven't received a single booking since last night, yet hundreds of purchases have been made from operators. The IT and integration teams have all been called in and are looking at it now, but you may want to contact Anders to see if he has any insight, I can't get hold of him at the moment."

"Ok, thanks for calling, I'll be with you just after 8am. Can you clear my morning of meetings please? I'll still go to my afternoon one, though."

During the tube journey, Leah went through in her head what could've caused the problem. Connectivity via API (application programming interface) was an integral part of the business, enabling booking systems to connect with

Global Tickets allowing customers to purchase tickets, not only for theatre shows but also for attractions and restaurants. No connection meant no business. This was bad, incredibly bad.

Leah drafted a number of messages which she knew would be sent when the WIFI signal appeared intermittently at tube stations. The first to Anders, urgent, contact me pls, the second to Georgia serious IT issues, could be a late one x and the third to her sister Hey, I'm in Brighton next week, fancy meeting up? Then, to take her mind off things for a short while, she crushed some candy for the last ten minutes of the journey.

There was a sense of panic in the office, as her team rushed around to use different PCs with mobiles glued to their ears.

"Hey guys," she called out. "I appreciate you're trying to get to the bottom of this, but I need you all in the boardroom in five minutes, please. We need a joined-up, and logical approach to this, which means a clear plan of action with each of you assigned different tasks, OK?"

Leah took a call from Anders. "Good timing, I take it you've heard?"

"Yeah, just catching up on messages and emails. Have you talked to the team yet?"

"Just about to," Leah replied, "anything apart from the obvious I should mention?"

"You know what you're doing, but just in case it is someone in the family, which I don't think it is, let's keep action points clear and person-specific. I'm just heading off to the airport, so can you call me with an update later?"

"Yeah sure."

Leah watched as the team started to filter into the boardroom; it was still early, so not everyone was in yet but, as the main people were present, she decided to get a head start in rectifying the situation. One hour later, she emerged from the meeting none the wiser. Martin, the IT Director, beckoned her over to his screens. Hakim, who sat at the desk opposite, offered to make Leah a drink.

"You can read my mind, yes please I'd love a tea, thank you."

"Sure thing. Martin anything?" Hakim asked.

"Coffee please mate, milk, two sugars."

Martin went to the API backend and showed Leah some incorrect configurations. "I think this is the main root of the problem. It seems as though every product code is out by one digit, which means not a single performance, attraction, restaurant, you name it, is correctly mapped. Looks like we're going to have to go back in and change everything one by one. We're on it though already, so hopefully within a few days, we'll be back on track. In the meantime, it's probably worth pulling in the sales and marketing teams to answer phones and emails to minimise any further disruption."

"Thanks," said Leah. She lowered her voice and moved closer to Martin behind the screen, "What are your thoughts?"

"I'm leaning towards human error, whether that's someone internal or someone within the API environment, but it couldn't have just happened. Don't worry, this is our family too, so we'll work for as long as necessary to get it fixed."

Hakim came over with Martin's coffee. "I put your tea in your office Leah."

"OK, thanks. If either of you need an extra pair of hands, just let me know, I'm happy to help out," Leah offered.

"We may well be asking you," said Hakim "but aren't you off to the Houses of Parliament this afternoon?"

"Oh, I am indeed Hakim, thanks for the reminder," said Leah standing up and wondering when she'd mentioned the location of her meeting previously in the office.

Chapter 19

Anne-Marie arrived at the hospital in good time, despite the traffic around Brentford being horrendous. She sat in her battered red Corsa mentally preparing herself for the visit. She'd received a call from the ward nurse advising that her mum's condition had deteriorated, and she should start to prepare for the inevitable.

Anne-Marie had always shown a great deal of respect for her mum but, as with any mother-daughter relationship, slanging matches, fights and shouting had been par for the course. Being the eldest of four children, she was often required to help dress, wash, feed and amuse her brothers, which she did willingly, partly because she didn't know any different. With her father working away most of the time at sea, Anne-Marie had to be strong for her mum and took it upon herself to learn things that were traditionally considered a man's job. She could wire a plug, unblock a drain, put up shelves, fix bikes, mend broken toys etc. Every time she carried out such a task, she'd make up a scenario in her head about living in a castle and fixing something for a princess or being at war and defusing a bomb. Her imagination would run riot and she would start to sketch out the scenes in her mind, adding characters and deciding what type of music would work well with which bit. By her teenage years, Anne-Marie owned a second-hand video camera and had made scores of short films about random things.

During careers advice at school, when asked what she wanted to do with her life, Anne-Marie simply replied make films, and, to her surprise, the advisor congratulated her and said great choice. He helped Anne-Marie choose the relevant A-levels, which eventually led to her being accepted into Manchester University to study

Film Making. She loved the course and revelled in the assignments and projects given to her. After living in halls of residence for the first two years, she decided for her final year that she'd prefer to live in a house share. Overhearing a group of other Year 2 students discussing accommodation in the union bar one afternoon, Anne-Marie joined in the conversation, not one for beating about the bush even then, and by the end of the evening she'd manage to secure a room in a house for the following year, along with four other people, two guys and two girls - one of which was Leah Pope.

Anne-Marie closed the car door and went to buy a car park ticket, debating whether to get one or two hours. Probably two, she thought; the machine asked her for £4.00. "Daylight fucking robbery," she said aloud.

She knew the route through the hospital off by heart, so went through the double doors, along several corridors taking lefts and rights, going up and down stairs, along more corridors with ease. She went over to the reception desk and talked to the duty nurse.

"Hi, your mum is looking forward to seeing you."

"Aye, that's good news. How is she doing … really?"

"Mrs McPearson's in good spirits considering what her body is going through. She's on constant medication which is sedating her body a lot more than her mind at the moment. That won't always be the case, though, so make the most of your visit."

She read between the lines and knew her mum's life was nearing its end.

"Hey mum, how are you doing?"

"All the better for seeing you, although you're not looking too good yourself; have you been at the bottle again?" said Mrs McPearson, in a harsher version of Anne-Marie's accent.

Anne-Marie chuckled, it felt like she had her mum back – direct and rude. "Aye, I've got myself a new boozer and am helping them with their business by drinking as much as possible."

Mrs McPearson frowned and patted the bed, indicating for Anne-Marie to sit down.

"So, tell me, what's going on in your life, how's work, have you found yourself a nice young man yet?"

She forced out a smile, trying not to get annoyed that her mum asked the same questions at the beginning of every visit. Anne-Marie stayed patient and always gave a different response. "Nice young men don't exist, mum, and work, well, you never guess who the new Chief Tourism Director is … Leah Pope!"

"Are you still letting that woman get to you? This has been going on far too long, you have to let it go and get on with your own life, do you hear me? One mistake twenty years ago and you're still obsessed with it."

"A fucking mistake, is that what you call it, she ruined my life, she stopped me from completing my coursework, which meant I failed the course, failed the degree, failed my career full stop. All because she couldn't admit she preferred women to men."

"Anne-Marie, you made a film about her and her sexuality behind her back and then expected her to give you permission to broadcast it to the world?"

"Are you saying it's my fault mum?"

"No, of course not, you were the better person, what you did for that wee girl was one of the kindest, most courageous and unselfish things a person could do. You sacrificed your own degree for someone else, someone who couldn't come to terms with who she was, someone who wasn't ready to face the truth about her sexuality. Just think what she would've done if you'd shared the

92

film? What would a vulnerable student have done, a woman coming to terms with who she is? What would you have done?"

Anne-Marie knew her mum was right. "Probably taken a cocktail of pills and vodka."

"Well, there you go then. You did the right thing and I bet there's not a day goes by when that woman doesn't think about what you did for her."

"Do you think so?"

"I know so. Now, my dear, can you get me some fresh water please, I'm parched?"

Anne-Marie picked up the empty plastic jug and headed out, thinking about what her mum said. When she returned with the water, her mum looked sleepy.

"Thanks, can you pour me a wee glass please?"

"Here you go," said Anne-Marie as she lifted the glass to her mum's cracked lips. "Shall I let you sleep now?"

"Aye, that would be good. You think about what I said, won't you, but don't think about it in the pub."

Anne-Marie smiled at the fact that even on her death bed, her mum could tell her what to do, as well as managing a little humour. She kissed her on the forehead and told her she loved her.

Chapter 20

Leah checked and then checked again the email inviting her to the second meeting of the series, she wasn't going to be late again this time. Definitely 15:00, with tea and coffee served from 14:30. Allowing herself plenty of time to reach Westminster, she arrived with ten minutes to spare. She informed the guard the reason for her visit and followed his directions to the security queue, which, to her relief, didn't look too long. As her turn to go through the scanner approached, she reached into her handbag and, in anticipation of being asked for ID, she took out her wallet. Smiling at the guard she put her bag and coat on the security belt and began sifting through her wallet for her driving licence. Bloody thing, she cursed to herself, where is it? Knowing her driving licence must be inside, she went through its contents one at a time, but for the life of her, she couldn't find it. The security guard saw her details on the manifest and was tempted to let her in, but rules were rules and he needed to verify she was who she said she was.

"I have bank cards," said Leah.

"Sorry ma'am, I need photo ID."

"I could 100 per cent swear that my driving licence was in my wallet …" Her phone beeped with a message from Ryan, the rep from the MET who she'd hit it off with at the previous meeting. *C'mon, you're holding up the queue.*

Thinking on her feet, she asked the security guard if he'd take somebody's word that she was who she said she was, someone of authority from the MET perhaps? He nodded, and before he could say anything, Leah repacked her bag and moved back in the queue to join Ryan, much to the bewilderment of others waiting. "You need to vouch for me with the security guard," Leah said, putting her hands together.

"What's it worth?" Leah saw Ryan's mouth form a cheesy grin.

"An IOU?"

"You're on."

The pair were shown through a series of corridors and doors, whilst Leah tried to rack her brains as to when she last saw her driving licence or used her purse. It must've been earlier that morning in her office. She remembered using her credit card to book a train ticket to Brighton. She sat at her desk and went through her cards and put them back ensuring they were all the same way around and in alphabetical order, which, according to Georgia, was one of her annoying habits. The driving licence was always placed in the first slit inside the purse opposite the bankcards. She remembered it being there as clear as day because the photo always made her chuckle and think of how, as a teenager, she and her friends went through a phase of spending most of their £2 pocket money on getting silly snaps taken in photo booths. Did she leave her purse on the desk when she talked to the team? She couldn't dwell on it now, though, and instead re-focused and put her business face on, but at the back of her mind, a little voice bugged her.

Chapter 21

Leah dialled Helena's extension. "Fancy going out to get some lunch?"

"Sure, can we go sooner rather than later, though?"

"Yep, meet you downstairs at midday?" As Leah put the phone down, she nudged the keyboard and noticed something underneath it. Her driving licence. She shook her head and berated herself.

Before Leah left, she made a point of turning off her PC, the password to which she'd already changed that morning; she also locked her office. When she walked past the other desks, the team gave her a wary look.

"Do you think it's someone internal that messed with the system boss?" asked Josh from behind his double screens.

"We haven't ruled anything out, so I suggest we remain a little extra vigilant and report anything either internally or externally that we think looks suspicious," Leah said as a frown came over her face, "Were you not in the staff briefing yesterday?"

"No, me and Noah were at one of the theatres."

"OK, that makes sense. When I'm back from lunch, why don't you and Noah pop into my office and I'll bring you up to speed."

Outside the front door, Helena took a drag of her cigarette. "Wretched things, I gave up a month ago, but my will power is non-existent at the moment."

"Hope work isn't stressing you out?" said Leah.

"Haha, no, I look forward to coming into work, it's far less stressful than having two hormonal teenagers to deal with. Beppe's?"

Leah and Helena were greeted at the door by the charismatic Beppe himself. "Eh, my favourite ladies, c'mon in and sit down," he said taking them to their usual booth in the corner, surrounded on the wall by photos of famous people who had eaten there over the years.

"Specials today are the sardines and also some lovely mushrooms in a garlic sauce for starters and then pasta dish, we have spinach and ricotta tortellini or crab ravioli. You want to order your usual carafe of pinot grigio ladies?"

Helena knew what Leah's answer would be so went ahead and ordered. "Thanks, yes a carafe would be good and two crab raviolis please."

"Perfecto," said Beppe.

"So, apart from the kids driving you mad, everything else OK at home, no more drama with hubby?" Leah asked.

"No, thankfully not, things seem to have calmed down. The more I think about it, the more I think men go through some sort of menopause as well as women. Hopefully the worst of it is behind us now, although it's been like having three kids for the last few months. Enough of me, how are things with you?

Leah shook her head with renewed disbelief and explained how she couldn't fathom how such an error in the system could have occurred. After discussing every possibility with Anders and their colleague in the US, none of them were any the wiser of how such a problem could have arisen especially as, if anything, they overspent on security.

"The only explanation," Leah reasoned, "is that it must be an inside job, and that scares me more than anything."

"Shit, but who? Who on earth on the team would do that? Could it happen by accident, could an intern change something by mistake?"

"You're thinking Noah, aren't you?"

"It did cross my mind."

"It's possible, but then again, someone else would've been able to track the error and know immediately which user it was, so I'm not convinced. I'm speaking with him and Josh later anyway as they missed the briefing on Wednesday."

The waiter brought over two bowls of steaming hot crab ravioli.

"Hmmm, smells delicious, thank you," said Leah smiling at the waiter. Pondering over whether to open up even more to Helena, she took a mouthful of pasta and gave a satisfying groan. Looking over and seeing her lunch buddy's warm, receptive face, she told her about the couple of recent incidents relating to her newly appointed role. The first when she was late for the meeting, despite having thought the correct time was synced to her phone calendar, and the second incident with the elusive driving licence.

"Sorry to burden you with this; now I've said it aloud it seems menial, and perhaps I'm just making more of it than I should; things just seem a little off-kilter at the moment, do you know what I mean?"

Helena gave a sympathetic smile. "Don't worry, that's what friends are for. I know it may sound silly, but start writing down what happens when, where and who's around; we can go through it together if you like, you may find that these things are happening at similar times or after certain situations." To move the conversation on to less stressful topics, Helena asked how things were with Georgia.

"Yeah, all good on that front, she lets me vent, listens to me, makes me laugh and makes me feel good about myself. To be honest, I don't know where I'd be without her."

"Is she living with you now?"

"Yep, and I wouldn't have it any other way."

***

Back in the office, Leah sent a meeting request for 15:30 to Josh and Noah, before taking a fresh notebook from her bottom drawer and, as Helena suggested, jotted down the details of recent events including the when and the where. With the list finished, she was even more convinced that someone in the office was out to get her. But why and who?

A reminder popped up on her screen indicating fifteen minutes before her meeting with Josh and Noah. She made a mental note of some of the questions she needed to ask them and read through their CVs. Noah's connection to Anne-Marie worried her and, something that she was acutely aware of, why had she seemingly gone out of her way to help her cousin get an internship with Global Tickets. He'd been there for two months, so the incidents weren't exactly a coincidence, but perhaps he thought he'd get his feet under the table first before starting anything. Leah thought about who he worked with and who she'd seen him hang out with at lunch and during social events. Josh, Hakim, Tomas ... all of whom had been working at Global Tickets for more than a year and none of whom, Leah had any issues with, either workwise or on a personal level. Leah saw her phone flash with a message from Georgia. *Fancy a Friday night drink after work?*

Good idea, are you OK to meet here?

Sure, see you around 6pm?

There was a knock at the door. "Come in guys, please sit down," said Leah turning her phone over. "Right, I know you weren't at the briefing on Wednesday, but can I assume you read the subsequent email from Anders?" Josh and Noah nodded in unison.

99

"Noah, you've been working in the IT team for the last couple of months, haven't you; did you notice any changes over that time, perhaps the server slowed down when you were running certain applications or any specific mapping difficulties when you've been working with API connections?"

Noah took a deep breath as if about to begin a long answer. "No, nothing seemed odd, everything has been normal."

Leah wanted to pry further. "What have you been working on over the last week?"

"I have been working with Hakim, we are connecting big new API agent in China. Their system and words are very different, so it is taking longer."

"I see," said Leah admiring his English, "what are the main differences?"

Noah then explained the differences and how he and Hakim were working through each stage systematically.

"The sales lady, sorry I forget her name, say this China client could be worth millions to us, so we should make them a priority for connection."

Leah continued to talk to them both for a further twenty minutes, after which time she felt sure that neither of them were responsible. By 4pm, her brain had reached a brick wall. She put a quick call through to Anders and then went out to the main room.

"Hey everyone, as I'm sure you're more than aware, this week has been tough, but hopefully, due to your efforts and hard work, we've come through the worst of it, so thanks to all of you. The office will be closing at 6pm sharp this evening, but the terrace bar will open shortly and will stay open until 5:30, so please take this opportunity to either escape early and beat the rush hour or join me for a drink on the terrace."

The office emptied in less than five minutes, leading Leah to think it wasn't just her brain that had reached its capacity for the week. Half the team decided to leave, and the other half were out on the terrace enjoying the complimentary drinks. Leah looked around, no sign of the three amigos, Josh, Hakim or Noah. Tomas, though, was behind the bar again.

"Hey, you don't always have to be barman, you know?" said Leah.

"I'm practising for the remake of Cocktail."

By 5:30, the terrace was empty, and Leah had the place to herself. She locked up and messaged Georgia to find out how long she'd be, and then went to tidy up the bar. Whilst the cleaners would wash up and clean, they weren't contracted to clear away bottles, so someone from the office would usually offer and tonight it was Leah's turn, and she didn't mind. Lost in thought, she gathered up all the empty bottles and knelt down behind the bar sorting them out according to their colour - clear, green, brown. She was so engrossed in the recycling she didn't hear someone walk through the office and into the bar behind her. A hand went onto her shoulder and she bolted up with shock, her head hitting the shelf with a dull thud.

"Shit, sorry, the cleaner let me in, I didn't mean to scare you."

Clutching her forehead with one hand, she turned to see Georgia and took her hand with the other. Her heart was beating so fast, she half expected it to pop out through her chest. "Jeez George, I thought my time was up!"

Georgia took Leah into her arms and for a moment, neither moved. Feeling more composed, Leah removed a bottle of cold wine from the fridge and poured two glasses. Before handing Georgia her drink, she pulled her close and gave her a long, deep kiss.

"Hmm I'll think I'll scare you more often," said Georgia.

"There's more where that came from George, but in the meantime, I want us to do some role play ..."

Georgia raised her eyebrows in anticipation, but her suggestive look went straight over Leah's head.

"Everything's pointing to someone in the office, someone in my family being responsible for the system error, and I need a pair of subjective eyes to have a nosey around the office into desks and drawers. Are you up for it?"

"OK, but by 7pm promise me we'll either be propping up a bar or I'll be naked on your desk?"

"That's a promise," said Leah, leading Georgia over to a row of four desks. "OK, I want you to look in the drawers of these desks and see if anything stands out as being unusual."

Georgia leafed through the piles of paper on each desk, and then did the same for the filing drawers and box files. There wasn't a great deal, but from what Georgia could tell, everything looked normal, lots of technical bumf, charts, mapping documents and several papers in what she thought was Chinese. The only thing that looked slightly out of place were some hand-drawn plans of the Apollo Theatre in one of the desks. The fire exits were highlighted and on the reverse side was a map of where they emerged on the streets. As Global Tickets was the leading wholesaler of theatre tickets, however, Georgia didn't think it relevant so didn't mention it to Leah.

"Anything?" asked Leah.

"Nope, but then again, I'm not familiar with IT jargon, and my Chinese language skills aren't quite up to scratch these days."

"Are they not, Georgina Asher?" said Leah in a head teacher's voice, "Well, you may need to come to my office then for your punishment."

***

When Leah and Georgia finally left the office, they were famished and decided to head straight home and order a takeaway. As they walked back hand in hand from the station, Leah thought how normal everything felt, as if she and Georgia had been living together for years. She gave Georgia's hand a contented squeeze. Leah unlocked the door and went inside. Georgia followed and hung up her coat. Leah lifted up the post and opened a letter addressed to her, it didn't have a stamp or postmark on it. Silently, she passed the note to Georgia.

There once was an old dyke called Pope,
Whose career went down a slippery slope,
She slept with people's wives,
And ruined their lives.
But soon she'll die, I hope!

The note played on Leah's conscience all weekend, she tried to put it to the back of her mind, but it was no good. She kept reading the words over in her head, but soon she'll die.

Chapter 22

On Monday morning, Georgia said goodbye and left for work, not before giving Leah another prolonged hug. Once she'd finally left, Leah looked at the clock and noted there were a couple of hours before she needed to leave for Victoria to catch the train to Brighton. She was tempted to drive but quickly decided against it; in her current state of mind, staring out of the train would be the safer option. Was someone really out to get her or was she imagining things? The arrival of the note swung the pendulum in favour of option A, but why? Hopefully, a few days away would bring some clarity. As much as she couldn't imagine life now without Georgia, she realised that she'd started to depend on her, it wasn't something she was used to and didn't feel it was a healthy trait to have. Leah had been brought up to be independent and self-sufficient. You are your own best friend, lover and partner, her mother often said, so learn to love yourself. With the Leader's dinner on Tuesday evening, followed by meetings and another dinner (which required a speech by Leah) on Wednesday, she looked forward to having a day and a half to herself, and she'd finally manage to catch up with her sister at some point – lunch on Thursday looking the most likely time, before heading back to London.

**

MJ couldn't sleep, so she decided she may as well get up early. Kate's message came through at silly o'clock, a sign that both sisters were thinking about their visit to their mother's grave. It would've been her 60th birthday. MJ made the 10:40 train, found a seat and put on her headphones; closing her eyes, memories of that fateful day came back in an instant. It still felt unreal, more like something she'd dreamt. The call from her father came through after school, whilst MJ was watching an episode of *Tipping Point* at her friend's house. She wasn't paying much interest to the call until those few words penetrated the phone and infiltrated her body … mum followed by collapsed and then may not make it. Her father now had her full attention, despite her gaze still being fixated on the arcade machine going in and out and coins hanging dangerously on the edge, would they fall, or wouldn't they? Would her mother cling on to life, or would it slip by?

As the train pulled into Wokingham Station, MJ saw her sister on the platform looking fresh and tanned from her honeymoon. She wore a baggy shirt over her culottes, so it wasn't clear whether a bump was beginning to form yet. The sisters gave each other a squeeze and walked over to their dad's car.

"How is he?" asked MJ.

"How are any of us?" said Kate, gesturing towards MJ's red eyes.

"True," said MJ, starting to well up again.

It was a tough couple of hours with a lot of tears, but also a lot of love and physical contact between them. As had become customary, they each took time on their own at the grave and then came together to lay flowers and sing happy birthday, a song they didn't manage to finish because of the outpouring of tears and snot running down their faces.

Afterwards, the three of them sat in the car and let their emotions subside before heading off to their usual pub for lunch. Kate tucked into a substantial chicken burger and sweet potato fries with gusto, whilst MJ, in contrast, held a fork and pushed her food around the plate.

"You're not pregnant as well, are you?"

Fat chance of that, thought MJ. "No dad, I'm just not that hungry."

His eyes widened as he remembered that his youngest daughter was due to have a rendezvous with a young man the week after the wedding. He asked about her date.

"He was a gentleman, hopefully we're going to go out again soon," MJ said.

"So, what's his name, what does he look like, where does he work?" asked Kate.

"He's in IT, a few years younger than me, and he's called Hakim."

"Hakim?" said her dad, his body leaning back on the chair, "What sort of name's that?"

"It's a sort of name for someone who was born in Turkey and grew up in Germany."

Kate's face brightened and a smile formed, the first MJ had noticed all day. "Hey, if you're serious about him, then we could both learn German together. Jochen has already said he'll be talking to this little one in German, so I don't want to be clueless about what he's saying."

It hadn't even crossed MJ's mind about the German connection until Kate said it out loud. It had been just over two weeks since she'd been out with Hakim and, although they shared some messages and talked about going out again, nothing definite had been discussed, which played on MJ's mind. Maybe she should bite the bullet and suggest dinner, perhaps on Friday? Life's too short, she thought, so headed off to the toilets and sent him a message. By the time she sat back down at the table, she'd received a reply. *Sorry, very busy with system problem at work.* Her disappointment was short-lived, as the phone beeped again immediately after. *But I have tickets for Wicked this Friday, will you join me?*

With a faint fluttering in her stomach, MJ turned to her sister, "He's invited me to the theatre on Friday."

* * *

When MJ arrived back at Victoria, she headed to the Eagle, even though her shift didn't begin for another couple of hours.

"You're keen," said Steve, as he cleared glasses from the front of the pub, "You OK?"

"Yeah, just fancied some company."

"Fair enough love; I'm around if you want to chat."

Graham sat in his usual place with both hands around his pint glass, "Alright, MJ, any words of wisdom for me today?"

"Sorry Gra, I'm fresh out of wisdom I'm afraid, any other requests?" said MJ, already feeling better being amongst her pub family.

Alex came out of the kitchen with a smile on his face and a bowl of food in his hands. "I need someone to give me their opinion on my new chorizo and chicken pasta dish, any takers?"

As if on cue, MJ's stomach let out an enormous rumble and, without needing to hear her answer, Alex asked, "would madam like any cheese to go with that?" and produced a small bowl of grated parmesan.

Steve joined them at the bar, pocketing his phone. "Blimey, that smells good."

"One of Alex's new concoctions, boss," said Graham leaning over as MJ twirled the tagliatelle on her fork.

"That was one of my mates on the blower, asking if I wanted some football stuff for the pub, shirts and photos and the like – he's got a spare room full of stuff he doesn't need anymore. I'm going to go down to Brighton on Wednesday and collect it; do you fancy coming with

107

me, Graham? We could stay over, make a night of it?" said Steve.

"Sounds good mate, let me check with the wife. Oh sorry, I don't have one anymore," said Graham, as he produced a deep Santa laugh and patted his ribs, "Yeah, it'll be a laugh; I'll pack my Union Jack shorts and handkerchief."

"You're so classy Graham, do you know that?" said Alex shaking his head, "Do you want me to look after the pub, boss?"

Steve looked at him and nodded. "You read my mind, is that OK? Roxy will need looking after too, so perhaps you could stay in the spare room?"

"Sure, no problem."

Steve looked at MJ munching her way through the pasta. "MJ's on shift that night too, so she can do the bottling up and sort the tills out for you."

"I'll help out on one condition," said MJ licking her lips.

"What's that?"

"You make me another bowl of this pasta, it's delicious."

Chapter 23

As soon as MJ started her shift, her mood went downhill rapidly. Graham left early for a change, Alex stayed in the kitchen churning out platefuls of food, and she and Steve were left trying to manage several groups of rowdy office workers. This is not what I need tonight, thought MJ to herself. Her sour mood continued, even when the suits started to disperse, as their tables were left in a complete mess. She picked up the cloth and C20 spray from the sink and was about to start cleaning when the door opened, and another customer walked in. She waited patiently as he removed his jacket and contemplated which stool to sit on. He eventually sat down and looked at the different beer taps and optics. MJ continued to wait as she looked around the pub in disgust. Dirty tables and a sticky bar were, beyond doubt, her main peeves when it came to bar work; it looked so bad in a pub, especially when there weren't many customers left. Still holding the cloth and C20 bottle, MJ snapped at him, "In your own time, mate, it's not like I've got anything else to do."

At the same moment, Steve walked past with a stack of empty pint glasses piled high in his hands, "sorry about that, she's having a tough day."

"Aren't we all?" responded Robin, removing his elbow from the bar, standing up straight and ordering a pint of London Pride.

MJ poured his drink and placed it in front of him, without saying a word or offering a smile. She walked back to Steve at the hatch, and he gave her a hug.

"Why don't you call it a day, and pop yourself on the other side of the bar. It's quietened down now, so I don't mind finishing off."

MJ, with reluctance, pulled herself away from Steve's comforting chest and moved around to the other side of the bar. "I'm sorry, today is the anniversary of …"

"I know," said Steve as he put a vodka and coke in front of her.

MJ sipped her drink, savouring the cold, sharp vodka and sweet coke. She poked the slice of lemon with her straw and swirled the ice cubes around the glass. After a minute or so, the coldness of the liquid made the glass start to condensate on the outside, which MJ took satisfaction in removing with her forefinger. Swipe, move the glass, swipe, move the glass. Lost in thought, she tried to work out how many strokes were required before the glass started to be populated again by little water droplets.

Robin walked up to the bar with his empty glass and glanced over to MJ. "Can I get you another?"

"Why not. Thanks."

"Same again?" asked Steve, opening the steamy glasswasher and putting the empty glass straight onto the tray.

"Yes, please, and whatever this young lady is having," said Robin, handing over a £20 note.

"On the house," said Steve.

Robin pulled up a stool and sat next to MJ at the bar. The pair soon began talking, and, before long, it turned into an impromptu counselling session. MJ discovered that Robin spent a similar amount of time nursing his wife through cancer as she had her mum, and their end stories were almost identical. They talked about how totally random things brought back vivid images and they could imagine being back in the room again.

"For me, it's the Olympics," said Robin "I spent the whole of London 2012 with her and, as a keen athlete, she'd want me to describe everything in immense detail, from how much the pole bent before firing the person over the bar, to the angle of the javelin as it left the thrower's arm. I can't bring myself to watch athletics anymore."

"Do you talk a lot about her to anyone else, your kids or friends?" asked MJ.

Robin shrugged his shoulders. "She received her diagnosis not long after we met, so we never had children, I'm afraid. I wish we had on many an occasion, just having someone else who knew her like I did, that I could talk to, would help. But then again, hearing what you've gone through, I wouldn't want to inflict that kind of hurt and pain on anyone else, so perhaps better that another child didn't lose their mother."

The two of them continued to talk with intermittent outbursts of laughter but also tears. MJ looked into Robin's eyes – they were a vibrant emerald green, but she could also see pain in them and wondered if hers looked the same. Perhaps those who have lost someone close gave off a certain kind of look, something ingrained in their eyes. Robin spoke with care, asking MJ questions about her mum with tact and diplomacy. She felt comfortable and opened up to him about how she often talked to her at night when she lay in bed.

"I'm grateful that the image I have of her is that of when she was alive and well, not as she neared the end. How about you?" said MJ.

"It depends on my mood, when I am thinking happy thoughts, then she always has her hair down and is wearing the biggest of smiles, but on the other hand if I'm having a bad day at work, for example, then it's the complete opposite. Were you able to share your pain with any siblings?"

I wish, thought MJ. "I have an older sister, and, to be honest, our relationship has never been the same since,

111

although it's getting better. When mum collapsed, my sister was in her final year at university in Glasgow, so I was left to deal with mum's condition, as well as looking after our dad, who didn't cope at all well. I thought family meant more than studies, so expected her to travel straight home, but she didn't."

"I'm sorry to hear that." Robin reached across and put his hand on MJ's shoulder. She appreciated his tenderness and got the impression that he genuinely did understand her pain.

They continued talking and sharing experiences whilst Steve kept their glasses topped up. After giving out an exhausted yawn, MJ looked up at the clock to see it display 00:15.

"Shit, is that the time?" asked MJ as she checked her phone and turned to see Roxy curled up asleep under her master, whose eyelids were struggling to stay open.

"Oh wow, sorry you should've kicked me out," said Robin.

"Hey, no, you were deep in conversation, so I thought I'd leave you to it," said Steve struggling to open his eyes.

"Well, thank you, I appreciate that," said Robin, and he turned to MJ, "Thanks for the chat."

They gave each other a hug, and Robin said goodnight and left.

"Fancy a coffee or something before you head back?" Steve asked.

"Thanks, but I better get a shifty on, I'm back first thing in the morning. Why don't you and Roxy walk me home, though?"

Roxy's right ear pricked up as she heard both her name and the word walk in the same sentence.

"You know who that was, don't you?" said Steve as he reached for Roxy's lead.

"Who, the guy I was talking to?"

112

"Yeah, that's the one I told you about, remember? The one in the Instagram photo you saw a couple of weeks ago?"

MJ's head had gone through enough in the last twenty-four hours, so she looked at Steve with a blank stare.

"You know, the guy who knows the woman that Graham's wife is with?" Steve could see the penny beginning to drop for MJ, so continued. "You saw the photo of him, the Scottish bird and Graham all sat together like a coven of witches deciding on which deadly potion they'd stir up in their cauldron to kill the poor woman off?"

MJ tipped her head to the side. "But you said he was quite abrupt and callous."

"Yeah, he was, seemed like a different guy tonight."

"You should've told me who it was; I could've done some more digging."

"That's exactly why I didn't tell you, nosey knickers. Everything seems to have calmed down where Graham is concerned, which is a good thing all round."

Chapter 24

As she strolled along the blustery seafront, Leah felt mentally strong. The gusts of wind against her face were a reminder to enjoy life and not to take anything for granted. As she tasted salt on her tongue from the sea spray, she knew that having time away from the office and London had soothed out some internal knots which had developed. She thought back to the previous evening's dinner. Conversation flowed with a considerable amount of time spent discussing technology; those around her agreed that the industry faced a transitional phase with both tour operators and suppliers having to adjust to a change in customer behaviour. Leah shared her recent experience of the system being attacked and learnt she wasn't alone, with a number of others saying that they'd been victims of cybercrime or that their computers had been hacked. In virtually all cases, it turned out to be someone internal with a grudge against the company who was to blame. Their comments perturbed Leah, and a negative mindset started to creep in again until a colleague from the US made a flippant comment about where she came from, if an employee held a grudge, they'd simply shoot the boss. Although it perhaps shouldn't have, the comment did lighten the mood, and by the time Rahul, the rep from India, downed a few whiskies and started telling his witty stories, the atmosphere relaxed, and the rest of the evening turned out to be a fun, light-hearted affair.

***

Graham arrived at the pub just after midday and made himself at home on his usual stool before ordering a pint from Polly. Steve emerged from the cellar and acknowledged Graham before fiddling with some beer pumps and adjusting a tap.

"Hey Polly," Graham said, sounding pleased with himself, "I've started to write limericks; do you want to hear the one I've written about you?" Not waiting for her to reply, he took out a piece of A5 paper from his jacket pocket.

There was a young woman called Polly,
Whose hair was as blue as a lolly.
She served beer in a pub,
And liked to dance in a club,
But before long she'd turned into a boy, oh golly!

Polly didn't respond and went to wipe down some tables. Before long, Steve indicated that he'd be ready to leave in a few minutes, prompting Graham to finish off his pint in a couple of large gulps.

***

Traffic was light and they managed to get onto the M23 in good time. The pair shared some banter about football and gossip about the locals before moving onto the staff at the pub. Graham said it was about time there was some proper totty working behind the bar, which Steve took with a pinch of salt.

"Well, if you carry on writing rude limericks about my staff, there won't be any bar staff left to serve you at all."

"I sent one to that bitch as well; you know the one who stole my wife."

Steve glanced over to Graham. "You are kidding? Why did you do that?"

"I couldn't resist it; she deserves to know what she is."

"How did you send it?"

"Hand delivered."

Steve could hardly believe what he was hearing. He pictured Graham squatting behind a bush waiting for Georgia to leave the house and then rushing up to the front door to post the note like some sort of weird stalker.

"Nice place she's got, must be worth over a million."

"Well, for your sake, I hope it didn't have one of those ring doorbell things with a camera on otherwise, you're toast."

Chapter 25

After a successful day of debates and presentations, Leah took the short walk back along the seafront to her hotel, breathing in the fresh air and thinking how good it would be to live near the sea. After a last run-through of the speech she was due to deliver that evening, she enjoyed a soak in the bath with a glass of wine. She and Georgia chatted on the phone and agreed to go to their favourite pub by the river after work on Friday.

By the time Leah was due to go back to the venue for dinner, the knots in her shoulders were no more, and she felt pumped about giving her speech to an international audience. Having been out for dinner with many of them the previous evening, she felt more relaxed about addressing the vast dining hall.

At the drinks reception, she took a glass of champagne and headed over to the table plan which was displayed on a giant easel. Table One, she noted, was nearest to the kitchen, which should mean the first to be served food.

"You're on the top table with me," said Rahul.

"Great, you can tell me some more of your travelling tales," said Leah.

A thunderous gong sounded and the guests made their way into the dining hall. Elegant but subtle in its decoration, the hall's lights were on low which gave off an atmospheric ambience.

The waiting staff in their pristine whites arrived at Table One, and all stood behind their guest until receiving the nod from the team leader, an indication that, in unison, they should place the food on the table. Leah smiled, thanked her straight-faced serving-staff member, and turned her attention to the starter – smoked salmon mixed with fresh yogurt, dill and capers on top of crispy

117

potato skins. Whether it was hunger or nerves, Leah wolfed the plate of food down and then, waiting for what seemed like an eternity until the others on the table had finished, she excused herself and sped off to the toilets to make sure she looked respectable and didn't have any menacing greenery between her teeth. Right Leah, time to make a good impression.

She didn't have to wait long before the loudspeaker welcomed her to the stage. As she rose from her seat, a couple of noisy waiters emerged from the kitchen, looking flustered. They were quickly followed by one of the chefs, whose whites had seen better days. They were far louder than was acceptable, showing no respect for the dinner guests. Leah was about to give them a glare when she realised what the cacophony was all about. Smoke started to escape from the kitchen into the hall, followed by a stream of panicked-looking waiting and kitchen staff. Behind them, angry flames were rising up and reaching out in all directions. The dinner guests were ushered away from their tables and outside to safety. Leah stood mesmerized by the dancing sparks and had to be pulled away by a hotel staff member who couldn't quite believe how fast the situation was developing.

With clouds of smoke cascading out of the windows, alarmed hotel fire wardens gathered guests in the assembly areas, clinging on to their clipboards with intent. As often as they'd prepared for such an incident, they never thought that they'd actually experience it. With her back to the sea, Leah looked on in bewilderment, her mind and imagination running riot. Rahul joined her.

"What a bloody nightmare, so sad for everybody, but especially you Leah - you didn't get to make your speech, I was looking forward to it."

118

"Thanks Rahul, me too."

Rahul said good night, leaving Leah to her thoughts. She stood for a few minutes, watching the fearless firefighters go about their work whilst intrusive onlookers tried to get photos to impress their friends with on social media. Her stomach churned as she pushed a theory to the back of her mind, surely this couldn't be related to the other incidents; setting fire to a hotel is going over the top, why hurt other people and damage a property and why risk getting caught? Another fleeting thought went through her head, what if she'd been talking to her nemesis? What if she'd been out for dinner with them the day before?

Leah needed to hear a friendly voice, and fast, before her demons grew even more. She took out her phone and called Georgia, but to her disappointment it just rang out. She wrote a text instead. Fire at the venue, I'm OK, but call me when you can x She then sent another message. Can we meet pls? Almost instantly a reply came back. Casino in 10 mins?

***

Steve remained annoyed with Graham for being late and didn't buy his I fell asleep excuse, especially as he'd turned up at the hotel bar looking flushed and out of breath. Still, it gave Steve a chance to chat to the lovely barmaid, not as lovely as MJ but a close second. He'd asked her about good pubs and she suggested they go to the casino as it was open late and offered good deals on Wednesdays. When Graham finally arrived at the bar, he seemed up for it and said he fancied a game of poker.

As they entered the casino, Graham stopped dead and pulled Steve back. He pointed towards a roulette table where, amongst four guys, sat a woman with long, blonde hair. Standing behind her lingered a face that had plagued

119

him over recent weeks. He watched as Leah placed her hands on the woman's shoulders, giving them an intermittent squeeze. She leant down, whispered something in the blonde's ear and gave her a kiss on the back of the head. Without turning around, the blonde moved her hand away from the chips and gave Leah's hand a stroke. "Shit the bed, look, that's the bitch who's fucking my wife."

"Bloody hell! Who's she with though, that's not Georgia is it, unless she's dyed her hair and lightened her skin?" said Steve.

"Bet she's doing that piece as well."

Sensing that Graham could cause a scene, Steve suggested they went somewhere else as they should still be able to make last orders, just. Graham didn't argue and left the casino looking dumbfounded, shaking his head and verbalising obscenities as he went, with every third word being bitch.

***

Leah moved away to the bar, where she propped herself up on a stool and ordered a bottle of Bud and chatted to the barmaid. "I can't watch," said Leah. "My sister is about to blow all of her chips on her lucky number 17." She distracted herself by looking at her phone and saw a couple of missed calls from Georgia, so sent her a quick text back saying that she'd hooked up with her sister but would call later.

"If that's her walking over here, I'd say from the look on her face that the premonition was right," said the barmaid, nodding towards Leah's sister, Jo.

"We did it ..."

"You ... are ... kidding!" said Leah.

120

Jo moved the Bud away from her sister and ordered a bottle of Moet. "So, what else is on your mind? I can read you like a book you know, even your text messages."

"Where do I start?" said Leah. "I'll cut to the chase; I think someone is out to get me." She told her sister about the string of recent events but, in the process, again found herself thinking that some of things sounded insignificant and trivial.

"Leah, the note is probably from a jealous rival just seeing if they can spook you, and the forgetfulness could be your age … didn't mum reach the menopause in her 40s?"

Strange that Jo mentioned the menopause, as it had crossed her mind. Saying things out loud to her sister did make Leah question herself. Maybe her memory was deteriorating, or perhaps she was just struggling to cope with running her company as well as taking on the new role. But the system error surely wasn't down to her; and what about earlier, the fire breaking out resulting in her speech being cancelled.

"Just wait, you'll be in your 40s in a few years, and then I'll take the piss out of you and your forgetfulness," said Leah deciding she'd put things behind her for now and enjoy sharing some laughter with her younger sister, not to mention helping her spend the roulette winnings.

Chapter 26

At the Eagle, despite a couple of manic hours early on, business had been slow, which enabled MJ and Polly to catch up on the gossip with each other.

"I'm glad that tosspot Graham isn't around, he does my head in," Polly said. "Did you know he wrote a crappy limerick about me?"

"No good then?" asked MJ.

Polly avoided answering, but raised her eyebrows, "I guess you're next on his hit list, so brace yourself."

At 10:50, Polly headed down to the cellar to collect the required bottles to restock the fridges. MJ rang the bell for last orders and watched as the last of the punters headed out of the pub. Some would be going home to an empty bedsit, others would visit their secret lovers, whilst some would have to care for an elderly parent. MJ often wished she could attach a tiny webcam to every customer to see if the picture she painted of them reflected the truth. The door opened and Andy walked in. Ah-ha, she thought to herself, he's someone else who interests me.

"Hey, you're just in time. Peroni?"

"Is the Pope Catholic?" said Andy.

With the fridges restocked, tables wiped down and chairs put up, Polly said her goodbyes and MJ joined Andy and Alex at the bar.

"Where's the boss tonight?" asked Andy.

"Gone down to the South Coast with one of the regulars to pick up some football stuff for the pub," said MJ.

"Yep, so I'm allowed to throw you out if you get rowdy," said Alex getting up to lock the front door.

MJ let Roxy out, who followed her usual routine of walking around the tables, sniffing out any discarded crisps, hoping for a dropped piece of sausage or pork crackling.

Andy stayed put and watched as MJ went behind the bar and began pouring him another drink.

"So, MJ, tell us more about your recent date?" asked Alex. MJ looked up and glared at him, she didn't want her love life broadcast, especially not in front of Andy. He looked taken aback.

"Aye, aye," he said, cursing himself for sounding like Anne-Marie again.

"Some Asian prince, who works for a ticketing company," said Alex.

"Does the lucky man have a name?" asked Andy.

"Hakim."

"Not Hakim Kahn?" Andy asked, his eyes widening.

"Yeah, why, do you know him?"

"Well, there can't be too many Hakims in London who work for ticketing companies, surely! Does he support Liverpool?"

"Yep."

"And did you go out with him a couple of Wednesdays ago?"

"Er yeah, why?"

"A few of us planned to watch the Europa league final together but he blew us out saying that something had come up."

Alex screwed up his face. "Makes you sound like his lunch."

"Very funny," said MJ, wondering why Hakim hadn't just said that he was going on a date. Rather than quizzing Andy about Hakim, a penny dropped in MJ's mind. "Is someone called Leah his boss?"

"Yeah, she's more than his boss though, she owns the company."

123

The three of them sat motionless at the bar taking in a rare moment of quiet. MJ then noticed a couple of messages on her phone. The first one, coincidentally was from Hakim, saying that he made a mistake about the theatre, it wasn't 13th June but 13th July. Oh well, she thought, that's not too long to wait, although she hoped she'd see him before then.

The second was from Steve, which she read aloud. *Just clocked the girlfriend in the casino, Graham's fuming. Hope all ok in the pub?*

MJ, sensing Andy's confusion, explained that the girlfriend is Leah – Hakim's boss.

"Sounds entertaining," said Alex. "Wonder what she's doing in Brighton … picking up women?"

Andy waved his finger, "Nope, there was some global tourism conference down there this week; she'd be there for that."

Was it more than a coincidence that Graham happened to be in Brighton at the same time as Leah? MJ pushed the idea to the back of her mind, as Steve instigated the trip and not Graham. Andy interrupted her thoughts.

"How did your date go with Hakim? Have you seen him again?"

MJ felt awkward. "Fine, haven't seen him since though, says he's busy at work."

"Yeah, that's true about work, sounds like their entire booking system went down, which for a company who relies on API connections is a pretty major deal."

MJ looked at Alex who turned to Andy. "Sorry, what are API connections when they're at home?"

Andy took a deep breath and explained about how they allow ticketing systems to speak with each other, and check for live availability for tickets on a particular day, time and even choice of seat. Customers can make bookings from anywhere in the world. "Global Tickets are completely screwed if they're having a problem with the API," said Andy.

Alex looked at MJ. "Imagine if customers from New York could order a Guinness and Strongbow for 2pm on Monday and the beer tap would automatically pour the drink at that exact time; you'd be out of a job."

"Scary thought," said MJ, but she was still thinking about Hakim working for Leah, "What do you think of her?"

"Who?" said Andy tilting his head quizzically.

"Leah."

"Leah, yeah, she's alright. I've taken a liking to her; she's clever and very quick-witted. Hakim says she's a cool boss as well, treats everyone as individuals and welcomes their ideas and suggestions however bizarre they may be. That's maybe why she's so successful, she takes chances."

"Your boss doesn't like her though, does she?" said Alex, "She came in the other day mouthing off about her."

"Is that when the news came out about Leah getting the role? Yeah, she really wasn't happy, that's for sure."

"But why doesn't she like her? I thought women stuck together in business?" asked Alex.

"No idea, but I think it could be personal," said Andy giving his pint glass a shake.

MJ looked at Alex and then at the clock.

"OK, one more and then we'll call it a night; we've still got to cash up and the dog needs her W-A-L-K," said Alex, deliberately spelling out the word to prevent a frenzy of tail wagging and barking. He poured Andy another Peroni, and MJ a vodka and coke, before getting himself a Bud from the fridge and making a note of the drinks in Steve's book.

MJ, like a dog with a bone, probed Andy some more. "What do you know about her personal life?"

"Are we still talking about Leah?" said Andy.

"Fess up MJ, you fancy her, don't you?" said Alex.

"I've never even met the woman. I'm just interested, that's all – Hakim works for her and one of our regulars found out that his wife is having an affair with her."

"Sounds like you know more about her than me. How did he find out?" said Andy.

"According to Steve, Robin, that older guy who's been in a few times, showed him a photo of Leah celebrating with her work colleagues and Georgia was next to her."

"Georgia, being Graham's wife?" asked Andy.

"Yep, you got it Sherlock," said Alex.

Andy made eye contact with MJ, before taking out his phone. "Let's have a look, it's probably on social." He tapped and scrolled, tapped and scrolled some more, "Nothing, not a thing, well just this official headshot of her and few images from her in the past, one with Anders, who she set up the company with, and one of her receiving a special award from Apple."

"Gwyneth Paltrow's daughter?" said Alex, the attempt at humour going straight over MJ's head.

"No, you goose, she worked for Apple, you know the tech giant."

"Shit … but look at this!" said Andy, getting up and moving between Alex and MJ to show them the Twitter feed. *Suspected arson attack interrupts international tourism conference at Brighton's Hilton Metropole Hotel.*

"I hope it wasn't Graham," said Alex, but neither Andy nor MJ laughed.

Chapter 27

Leah and Georgia had arranged to have dinner at their favourite pub by the river. The evening sun glowed over the Thames creating a haziness above it. Georgia managed to get a table in her preferred corner spot overlooking the river with a view of everyone outside; she liked to keep an eye on people and see if anyone was gossiping about her.

Despite being with Leah for a number of months, she still didn't feel 100 per cent comfortable being out and open about their relationship. When they were alone, there were no concerns, and her body didn't object to being intimate with another woman's. However, in public, her head and body weren't in sync, and she found it difficult to relax when she sensed Leah's hands about to caress her back or her light breath advancing on her neck. It made her feel nervous and she imagined hundreds of disapproving eyes looking at her. In reality, nobody gave two hoots about her and were more interested in their own love lives, arguments or family problems. She was getting better though and hoped it wouldn't be too long before she could behave with Leah in the same way as she did with Graham.

Her mind then drifted towards Graham's Jekyll and Hyde type of behaviour, aggression turning to self-loathing, turning to craving love and attention. She used to dread him coming anywhere near her after his aggressive outbursts; how could he be so nasty and spiteful one minute and want to ravish her body the next. It made no sense to Georgia. Fingers crossed, so far with Leah she'd seen no significant mood swings or personality changes, impressive considering what she'd gone through over the last few months … campaigning, debating, becoming Chief

Tourism Director, at the same time as running her own successful business. Even with the recent tech problems, she had remained positive and still made time for Georgia, even if she did always turn up late. Today, it was nearly forty-five minutes, which meant that Georgia was already on her second large glass of Sauvignon. Leah waltzed across the beer yard smiling that booming smile and flashing her deep, dark eyes, making Georgia's heart melt and forget, for a millisecond, that she'd soon be leaning over her and kissing her, changing the melting heart to a freezing up one.

"I'm so sorry, the tech experts have been in."

Georgia smiled, knowing Leah always spent a while getting her workday off her chest before she could relax.

"It's fine; the sun's out and I have a glass of wine. Anyway, how did they get on, do you know what happened yet?"

"They were there all afternoon and say it looks like a professional job. It's a complete mess."

"Shit, Leah, I'm sorry, is it something you can sort out easily?"

"I wouldn't say easily, but I have a great team around me who have been working 24/7 to get it sorted. They've made a lot of progress but, in the meantime, the sales team are having to make bookings manually. M a n u a l l y ... I mean we haven't done that since the 90s."

Leah had been trying to grab the waiter's attention whilst she spoke, but failed miserably, so she stood up. "I'll go into the bar – it will be quicker."

"Before you go, can you just sit down for a second, I need to tell you something."

"Sure, what's up?"

"Well, you know it's been hard for me to talk about my past ... well, I'm ready to tell you now."

Leah took Georgia's hands and gave them a squeeze. "I'm listening, George."

Calmness went out of the window and she just blurted out the words festering in her mouth. "I've never been in a relationship with a woman before, and I'm married, well, technically, anyway."

Leah sat motionless, staring at Georgia, not saying anything. Then, a small grin grew at the corner of her mouth, breaking into a full smile, "Don't worry, I already knew! And it doesn't change a thing, I think it might make me love you even more, if that's possible?"

Georgia tried to speak but no words came out. She drank a gulp of wine. "How did you know?"

"I'm very perceptive, it's one of the reasons I am where I am today. I can also tell that you've already put away a few glasses of wine and need some food, am I right?"

"You know my body too well," Georgia said, with relief.

"Sure do, inside and out."

Chapter 28

Andy said goodbye to his colleagues and left the pub just after 9:15, feeling smug that he'd resisted staying for another round of shots. He had been in the pub since 5pm, though, and consumed four pints as well as two sambucas, so knew he shouldn't be feeling holier-than-thou. Still, with his flat mate working nights, he'd be able to cook himself a half decent meal and would make enough for Phil to have whenever he returned home. Pasta and lots of it if he was cooking for Phil, who had the metabolism of a 12-year-old. As he walked to Victoria Station, he made a mental note of what he needed from the shop but, as he turned the corner to go into the station, he saw crowds gathering outside the Apollo Theatre. He frowned and checked his watch, 9:25pm, way too early for the theatre to be emptying out, it must be a fire alarm.

Unknown to Andy, inside the theatre a tsunami of confusion and chaos washed through the auditorium. The interval had started like any other, some people rushed to the toilets whilst others queued for ice creams, lots of mobile phones were turned on and messages checked, just like any other night. The five-minute warning bell sounded and people started making their way back to their seats. The green witch emerged onto the stage, just as she always did after the interval, and broke into song with the majestic orchestra accompanying her dancing around the brightly decorated stage. The cymbals became louder, and a deep rhythmic drumming started to crescendo. All of a sudden, several loud shots, one after another, could be heard, the audience gasped as the witch fell to the ground with a small eruption of blood coming out of her temple.

"That didn't happen last time," whispered one woman to her husband. He turned his head to her and spoke in a low voice, "Looked pretty real though."

It didn't take long, for people to realise that one of the ushers was lying on the floor near the emergency exit, with blood pouring out of her chest.

"She's been shot!" someone cried.

There was screaming, and people started running towards the exits.

"Help!" shouted a middle-aged man in a suit, as he crouched over the usher's body, trying to stem the flow of blood.

Panic started to take hold and a crowd formed around the usher, whilst others rushed past not giving the dying woman a second glance. Not knowing where they'd emerge, groups of the audience started to climb the several flights of concrete stairs until they reached a large green door and pushed down the metal bar before fleeing to safety. They burst out into the street, much to the surprise of the punters enjoying their drinks outside Wetherspoons. More and more people raced out of the emergency door and onto the street, scattering in different directions; some went into the pub, others ran towards the tube station and some just crouched down in bewilderment.

Andy froze, unable to take in what was happening, when his eyes were drawn to a teenage girl who ran out into the road, her auburn hair striking as it glistened against the streetlight. He felt a silent scream form in his throat as he realised that her auburn hair was indeed red, because her skull had been shattered by a bullet. The girl collapsed, her dead weight causing her to thud onto the road. There was more screaming, as a passer-by spotted her body. A small group knelt with the teenage girl doing what they could to help, but it was no good – life gradually ebbed out of her body.

Andy stepped out into the road bewildered, as several police cars and an ambulance screeched past, almost knocking him down. By now his heart rate had increased to a ridiculous level and his adrenalin pumped like mad. Not knowing what to do, he stood motionless as he watched well-drilled police officers clear the area and put up blue and white crime scene tape as more and more emergency service vehicles arrived, their sirens excruciating. Andy began running towards the tube station, eager to get away but, as he got near, he saw an armed officer blocking the doorway. In a fluster, he turned and began running in the other direction, away from the crime scene. Why was he running and why did he feel so panicked? He needed something to settle his nerves.

***

Anne-Marie had been in the Eagle for just over half an hour and was standing at the bar when Andy walked in looking as white as a sheet. "Dear Lord, Andrew, what the hell has happened to you?"

"Something's happened at the Apollo, it looks bad." Andy described what he'd seen and had the attention of everyone at the bar.

Steve called over, "Mate, sit down, I'll get you a drink before you pass out."

Anne-Marie pulled out a stool and guided Andy onto it. "He'll have a whisky. Make it large."

Steve put the whisky in front of Andy and then checked his phone for any news about the incident. There were two WhatsApp messages, one from the local pub cluster group, and the other from the police group forum. The

132

message on both gave the same brief statement.
Suspected shooting at Apollo Theatre, stay vigilant.

Chapter 29

Georgia blushed, a happy and in love kind of blush. By the time they'd finished the second bottle and eaten a couple of juicy burgers, she lay back in Leah's arms and conversation moved away from work. Her inhibitions became neutralised by the alcohol and she no longer minded Leah's hand touching her bare skin or her lips making contact with the back of her neck; in fact, she couldn't get enough of her.

Just as they were about to kiss, Leah's phone buzzed; she swiped to the left and turned back to Georgia, but the phone started ringing again. "Sorry, I better take this." She stood up and made her way out of the yard to hear more clearly. "No no no, shit, how many?" It was Anders, her co-director. He told her about the suspected shooting at the theatre and the reports that at least three people had been killed, including one of the actors. Leah went back to Georgia. "George, we have to go."

Georgia turned around and, by the look on Leah's face, she knew it must be bad.

***

They exited Turnham Green Station and headed towards Chiswick High Road, unable to comprehend what had happened.

"I think we need another drink; I'll pop into Sainsbury's. Is there anything else we need?" Georgia asked.

"A bottle of red would be nice, oh and I think we need milk too. I'll head home and open the windows to get some air in the place, see you in a minute."

Georgia turned and headed towards the shop. It was a lovely evening, which seemed to be reflected in people's moods, as she only saw happy faces. It seemed a world away from what had happened back in the West End. She flashed them a smile and then she thought of Leah having to face what seemed like problem after problem at the moment. Browsing the wine shelf, she contemplated an expensive bottle of French vs a cheaper New World. Better stick to something I know Leah likes, she thought, and she deserves something nice. As she stood in the queue, she listened to the local radio station playing in the background as the 11pm news began. The shooting at the theatre dominated the headlines. Georgia only heard the opening line At the Apollo Theatre... before something clicked in her head and she took out her phone and started to text Leah.

"Excuse me, miss?" said the shop assistant trying to get Georgia's attention.

"Oh sorry," said Georgia, leaving the message in the drafts folder and putting the phone back in her pocket; she'd just have to tell Leah when she got home. Declining the offer of a plastic bag, Georgia carried the 2pint milk bottle in her left hand and the bottle of wine in her right. She reached the zebra crossing, checked both ways and stepped out. Out of nowhere came a pair of blinding headlights. They continued at speed and took Georgia out with one sweeping movement and continued off into the distance. Like a gymnast carrying out a complicated dismount, Georgia's body turned and flipped before landing with a slap and a crack on the road. The milk and wine hit the road a nanosecond afterwards and shattered, the red and white liquids flowing into each other creating a stream which resembled melted raspberry ripple ice-cream. The flow thickened as body tissue and slithers of bone joined and created tributaries making their way down to the curbside.

Back at Vernon Close, Leah opened the kitchen cabinet door and took out a couple of red wine glasses. She glanced at the front door and then at the clock. The phone rang and, without looking at the screen, she answered it. "What's keeping you? Don't tell me they've run out of wine?" But it wasn't Georgia, it was someone from a radio news channel, whose first name she didn't quite get. He asked for her comments on tonight's theatre shooting. She was about to tell him to do one, but the sound of sirens nearby stopped her mid flow.

"Hello, Ms Pope? Do you think that theatres are safe, or do you think the killer's still out there?"

Leah's heart rate started to gallop as she heard his words being repeated over and over again, do you think the killer is still out there, the killer … killer still out there, killer …

The sirens were getting louder. Without closing the door behind her, she walked out of the house like a zombie, phone still connected and in hand, and followed the sirens. As she turned the corner, carnage covered the road, set out like a stage in front of her, featuring flashing lights, dramatic noises and a cacophony of voices. Her stomach twisted, impulse took over, and she ran, screaming Georgia's name, into the middle of the main scene. Police and paramedics turned as they heard her wailing scream and tried to stop her, but she couldn't hear or feel them. She kept on trying to run, she needed to get to Georgia, but she seemed to be getting further away with every step. With her energy sapped, she finally slumped down on her knees, hands over her head. She wanted to sink far, far away and only emerge when she was back in her bed with Georgia.

A member of ambulance staff moved her away to the side of the road, where a young officer managed to coax her into a nearby café. The policeman sat Leah down with her back to the window and encouraged her to lift her head, so he could talk to her face to face. Leah found some inner strength and looked up just as the officer was joined by an authoritative looking woman who introduced herself as DI Madeline Johnson.

"It's my partner, isn't it? She's dead, isn't she?"

"I'm sorry, Miss ..." began DI Johnson.

"Call me Leah."

"I'm sorry Leah, we haven't made a formal identification yet."

***

The reporter couldn't believe his luck that the phone remained connected; he had heard everything and couldn't wait to break the news. Whenever he called for a quote or comment, he'd record the conversation and tonight was no exception. He ran the call again, summarising the conversation before emailing it on to the senior editor. This should move me up the ranks, he thought. His phone rang just five minutes later.

"Good work Jamie, we're running the story on the midnight bulletin."

Jamie sat in his front room, turned on the radio and waited. As it approached the hour, the three beeps rang out and the brief news jingle played.

Good evening and welcome to the news at midnight. Just hours after a fatal shooting at one of London's top theatres, the partner of the newly appointed Chief Tourism Director, Leah Pope, is reported to have been killed in a hit and run incident. Our reporter on the scene described the incident as targeted and callous. We'll bring you further details when we have them...

The radio played in the café, too. DI Johnson looked at Leah, whose mouth gaped in disbelief. She held up her phone, realising what had happened before pushing it away from her and sliding it across the table into the lap of the DI.

"I hadn't turned it off," said Leah. "I received a call from a reporter moments before the accident."

DI Johnson excused herself and went outside, beckoning over a colleague from the crime scene and handing him a piece of paper with a phone number on. "Get on to the vermin at this radio station and find out whose number this belongs to; tell them if they mention Leah's name again, there will be major consequences."

"Yes, Ma'am."

DI Johnson returned to the café and assured Leah that her name wouldn't be mentioned again. She asked if Leah had anyone that could come and stay with her, and then requested the police officer take her back home saying that she'd join them soon.

Anders, reliable as ever, arrived within the hour. DI Johnson let him into the kitchen and talked in a low voice. "Needless to say, she's in a bad way, so I thought it better if someone could stay with her."

"No problem," said Anders looking over with concern at the curled-up ball of a human on the sofa. "What happened?"

"Hit and run by the looks of it, the team will be checking through CCTV later, but reports from witnesses say that a car came speeding along the road, didn't attempt to slow down and sent the poor woman flying high into the sky; she didn't stand a chance."

"Did Leah see it happen?"

"No, I don't think so, but the way she's reacting I'd say she arrived before the body was covered, so she would've witnessed her girlfriend's body in bloody pieces."

***

Leah felt removed and empty, she couldn't formulate logical thoughts in her brain. Was she perhaps the one who had been killed and not Georgia? The light felt bright, and she could sense she was floating, was this how people felt when they were about to enter heaven? She wanted to go through those towering golden gates, she wanted them to open for her to walk through. Where were the fluffy clouds? Why couldn't she see angels? And why could she hear Anders nearby? And who was the other person with Anders? Was it Georgia? Yes, yes, it must be. She took a long deep breath and rubbed her eyes. Maybe she'd been drugged? She urged her brain to work … she was in the pub with Georgia, they'd been drinking wine and then she remembered receiving a phone call. A killer. Someone called and asked if the killer was still out there. The words, the information swam around in her brain, she couldn't cope, what was happening to her. She felt sick.

Anders and the DI rushed over to Leah, Anders with a bin and the DI with a glass of water. They consoled her like parents of a drunk teenager, one rubbing her back and the other saying that everything would be OK. After the sickness, came an angry outburst, which morphed into sad wailing, followed by an onslaught of tears that seemed never-ending. The thirty-minute episode left Leah drained in every way. Anders found a light blanket and draped it over her, stroking her head before giving her a heartfelt kiss. He told his family he wouldn't be back that night, and they were 100 per cent supportive. His wife knew Leah from the early days and had enormous respect for her. She told Anders to stay with her for as long as it took.

DI Johnson watched on in sympathy. She'd seen a lot of grieving families, but for some reason, she felt real empathy for this woman. But right now, she had a job to do, and it was a relief when the emotional episode subsided, and Anders returned to the kitchen and sat himself down on a stool at the breakfast bar. "I won't take much of your time, but I need to establish what's going on here."

"Ask me anything, I want this scumbag caught as well," said Anders.

The DI went through the usual questions and started to formulate a picture in her head. She couldn't help thinking that the victim here could be Leah herself, especially given the recent system bug and that night's theatre shooting. Without doubt though, the first person that needed to be questioned was the husband of the deceased. She'd see to that personally in the morning.

Chapter 30

The racket from next door's kids seemed to start earlier and earlier every day. Not just the kids either, the parents seemed to have voices as loud as fog horns too. The kids would do something wrong and they'd get yelled at by the parents, the kids would yell back louder, which would prompt the parents to go in a decibel higher. If he wanted to start bringing women back, they wouldn't stay long if the neighbours continued like this. Not that he wanted anyone to make themselves at home quite yet though; he wanted to play around and have some fun first before he could contemplate having someone permanent in his life again.

Brighton proved to be a great deal of fun, to begin with anyway – he had paid for a prostitute to come to his hotel room for a couple of hours of pleasure. Maybe he should've told Steve, but he didn't want any disapproval to ruin the evening, although that blonde bitch in the casino managed to ruin it anyway. He should tell Georgia what he saw – she had a right to know. He should send her a text message and ask to see her, perhaps she could come to the house on the premise of picking up some of her things.

As he reached for his phone, he heard a tremendous bang from next door and imagined one of the kids being given flying lessons off the top bunk. Then he heard a knock at the door, followed by a ring on his doorbell. Maybe the neighbour was coming round to say they'd killed one of the kids ... or perhaps the other way round. He pulled on a Budweiser t-shirt over his boxer shorts and went downstairs to the front door. Not bothering to check first, he opened the door to a couple of formal looking figures.

141

The first a tall, slim man in his 30s with a receding hairline, and the other a tanned woman, her hair unkempt but wearing a smart tailored trouser suit.

"Mr Graham Fisher?" said the woman as she flashed her police badge. "Can we come in please sir?"

Shit, what was this about, perhaps they knew about the limerick or, maybe the bitch had a camera on her house, like Steve said, but why come so early? "Yes, that's right, please come in."

"Thank you, sir."

Graham led them into the lounge and offered them a drink, wondering where the sudden manners came from. "What's all this about?"

"Can you confirm your relationship with Georgia Asher?"

Without hesitating, he said, "She's my wife, and she's called Georgia Fisher, Asher is her maiden name."

"I'm sorry to inform you Mr Fisher that your wife was involved in a hit and run accident late last night and was killed on impact."

Graham opened his mouth, but nothing came out, not even an expletive. He looked at his phone, he had just been about to text her, the message was still on the screen.

"Mr Fisher, do you understand what my colleague has just told you?" said the male officer.

"I ... er... um ... so you're telling me that my Georgia is dead?"

"As far as I understand it Mr Fisher, she was no longer your Georgia, was she?" said the DI. "Hadn't you two separated?"

Graham's face started to redden, what does she mean she wasn't my Georgia, what sort of insensitive comment is that, he thought to himself. Who does this woman think she is talking to me like that?

"Mr Fisher, where were you last night between the hours of 8pm and midnight?"

"I was here."

"Anyone else with you?"

"No, as you pointed out, my wife has left me." He didn't like this woman one little bit, asking him questions like that, it's his business who he invites into his house, not hers. Then the penny dropped, were they implying that he had something to do with her being killed? He'd have knocked over that bitch Leah without a second thought, but not his Georgia, and she was still his Georgia whatever they said. Tears started to build up, but he fought them back.

"Can you think of anyone who would want to hurt your wife?" the officer asked.

"No, she didn't have any enemies."

"What happened when she left you, Graham, were you angry?"

He wanted to yell and shout, hurl obscenities, but he knew that wasn't going to help his case. He tried to remain civil. He wanted these pigs out of his house as soon as possible. "I was upset and angry, yes, wouldn't you be? She left me for a woman, which in my eyes, as a man, is the ultimate insult."

"Have you ever wanted to get revenge on her?"

"Yes and no, but I'd never hurt her, she was the love of my life and as much as I hate her for what she did to me, there's no way I'd lay a finger on her, do you understand?"

"Thank you for your time, Mr Fisher, I'm sure we'll be back to speak to you again."

"Sorry for your loss," said the PC.

Graham shut the door and slid down to his knees with his back against the door and sobbed.

143

Chapter 31

MJ spent the previous evening at home and watched the story unfold both on TV and on social media channels. Shortly after the news broke, she received a call from her dad, checking she was OK. She reassured him that she was safe and sound, lounging around on her sofa eating popcorn. The minute she put the phone down it started ringing again, this time it was her sister checking up on her. At least she knew her family cared.

Later on, she headed over to the pub, slowing to a snail's pace as she neared the theatre. Although not directly en route, she went past the crime scene but there wasn't a great deal to see, just blue and white crime scene tape cornering off the entrance to the theatre, and also some barriers and a tent in the middle of the road. There was still a large number of police officers though.

She knocked on the front door of the pub and heard Roxy bark and come bounding to the door. The dog rested her long front legs on the windowsill and flashed her sharp teeth. A definite deterrent for anyone who didn't know the soppy hound was more likely to wash your face than bite it. Steve appeared, and as usual had a tool in his hand, this time a hammer. He opened the door and Roxy bounded out to greet MJ before running around in a circle and going back into the pub again, disappointed that it wasn't a new person to lick.

"I don't know who looks more menacing, Roxy flashing her sharp fangs or you with that hammer."

"Well, after last night's shooting, I hope we both do."

"Yeah, I watched it on the news, do you reckon it's terrorist related?"

"Dunno, could be. Your mate Andy saw the immediate aftermath though, walked in here looking like he'd seen a ghost, poor lad."

"Really? He wasn't at the theatre though, was he?"

"No, but I think one of the victims managed to get out then collapsed in the road, her skull was shattered by a bullet. Andy saw her!"

"Jesus, poor guy."

MJ and Steve set up the pub and then sat down with a couple of bacon sandwiches. They'd just taken a bite, when Roxy's ears pricked up and she ran to the front door.

"Postman?" said MJ hopping down from her stool.

"Wait," said Steve, "let me." He took his hammer and looked over at MJ smiling, "Just in case." The hammer wasn't required though … it was just Graham.

"Great timing, mate." Steve walked back to his stool and continued to munch on his breakfast, with MJ noticing that Graham's face looked completely void of colour.

"Big one last night Gra? You look like death warmed up."

"It's Georgia, she's dead!!"

Both Steve and MJ stopped mid mouthful, their butties destined not to be finished.

"What? No? How come?" asked Steve.

"Hit and run, she didn't stand a chance."

MJ took the half-eaten sandwiches back to the kitchen before going behind the bar and getting Graham a pint.

"What did the police say? Do they have any idea who did it?" asked Steve.

"The fuckers were at mine first thing this morning questioning me, looks like I'm their number one suspect."

"That's bollocks mate, you may be a twat with a bad temper, but you'd never kill anyone let alone someone you used to love."

Say it how it is, thought MJ busying herself behind the bar leaving Graham to talk to Steve. What a night, first the shooting and then the hit and run. Despite finding out that Andy witnessed the aftermath of the shooting, she thought it only right, given their in-depth discussion a few days earlier, that she let him know what had happened to Georgia.

***

Andy watched as the teenage girl walked towards him with a gaping hole in the side of her face, she tried to say something to him, but he couldn't decipher what. She smiled and put her fingers through her dark curls, which came away from her head and turned to red liquid. She raised her other hand and repeated the process, but this time a part of her scalp came away, then flowed red. She continued trying to say something to him, but he still couldn't hear, so he called out to her.

Phil opened the bedroom door and saw his flat mate sat bolt upright in bed, dripping with sweat and calling out something incomprehensible. Phil had taken part in numerous courses over the years working for the MET, including how to recognise and understand PTSD. Sleep disturbances or the inability to sleep were key indicators that someone was suffering and, given what Andy witnessed outside the theatre, it was fully understandable.

Andy appeared in the doorway looking like he'd just come back from a twenty-four-hour bender – red eyes, rough stubble and dishevelled hair. His white t-shirt was tie dyed with sweat marks and Phil thought there was an unsavoury smell coming from his room.

"I can't get the image out of my head, every time I close my eyes, I see the girl, her face and skull are disintegrating right in front of me."

Phil, grateful that Andy acknowledged what he was experiencing, gestured for his flatmate to sit down on the sofa, "Do you want a tea?"

Chapter 32

Anne-Marie received a call from the hospital advising that her mum's health had taken a turn for the worse overnight and they didn't expect her to make the next twelve hours. Over the last couple of weeks, Anne-Marie watched her mum become weaker and weaker, but taking the call from the nurse, still hurt in the pit of her stomach. She phoned her brothers. Two of them lived with their families overseas, so she didn't expect them to travel over but she hoped her youngest sibling, Gareth, would be able to drive down straight away as she knew things were near the end. She then sent a brief message to her senior director, as well as Andy, letting them know that her mother's death was imminent and that she would be off work for the next few days.

Anne-Marie left her house and tried to figure out where she'd left the car the evening before. "For fuck's sake woman, where did you park?" she reprimanded herself, much to the amusement of an early morning dog walker. After walking along a couple of adjacent streets, she saw the little red rust bucket. "There you are," she said as if talking to missing cat.

It was a short fifteen-minute drive from Ealing to West Mid Hospital. Driving over to her mum's warden-assisted housing in Strawberry Hill most Sundays, she'd pass West Mid Hospital and wonder whether she would end up there one day. It never crossed her mind that her mum's life would end there. At the car park, she argued with the ticket machine, this time shouting at it, "You fucking tell me how long my mum is going to stay alive for, stupid machine." She put in ten pounds worth of pound coins which she'd robbed from her piggy bank and shouted back at the machine, "If she dies in less than six hours, I want my money back."

A stillness surrounded the ward, a sign that she'd even beaten the breakfast trolley making its way around the wards distributing soggy toast and tepid tea.

The usual ward nurse appeared and offered a compassionate smile to Anne-Marie. "Come through, she's in no pain at all, but her vital organs are all slowing down, so she's entering the final part of her journey."

Anne-Marie blinked away the tears as she saw her mum, a fraction of the woman she was a few months ago when she'd been admitted, lying there, old and frail. She agreed with the nurse though, her mum looked comfortable and not in any pain. Anne-Marie did what she always did, she sat next to her on the bed, held her hand and talked to her in a soft voice. On feeling Anne-Marie's warm hands, her mum's head turned and locked eyes with her daughter. She opened her mouth and, barely audible, came the words no more grudges followed by the name, Leah.

She drifted back off to sleep and Anne-Marie wondered if that was it, game over, but a glance towards the machines told her that life still existed. The door opened and in walked her brother Gareth. "That was fucking quick."

"I've been working near Heathrow, how is the old bird?"

"Clinging on to life, she'll be pleased to see you."

Gareth went around the bed and sat down. Each of them took a hand and began stroking their mother's wrinkled skin. Her eyes flickered open and went from Anne-Marie to Gareth, she tried to talk but just managed the word love before her eyes closed again and her body relaxed. Then came the long dull sound from the machine, the sound of life ending.

The nurse waited outside and offered her arms for a hug, which Anne-Marie accepted with vigour, nearly crushing the poor woman. Not being released, the squashed nurse rasped, "she was waiting to see you before she went, she wanted to tell you something."

"Aye, that she did my dear," said Anne-Marie.

Chapter 33

Anne-Marie woke the next morning with a sense of sadness, as it dawned on her that she had watched her mum's life slip away less than twenty-four hours ago. As usual, she knew she would be the one left to pick up the pieces, organise the funeral and sort out the will. That would wait for now though, she needed to look for something, but first things first, her stomach needed to be fed and watered. She wished she could be like the people on TV who always lost their appetite at the first sign of grief or adversity. Anne-Marie took great comfort in food, regardless of which emotional journey she was on. Food hadn't always been a comfort though. As a child, eating was just something she did three times a day, but before long she found herself cooking meals too. By the age of nine, she could peel potatoes like a pro, not to mention slicing carrots and making gravy. In fact, before she left primary school, she took responsibility for making the Sunday roast. Her body remained small and wiry until late on in her teenage years; she often stood in front of the bathroom mirror and wondered whether puberty even existed. Looking back now, it was only after she failed her degree that she took any pleasure from eating and when she did, her body started to change, as if her hormones were playing a ten year catch up game.

The impressive American style fridge looked out of place in the small galley kitchen, but Anne-Marie insisted on getting it, even though the builder had to remove a whole kitchen unit in order to accommodate it. She peered into its vast space and examined the contents of the assorted plastic containers, like a scientist checking out their Petri dishes. The spaghetti bolognese looked good, but even for her it felt a bit early to be having pasta. The last container to be opened featured a pair of handsome looking sausages. Anne-Marie licked her lips and took out the container. She remembered cooking them a couple of days ago, so they'd just need a quick heat up in the microwave. She moved over to the bread bin to see what carbohydrate delight she could wedge the sausages between. Ahhh, perfect, a large chunk of a semi-fresh-looking baguette would do nicely, she thought reaching to turn the digital radio on.

The clock showed 08:58, which meant the news should be coming on any minute. Perhaps there would be an update on the theatre shooting, the tourism industry could do with another terrorist attack like a hole in the head, so she rather hoped that a delusional actor, wanting to make a name for themselves, was responsible. *It's been five days since the theatre shooting …*
Has it been that long, thought Anne-Marie realising that she'd been so caught up with her mum that she hadn't engaged with any media in the last few days. The news reader continued, *Police are saying that whilst they're not ruling out terrorism, they do think there's a connection with the hit and run incident that took place in Chiswick the same night.*
"What the f …?" said Anne-Marie.
The police are continuing to investigate the accident which resulted in the instant death of a 39-year-old woman. The victim's partner is said to be helping police with their enquiries as there have been a string of other possible related incidents targeting the successful businesswoman who owns a major ticketing company.
"Leah fuckin Pope!!" said Anne-Marie, looking up to the ceiling. For the first time in her adult life, Anne-Marie pushed her plate of food to one side, her appetite lost.

152

She opened a cupboard and pulled out a large cardboard box with 'UNI' written on the top in red pen. Back at the tiny kitchen table she opened it. She knew exactly what she was looking for; a VHS tape, 180 minutes still in a pristine plastic case. It was lying underneath the bright yellow leavers t-shirt. She clicked open the lid and removed the tape. The yellow rectangular sticker displayed the text Tangled Up in Blue by Anne-Marie McPearson, 11/05/00. As she held the tape in her hands, she thought about how it had affected her life; a failed degree, an eating disorder, the inability to hold down a relationship, low self-confidence and so the list went on. She continued to hold the tape and could hear her mother's voice from within it no more grudges. All this time, she'd been blaming Leah for everything, but now the answer stared her in the face, the tape is responsible. Give Leah the film and move on with your life.

As nobody had video recorders anymore, she had to google companies who could transfer the tape onto a DVD and, with luck, found one just around the corner. Anne-Marie dropped off the tape later that morning before taking the E3 bus to Turnham Green. Feeling like a weight had been lifted from her shoulders, she knew what had to be done. She didn't expect it to be plain sailing; she knew Leah would be grieving – they would have that in common. She decided, however, she wouldn't burden Leah with her grief.

Anne-Marie followed Google Maps on her phone and within ten minutes found herself walking up the pathway to Leah's smart terraced house. One of the neighbours came straight out and pleaded with her.

"I know she's going through a rough time, but there's only so many times I can hear the same song over and over again. She's playing it 24/7, so if you could have a word, it would be appreciated."

"Sure, leave it with me," said Anne-Marie. As she rang the doorbell, she could hear the song in question, Tangled Up in Blue, and shivers went down her spine. The music stopped and the front door opened. Leah looked worse than she imagined. No sign of her usual exuberance or lust for life and her body looked as though it hadn't been fed for a week.

"Good God, woman, let's get you sorted out."

Leah put up no resistance, no response at all really, and let Anne-Marie inside. She then reverted back to the same position she'd been in for the last week – on the corner of the sofa with her knees up to her chest. Over the last few days, Leah's knees had become her comforter as, whether in bed, on the sofa or a kitchen chair, detaching herself from her knees felt like a wrench; without them vulnerability encroached her. She reached out to the remote to unpause the music on Spotify, but Anne-Marie took the opportunity to save the neighbour from having a breakdown and removed the remote from Leah's hand. She couldn't face that song again either.

"Why is all this happening to me? What have I done wrong? Why would someone hate me that much?"

This is where Anne-Marie would have to tread with care. "Leah, they don't know if there's any connection yet, it may just be a sick coincidence."

"And why Georgia, what did she do to anyone, except make me happy? What makes the situation one hundred times worse is the fact that I can't talk to anyone about it."

"Why not?"

Leah took a deep breath. "Well, for starters, my parents still don't know I'm gay."

154

"They still don't know? Jeez Leah, what's wrong with you? Are you saying that for the past twenty something years, you've been lying to your parents about who you are?"

"There's just never been a right time."

"Fuck sake, you're 40 years old and your parents are what, in their 70s? 80s? Surely they're not going to disown you if they find out you love women and not men. It's not a fucking crime, is it?"

Leah didn't respond but took its content to heart. She continued, "And secondly, Georgia was married but it seems as though her husband is in denial and won't accept the fact that she and I were together; he's carrying on as the victim and traumatised partner. I won't be able to attend the funeral and can't give her parents a hug and tell them what an amazing daughter they had. It's like I didn't exist, yet here I am surrounded by her clothes, her things, her smell. I keep imagining that she'll come downstairs any minute and walk over to me, I can see her smile; I can feel her breath."

Leah's eyes welled up and Anne-Marie reached out and took her in her arms like she did with her younger brothers when they'd fallen off their bikes and let her cry and cry and cry. She cried more than a week's worth of tears, the release of grief overwhelming and, when she managed to peel herself away from Anne-Marie's voluptuous chest, she was exhausted.

"Why don't you go to bed and get some proper sleep? I'll tidy up and sort you out something to eat, by the looks of it, a decent meal hasn't passed your lips in days."

Leah didn't argue and hauled herself off to bed. She put her face into Georgia's Chicago Cubs shirt and breathed in the last remaining smidgeons of her scent, an aroma which was becoming fainter every day.

Anne-Marie spent the next few hours occupying herself in Leah's house. She checked out the kitchen cupboards and found some lasagne verdi slices and a jar of bechamel sauce. The dates were fine on both, so she put them on the kitchen worktop and went to the fridge to see what she could put in the lasagne. The contents were a complete disappointment, curdled milk, a jar of Marmite, margarine and some mouldy cheese. Shaking her head in disbelief that anyone could treat a fridge with such lack of respect, Anne-Marie collected her handbag and hunted around for some front door keys, which she finally found in the front door. "Silly woman," she said to herself.

She walked back up to the High Street, where she'd clocked Sainsbury's earlier. Not sure whether Leah might be vegetarian, Anne-Marie decided to go with aubergine, peppers and mushrooms for the lasagne. She added some cheese, milk, bread rolls, a bunch of fresh flowers, a pre-prepared salad and an apple strudel. That would go well with the tin of Ambrosia custard she had noticed in the cupboard. In the aisle behind her she could hear two shop assistants chatting whilst restocking the shelves. She tuned into their strong indeterminable accents and listened to one of them telling her colleague that she had been interviewed twice now by the police as she had been the one to serve the victim and had seen the collision.

"I didn't tell them though about those two guys who were in here the day before discussing which woman they needed to deal with, they looked quite menacing, so I'm not going to risk my life by mentioning anything."

Anne-Marie raised an eyebrow and continued to listen in whilst comparing the origins of vegetables. She would tell Leah at a more suitable time; she didn't need this now. When she got back, the same neighbour who she had

156

seen earlier, opened her front door and said thanks for turning the music off and asked after Leah.

"Not too good I'm afraid, but with any luck, after a good cry, a sleep and a substantial meal, she'll be okay."

"I bet she's glad she has a friend like you to take care of her," said the neighbour.

Inside, Anne-Marie huffed her way up two flights of stairs and looked in on Leah, who continued to sleep like a baby.

A couple of hours later, Leah woke from her deep sleep to the smell of cooking permeating around her house. Anne-Marie heard the creak of floorboards and started to climb the stairs but stopped on the first floor and shouted up to the bedroom.

"Get yourself showered and then come down for your tea."

Whilst Leah did as she was told, Anne-Marie had a nosey in the other rooms on the floor – a study, a bathroom and a double bedroom. So why on earth do you choose a bedroom on the top floor when there's a perfectly good one here? Anne-Marie was happy with her first floor converted flat in Ealing, which had everything on the same level.

Leah came downstairs looking a little more refreshed, and her mouth dropped when she came through the doorway. In front of her was an immaculately clean kitchen, dining room, lounge and conservatory. Cushions plumped, fresh flowers on the sideboard and a cool breeze circulating through the open windows and door to the garden.

"Sit yourself down. I didn't know whether you are a meat eater or not, so just in case I made it vegetarian," said Anne-Marie donning gloves and removing the baking dish from the oven. She set it on the placemat in the middle of the table and watched as Leah inhaled the smell and watched the browning cheese gently bubbling.

"This looks and smells heavenly," said Leah, watching as Anne-Marie brought over a salad bowl and plate containing some fresh rolls. Anne-Marie rubbed her stomach – she hadn't eaten all day. The copious amounts of food on the table would be enough to feed a football team, so no need for her to worry. Leah tucked in with gusto and didn't stop until she couldn't move. Anne-Marie instructed her to go and sit down on the sofa, whilst she put everything away and loaded the dishwasher. She then joined Leah on the sofa.

"How are you feeling?"

"Full," said Leah managing her first smile in a week. "Why are you here?"

"I'm still asking myself that question. I'll be honest with you, I'm not your biggest fan, but I've come to realise that I've been living in the past for twenty years and I need to move on. I've been holding you accountable for everything that's gone wrong in my life. Ever since I failed to submit that film all those years ago, you've been my scapegoat for my lack of confidence, my eating problems, my lack of self-esteem and my inability to hold down a relationship. I've blamed it all on you, but not anymore, I need to bury the hatchet and move on with my life."

Leah couldn't speak, her face displaying genuine shock. "I had no idea."

"Aye, that wee tape has got a lot to answer for, which is why I'm giving it to you."

"You still have it?"

"Aye, but not for much longer, it's being converted to DVD and then I'll let you have both. I'm hoping that I'll be able to move on and won't have the curse hanging over me any longer."

"I'm so sorry," said Leah with tears rolling down her face, "I am eternally grateful for what you did for me back then, but in all honesty, I had no idea it had affected you like this. Why didn't you tell me, why didn't you shout at me, hurl abuse or even retaliate? You seemed so calm and just took it on the chin, saying that university degrees were overrated anyway. It's something I'm reminded of every time I do an interview. I can't believe you've been bottling it up all this time."

With roles reversed, Leah took her turn to offer a hug and watch as Anne-Marie broke down in floods of tears.

"Hey," said Leah, "these are the first clean clothes I've worn in a week, don't go wiping your snotty nose on them."

Anne-Marie pulled away and took a tissue from her pocket.

"That's more like it," said Leah.

"Will you do something for me, well three things?" asked Anne-Marie with her serious face on. "You're a talented, well respected and admired woman, why do you think Georgia fell for you? She'd want you to do what you do so well, so promise me you'll pull yourself together and get back out there, and represent our industry? Georgia would've wanted you to show your strength, confidence and humour to the world and that's what I want too, and you still owe me one if you remember? And tomorrow you are going to get yourself over to the pub where Georgia's ex goes and demand to speak to him, tell him how you feel and I'm sure you'll be able to go to the funeral and pay your respects. Thirdly, tell your parents who you are."

"You don't want for much do you? OK, I promise you I will do all three, although I have no idea who the man is or where he drinks?"

159

"Aye good point, luckily I do – I'll send you the details. Right, before I go, I'm going to help myself to some apple strudel and custard, do you want any?"

"How can I say no?"

***

As she waited for a bus back to Ealing, Anne-Marie wondered if she should've mentioned the conversation she overheard in Sainsburys, but as Leah seemed to have responded well, she didn't want to give her any setbacks, she would mention it at some point though. The next bus wasn't due for another seven minutes, so she took her phone out and noticed a message from Andy, How u doing? I'm off to the Eagle if u fancy a pint? Now there's an idea, she thought as she crossed back over the road and headed in the direction of Turnham Green Station; all being well she'd be in the pub within half an hour; how she hankered after a drink, a whisky perhaps.

As she travelled east, she thought how satisfying it felt being kind and helping someone. She was determined to carry on with the "new and improved" Anne-Marie.

Chapter 34

There were only a handful of punters in the Eagle. Steve was sat with Graham, who had been in every day since the news of Georgia's death, but otherwise it was quiet, which pleased MJ. She was still coming to terms with the events of the last week and was just content to clean glass shelves and optics and let her mind tick over with thoughts. Rumours were floating about that the road accident was somehow connected to the theatre shooting but MJ couldn't quite get her head around how. Hakim also occupied her thoughts. She looked at the WhatsApp messages between them. Her latest one was last seen today at 16:01, why not just send something back? Scrolling up through the messages she re-read a text from him and did a double take at the original date he'd invited her to the theatre – 13th June, the date of the shooting. Surely just a coincidence?

As she finished scrubbing away some congealed cordial from the corner of a glass shelf she stood up and came face to face with Andy and jumped out of her skin. "I didn't hear anyone come in, you scared me!" said MJ, composing herself. She poured Andy a pint of Peroni and, with the bar looking spotless and the bottling up already finished, she poured herself a half, and made small talk with him – there were worse ways to spend a spare few moments. He explained that his doctor told him to take some time off work after what he'd witnessed the previous week. MJ remembered Steve telling her how Andy's face looked as though someone had syringed all the colour out of it when he walked through the door. He was looking better today. The colour had returned, and MJ found herself appreciating his boyish looks, a touch of the Tom Daleys she thought.

Andy looked up and gestured towards Graham at the end of the bar, "What's he said?"

MJ leant in between two pumps so she could keep her voice down, "Not much, he's still gunning for Leah though, thinks it's her fault."

"I don't like it," said Andy "he's got a temper on him, he holds a grudge and has said he wanted to kill them both. It doesn't look good."

The door opened and in walked Anne-Marie looking flushed. Andy stepped down from his stool and gave her a long hug. MJ looked perplexed and wondered if she'd known someone injured in the shooting; after all, she wouldn't be upset about Georgia. Anne-Marie put her bag down underneath the stool next to Andy' and headed off to the toilets.

As if reading MJ's mind, Andy said, "Her mum died a few days ago."

MJ nodded and promised she'd talk to her later to offer her condolences. She took a Peroni glass from the shelf, but Anne-Marie came back shaking her finger.

"Thanks, but I am full up with lasagne and apple strudel, so it's a whisky for me, Glenfiddich please, straight, no ice."

Andy made some comment about lasagne and apple strudel being an odd combo and the two of them seemed back to their normal banter. Not long after, they were joined by Robin, who gave Graham a death stare as he walked past him on the way to the toilets.

MJ took a Pride glass from the shelf and began pouring his usual drink but didn't get far before the ominous spluttering sounds started emanating from the tap indicating that a barrel needed changing. Like the father of a crying baby, Steve knew the sound of an empty barrel and looked up, but MJ was already scampering down to the cellar.

Looking around the bar and seeing the presence of the three Leah-haters, Steve got off his stool and headed down to the cellar to have a word with MJ. She told him that Anne-Marie's mum died earlier that week too, which could add fuel to the fire. They would have to be on guard.

For a while, the pub remained calm with a sombre atmosphere as death and loss became the main topics of conversation. Anne-Marie, however, became louder the more she drank, aggressively pointing her finger at Andy telling him to make more of an effort with his mum.

"When she's gone, she's gone Andrew; you'll regret it you know."

Robin, no stranger to grief, joined in too and MJ could sense unease growing in Andy's head.

Graham stood up to go outside for a cigarette but stopped as he walked past to offer his contribution to the conversation. "If you ask me, we should appreciate everyone, you never know when your time is up, take my wife for example."

"And whose fault is that?" said Robin.

Graham's shoulders immediately went back and he sucked in air through his teeth. "What did you say?"

Uh-oh, thought MJ, sensing the wind picking up.

"You hated her for leaving you, I mean if my wife left me for a woman, I'd want to kill her too."

"You think I mowed her down?"

"Well, you did say in here before that you wanted to kill them both?"

"Figure of speech, you twat."

Steve called over to Graham and told him to go out for a smoke. Like a compliant schoolboy obeying his

163

headmaster, Graham went outside with his packet of Marlboro Lights and could be seen shaking his cheap lighter, trying to get it to work.

Anne-Marie had been quiet throughout the exchange but looked up from her whisky glass and asked Robin why he was goading Graham and told him he should give the man a break. Andy walked over to MJ. It had occurred to him that he should try and get Robin's phone to see who sent the photo of Leah to him.

"Yeah, good idea, be subtle though, things could boil over at any minute," said MJ.

"OK boss, watch the super sleuth in action."

MJ looked on as Andy waited for Anne-Marie to go to the toilets again so he could ask Robin for his phone. It could be a while, thought MJ, with Anne-Marie on the whisky she wasn't drinking her usual volume of liquid. But after less than twenty minutes, Anne-Marie moved off the stool with a thud and meandered off to the toilets.

"Hey Robin," Andy said, "I've been thinking about what you said, and I want to talk to my mum now. As I left my phone at home, is there any chance I could use yours please?"

Good work, said MJ to herself as she saw Robin unlock and then hand over his Samsung Galaxy. Andy thanked him and disappeared out of sight.

Robin called MJ over and looked at her with a sympathetic smile. "Sorry if all this talk about mothers and loss of life is hard for you, I know you're still hurting."

"Thanks, I appreciate that." What a genuine guy thought MJ, he'd have made a good parent.

The rest of the evening continued in a similar vein with not a lot of laughs being shared. Robin left first, followed a few minutes later by Anne-Marie, with Andy hanging around to walk MJ home. Whilst Steve didn't look overjoyed that someone else seemed to be muscling in on his job of protecting MJ, he knew Graham needed looking after too, so didn't try to object. With the pub being virtually empty, he suggested she get off early.

Once they'd said their goodbyes and were out of the door, Andy fidgeted like an excited kid. "OK, I found the photo and I know who sent it."

"And?"

"Boy1"

"Boy1? Is that it?"

"I couldn't memorise the full number, but it ended in 1990, easy to remember as it's the year I was born."

MJ didn't want to quash his excitement, but she didn't think Boy1 and 1990 helped much in their quest to find out who sent the photo in the first place. Still, she didn't want to upset him, so gave a coy good work and moved him off the subject. "What's the story with your mum?"

Andy went quiet before saying, "Do you mind if we leave it for another day?"

"Sure," said MJ reaching for her keys, "Well, this is me … do you want to come up?"

"Thanks, but I should be getting back, perhaps another time?"

***

Andy surprised himself, why didn't he take her up on the invite? Not the right time, a little voice inside him said. He turned back in the direction he'd just come from and walked towards Victoria Station to catch the train for the short journey back to Clapham Junction. Walking along the road minding his own business, Andy thought he recognised someone up ahead. It was the same girl he saw every night, her head disintegrating and turning to red liquid. He called out to her and she began walking towards him, but as she neared, her face was no more, in its place, a pool of blood.

Chapter 35

Steve knew instantly that the woman walking towards the bar was Leah. He got MJ's attention and nodded towards the visitor. "Hi," said Steve, "what can I get you?"

"Just a coke please," said Leah, "is there someone here called Graham? I'd like to talk to him."

"Do you think that's a good idea?"

"I'm not sure, but for my own sanity it's something I need to do."

"I understand. Look, let me go and have a word with him. You may hear a few obscenities, but he'll calm down and then hopefully will come and talk to you."

"Sounds like a character."

"You could call him that," said Steve warming to the woman, "take your drink and go and sit down, I'll see what I can do."

Leah reluctantly removed her sunglasses to reveal a pair of dark puffy eyes. She reached into her bag and took out her purse, but Steve waved it away indicating the drink was on the house. MJ shimmied over to Steve with widened eyes.

"She wants to talk to Graham!" said Steve.

"Do you think that's a good idea?"

"That's exactly what I said, but I think she needs closure. Right, here goes," said Steve heading to the end of the bar, where Graham was perched.

Graham's compassionate leave following Georgia's death meant him arriving in the pub everyday just after lunch. Despite spending even more time there, his alcohol consumption didn't seem to be dramatically increasing. Contrary to what a landlord might usually think, Steve was pleased. He cared about Graham and, during his time at the helm of the pub, their relationship changed

167

from being just landlord and customer to friends. Over the last few days, Steve the landlord had morphed into Steve the counsellor. Graham was not only dealing with rejection, but also death. As much as he hated Georgia, deep down he probably still loved her. Steve had no idea what his reaction to Leah would be, but he had to at least try. With MJ on high alert and Alex in the kitchen, they would be able to stop Graham if he went ape.

"Hey, can you do me a favour and hear me out first before saying anything please?" Steve asked, as he placed an arm on Graham's shoulder.

"Er, yeah of course, who do you think I am?"

"Someone who is grieving and has every right to be angry."

"What is it then, spit it out."

"Someone has just walked in the pub and wants to talk to you."

"If it's another bloody journalist, they can do one."

"Hey, I said hear me out first."

"Sorry."

"The woman Georgia was seeing is in the pub and wants to talk to you. I know she's probably the last person you want to see, but it may just help lay a few demons to rest, mate. Do you think you can face her without making a scene?"

"Christ, I wasn't expecting that. Where is the bitch?"

"You can start off by not calling her that; her name is Leah."

"Sorry Guv."

"Will you speak to her?"

"If you and perhaps MJ come over too, I can't do this on my own – and I'm less likely to kick off as you put it, if you're both there."

Steve looked over to MJ.

"Fine by me."

"OK, let's do this and let's all be civil, please, the woman is obviously grieving too."

The three of them, with Steve in front and MJ at the back, walked towards Leah, who rose to meet them. Steve introduced Graham to Leah, who offered a handshake which was rejected. MJ introduced herself quickly and offered a friendly handshake in order to defuse the situation. She couldn't help giving Leah a once over as she did so. Dressed in black jeggings and a lightweight cream top with sleeves just below the elbow, she looked casual yet smart. Her body language gave off an air of confidence and strength, yet her face displayed sadness and hurt. MJ and Leah sat down together on the banquette seating, Steve and Graham on the chairs opposite.

"How did you know where to find me?" asked Graham.

"It doesn't matter, but I'm glad I did. Thank you for agreeing to talk to me."

"Were you with her when she died?"

"Not exactly. We were going home, and she stopped off to get some things from the shop. I went on ahead and after a few minutes I heard the sirens and knew something had happened. I went out to the main road and there she was, lying like a rag doll on the road."

Leah started welling up but took a deep breath and composed herself. Under the table she took hold of MJ's hand.

Graham was looking to the side, but MJ could see tears starting to form in his eyes too. She wondered if Graham had picked up on how she said we were going back home indicating that Georgia had been living with Leah for a while.

"I'm glad I didn't see her face though, I'm lucky the image I have of her is still perfect and that's what I cling onto every minute of the day."

Graham stood up, "I can't deal with this." He rushed outside wrestling with his pocket to find his lighter. Steve went after him.

"He'll come back," said MJ still with her hand being held so tightly she feared her circulation would be cut off soon. "He only found out about you a month or so ago, so I don't think he'd come to terms with it before, you know…"

"Before she was killed?"

"Sorry."

"It's OK. Tell me, now he's not here, was he angry when he found out about us? You don't think he would've had her killed on purpose do you, sorry to ask, but other stuff has been happening around me and I sometimes get paranoid that I've upset someone."

"Graham gets angry easily, so yeah he was pretty mad after she'd told him about you. I wasn't here, but Steve said things got heated and he was hurling abuse."

"At Georgia?"

"No sorry, I think he came to the pub after he'd seen her and was just swearing at anyone he saw."

"OK, so you don't think he'd want to hurt her?"

"No, I don't, but he does have a temper on him, so I couldn't say for sure. Did she talk about him to you?"

Leah paused. "Actually, she only told me about him on the evening of the accident. I knew though, as I noticed her wedding ring the first time I saw her. I just thought she'd tell me when she was ready. But now I wished I'd asked her sooner, found out more about him, so at least I understood why she didn't want to be with him anymore."

Steve and Graham soon came back inside and sat down in the same places. Graham looked at Leah and apologised, albeit reluctantly.

"Did you want to say something in particular as I take it this isn't a social call?"

"Yes, I want to ask if I can be at the funeral. I need to say goodbye to her properly and, out of respect, I didn't just want to show up. For God's sake, I hadn't even met her family."

Graham put his hands behind his head, leaned back on his chair and grinned. "Didn't know her that well then, did you?"

Leah didn't rise to the bait; she'd had to deal with people far more smug before. "Look, I'm just asking if I can come along and show my respects."

"Her family will ask me who you are and what am I supposed to say? That their daughter was cheating on me with a fucking lesbian?"

"Graham, enough," said Steve firmly.

"Why don't you bring your other girlfriend?" said Graham sitting upright and shaking a finger at her.

Leah frowned and hesitated before asking, "What do you mean, other girlfriend?"

"He's talking rubbish, just ignore him," said Steve, not wanting to get Graham worked up.

"No, no, I want to hear what he means, go on."

"The woman we saw you with in Brighton the other week in the casino," Graham continued, "your hands were all over each other."

"Have you been stalking me?"

"Are you denying it?" asked Graham, leaning across the table moving his pint glass nearer to Leah. "How many women do you have on the go?"

171

"I can get the police onto you if you've been following me."

MJ was concerned where this was going, so was thankful when Steve stepped in.

"I had to collect some stuff for the pub in Brighton, Graham joined me. We had no idea you'd be there, let alone in the casino."

By now Graham was tapping the beer mat irately on the table. "Are you going to answer my question or not?"

"Oh, for God's sake, that was my sister, we hadn't seen each other for months! We'd won £700 on roulette … not that I need to explain anything to you. I was in love with Georgia, we were in love, she meant the world to me and now she's gone. I'll be eternally grateful though that we even met in the first place and had six amazing months together …"

Graham's face reddened and his eyes grew intense. "Six fucking months?"

Oh god, thought MJ, why did she have to go and say that?

"You're telling me that you had been fucking my wife for six months?"

Steve turned to Leah. "I think you better go; give your details to MJ outside and we'll be in touch."

MJ took Leah outside and walked down to the main road with her. Leah put her sunglasses back on, flicked her hair back and shook her head, "Sorry, I shouldn't have said that, it was stupid of me."

"Hey, don't worry, I get more expletives from Graham on a regular Friday night when the head on his pint I've just poured is too big. Listen, why don't you give me your number?"

Leah handed over her business card. "Thanks, and sorry for nearly breaking your hand under the table. I hope I didn't leave any lasting damage?"

"No broken bones, take care." MJ put the business card in her jeans pocket and watched Leah as she walked down the road.

Back inside the pub she found Steve and Graham having a heated argument. Graham stormed out and lit a cigarette.

"What was all that about?" said MJ.

Steve explained how when they'd been in Brighton and had arranged to meet in the bar, Graham rocked up two hours late and said he'd fallen asleep. It was around that time that a fire broke out in the kitchen at the hotel where Leah's event was being held.

"But I arranged the trip," said Steve, "so how would he have known that Leah would be there?"

"He knows a lot about her Steve, where she lives, where she went to Uni, date of birth. Are you having doubts about him?"

"I don't think he'd harm anyone but something's not right."

A few minutes later, Graham walked back in the pub, his head held low and shoulders forward. He asked MJ for a whisky whilst shaking his head and mumbling, "six fucking months!"

Chapter 36

Leah flicked on the TV, she couldn't stand the quiet and, after being reprimanded by her neighbours for playing the same song on repeat, she opted for quiz shows to nullify the silence. She took her sunglasses off and looked in the mirror aghast at the pair of puffy eyes looking back at her. Sort yourself out woman, she said to herself, reaching into her handbag for her eye drops and concealer. You heard what Anne-Marie said, stay strong, grieve yes, but be brave, show the world what kind of person you are. You're a winner, make Georgia proud of you.

One of today's *The Chase* contestants was particularly unintelligent and getting on Leah's nerves. The host asked the next question, 'From which country does the furniture store IKEA originate? Is it Sweden, Singapore or Switzerland?' At the same time, the doorbell rang, and Leah went to open the door. The contestant pressed Singapore.

"Honestly, woman, just do one, what's the point of even turning up when your brain's the size of a gnat," said Leah.

"Well, that's not a very nice way to greet an officer of the law is it now, Ms Pope?" said DI Johnson with mock seriousness. She couldn't help but laugh, which in turn produced a proper smile from Leah. "Can I come in for a minute please?"

"Sure. You know where IKEA originates from, don't you?"

"Sweden. Listen, strictly speaking I should be giving these to Graham, but I like you and it's clear that you meant the world to Georgia, so I took it upon myself to bring you her things we took after the accident," said DI Johnson passing Leah a clear plastic wallet. "I'll leave you to go through them on your own."

Leah didn't notice DI Johnson leave, instead she sat down at the breakfast bar and slowly opened the plastic bag, taking out the items one by one. She handled everything with great care, running her fingers across each surface and raising them to her nose to see if there was any trace of Georgia. She left the battered phone until last and was hesitant to touch the screen. Nothing happened. It was dead. Not knowing whether it was a good idea or not, Leah reached for the iPhone charger and connected it to Georgia's silver iPhone. As she waited for it to start up, Leah turned back round to the TV and changed the channel over to the news, which continued to focus heavily on the shooting at the theatre. The reporter was outside the Apollo.

A police statement says that the attack didn't follow the usual pattern of terrorism and nobody has yet come forward to take responsibility. Investigations continue, and the police are asking for anyone in the area from 7pm onwards who may have taken photos to come forward as the perpetrator may have been caught in the background. In the meantime, tourism experts have been reassuring visitors that theatres are safe.

Leah tutted, she'd seen bookings plummet since last week, so the message clearly wasn't getting through. She'd make sure that when she was back at work properly, it was the first thing she would address. An incoming WhatsApp message alert made Leah's heart jump, until she realised it was on her own phone and not Georgia's. She reached across and read the screen, the message was from MJ saying that Leah had the go-ahead to go to the funeral but only if she was discreet and went with MJ. Leah, feeling relieved, exhaled a deep sigh but the air she inhaled back in was riddled with grief and sadness. She turned her attention to Georgia's phone,

175

and on the third attempt got the passcode right, 811010, Georgia's date of birth backwards – she knew her so well, she thought. She was greeted by a pair of happy faces pressed together, joyous smiles and glistening eyes. It was the same picture Leah had as her wallpaper. She kissed the cracked screen before clicking on Messages. There weren't many, as Georgia was quite particular about deleting and filing messages when she no longer needed them. There were some from Leah and a few from her work colleagues. There was little of interest in the Sent box either, so Leah moved on to checking the Draft folder. There was one message, and it was composed just minutes before she was pronounced dead. Leah's heart started to beat faster. She opened the message. *I saw detailed plans of the Apollo Theatre in your office …*

Chapter 37

MJ arranged to meet Leah outside M&S at Charing Cross Station. She was a little apprehensive about going to the funeral, especially as the last one she went to was her own mother's. She needed to be the strong one today, though, as she'd given her word to Graham that Leah wouldn't make a scene. Graham said that things would be informal, so MJ dressed in her usual black jeans, converse trainers, blue shirt and black leather jacket. She also made sure that her sunglasses and scarf were packed, necessary items for a funeral when the tears started to roll.

At Charing Cross, Leah's bobbed blonde hair could be seen as soon as MJ entered the concourse. MJ raised a hand and gave a smile; Leah greeted her like a friend and removed her big sunglasses. MJ noted Leah looked considerably better than the last time she saw her.

"Good to see you again, thanks for doing this, I know it's not an ideal way to spend a Monday afternoon."

"It's no problem," MJ said with a reassuring smile.

Leah bought two return tickets to Tunbridge Wells and they headed to the platform. The midday train was quiet and the journey went quickly, with Leah being very open as MJ asked questions about her career and how she set up her ticketing company. MJ wanted to keep her distracted and off the subject of Georgia for as long as possible.

"Funny, but I went on a date with someone from your team a few weeks ago."

"Really, ooh, let me guess … man or woman?"

"Man."

"Under or over 30?"

"Under."

"Native English speaker?"

"No"

"OK, I've narrowed it down to a few, but you may as well tell me?"

"Hakim."

"Hakim Khan from IT? Aw, he seems like a good guy. A little quiet, but I've never seen him outside of work though, what's he like?" Leah asked, appearing pleased to be having such a normal conversation.

"Well, I thought the date went well but I've not really heard from him since, although he did say that there'd been some bad tech issues with your system?"

"Yeah, that's true – sorry if I've been overworking him."

"No, of course not, I'd just prefer him to tell me if he's not interested, that's all, but you know what men are like." Leah raised her eyebrow and MJ apologised, realising what she'd just said.

"Hey, you don't need to go out with a man to know what they're like," said Leah with a chuckle.

"True," said MJ, "do you think it's less complicated going out with women?"

"It's just the luck of the draw I'm afraid, male or female. You'll find someone who you just click with; in the meantime, enjoy trying on shoes of all varieties until one day you find a pair you'll never want to take off."

"Wise words," said MJ. "Hakim has invited me along to an event on Friday … if he remembers. Will you be there?"

Leah nodded, "Yes, it's a big industry awards gala. It's one of the events of the year and I'm presenting the awards."

MJ apologised again, "Sorry I didn't realise. It sounds like a big deal!"

"Why should you apologise, it's fine. It should be a good event, though."

The train began to slow.

"Right, here we are, deep breaths. Just to warn you, your hand may be subject to even more squeezing today, and your shoulder may bear the brunt of my tears," said Leah. They climbed into a taxi and travelled the three miles to the church. Before getting out of the taxi, both women put on their sunglasses and wrapped their scarves around their heads. On seeing their reflections in the car window, they realised they looked more like Thelma and Louise than two people trying to be inconspicuous and blend into the background, so MJ removed her scarf and tied it around her neck. They held hands and walked to the entrance with their heads bowed. As they neared the church building, Leah's pace slowed to a crawl.

"It's OK, you can do this. Keep your head down, keep squeezing my hand and we'll find somewhere to sit at the back." MJ sounded strong, but she was having a wobble too.

Leah bowed her head and looked like she was taking a never-ending prayer, whilst MJ checked out the other mourners, trying to establish who belonged to whose family and who should be avoided afterwards. Graham sat at the front, with possibly his parents and sister. She assumed that the people on the other side were Georgia's parents. She felt someone from behind put their hands on her shoulders, making her jump – Steve; he then put his hand on Leah's back and gave her arm a squeeze, before moving towards the front and taking a seat behind Graham.

The next twenty minutes were excruciating, both physically and emotionally. Every time her hand received a squeeze, MJ thought Leah was going to get up and interrupt. When Graham took to the microphone, MJ became even more nervous and put her arm around Leah.

179

When the service ended, MJ suggested to Leah that they make a swift exit. They walked around the church until they came to a bench slightly hidden from view. Leah removed her headscarf and sunglasses and looked up to the sky. MJ didn't say a word, she sensed she was having a moment, saying goodbye to Georgia, so let her do what she had to do. When Leah had finished, she put her head on MJ's shoulder and sobbed for a full ten minutes, all the time not letting go of MJ's hand, which by this time had been left numb and bruised.

"Let's go," said Leah abruptly, "I've said my goodbyes; she's still inside me and always will be."

"Leah, can I ask you something?"

"Sure," said Leah looking worried.

"Please can you let go of my hand now?"

***

The return train journey was calm. Leah slept, leaning her head on MJ's shoulder. MJ didn't mind though, it felt like looking after a child, just as her Auntie Annie had done for her at her mum's funeral. Back in London, the pair made their way to Victoria where they said their goodbyes. MJ asked Leah to text her when she got home to make sure she was okay. Leah nodded, and thanked her for having been such a support.

Emotionally drained, MJ headed to the Eagle, went straight behind the bar and served herself a vodka and coke. She plonked herself down on a bar stool and looked at her left hand, which was visibly bruised. Steve hadn't stayed on for the wake either, and had somehow beaten her back to Victoria.

"Battle wound?" he asked, giving her a sympathetic look. "You did us proud today."

"I don't want to do it again in a hurry, that's for sure, but I like Leah, her sense of humour is endearing, even when she's facing adversity."

"Ey, you're not turning the other way, are you?"

MJ shook her head. "I didn't say I wanted to sleep with her, did I? Can't I compliment a woman without your mind thinking of only one thing?"

"Just messing."

Feeling slightly annoyed by the comment, she gave her head another shake. "What a day, I don't think I can deal with many more dramas. Actually, I think I'm going to head home and crash out."

Polly was behind the bar and tried to get MJ's attention. "Hey, before you go, is there any chance you can cover my shift on Friday evening?"

"Sorry, no can do, I've got a date with a posh frock and an Asian prince, otherwise I would have done. We're going to a fancy awards gala dinner."

"You're not still serious about that guy, are you?" asked Steve.

"I don't know, I'll tell you after Friday. See you later." MJ swigged the last of her drink, gave a weary salute and left. Polly looked over at Steve's screwed up face. "If you're worried boss, why don't you offer to drive her over to the hotel, she's bound to come in here for a drink before-hand. You may even get to see the guy again for yourself and warn him not to lay a finger on her."

Steve paused for a minute. "Hmm, maybe you're right," he replied before reaching for his phone and typing Does Cinderella want a lift 2 the ball on Fri eve? He hesitated with his finger over the Send button.

"Boss," Polly said, "stop thinking about her and come and help me serve?"

Chapter 38

Anne-Marie saw Andy's text and replied, *Of course I'm going to the awards dinner, I may win that lifetime achievement award this year!* He replied with a smiley face and a thumbs up.

Right, first things first, she thought, and headed to the video shop. Five minutes later she stood outside with sweat running down her forehead. She moved to the shade and wiped her head with a tissue, the heat was almost unbearable. The organisers of the event must have a direct line to the powers that be, thought Anne-Marie, she couldn't remember an event in recent years when the weather hadn't been glorious. At the same time, it reminded her of her size and how she wished she could wear a light strapless dress to the event like so many of the others. Instead, she'd wear her thick layered maroon dress which hid many of her folds and lines, with a cardigan over the top, covering her whale-like arms. By the time she'd arrive at the event, her legs would be chafing and sweat glands would be starting to enjoy the party. At least she wouldn't have to get ready at home or in the office this year, Leah had asked if she could be with her at the hotel beforehand and she could use her room to get ready. She couldn't let Leah down, so agreed to meet her around 5pm and have a drink beforehand.

With the sweat having stopped dripping down her face, Anne-Marie walked into the small box room of a shop and handed over her receipt to an elderly woman, who looked out of place surrounded by gadgets.

"Thanks love, Adrian has just popped upstairs, but he'll be back in a jiffy. Why don't you take a seat, would you like some water?

Anne-Marie thought that she must look just as bad as she felt. She nodded her thanks and sat down. Whilst waiting for her water, she heard a door in the back open and then close. The man, who had the same pointy nose as the woman, must be related, so Anne-Marie deduced it to be Adrian.

"Ah, yes, hello Miss, er McPearson, you've come to pick up your video and DVD, haven't you. I hope you don't mind me asking but did you make the film yourself?"

Taken aback by the question, Anne-Marie hesitated.

"Urrm, yes, around twenty years ago, so I can't remember it much."

"Ahead of its years I'd say, it's brilliant, the viewer perceives they're watching it in black and white, but the colours running through the emotion-based scenes are genius. I suggest you watch it again, it's a work of art."

Anne-Marie smiled back at Adrian, who grinned like a Cheshire cat. She paid the £20 and left the shop in bemusement. When she got home, she toyed with the idea of playing the DVD, but decided against it, it would be too painful. Instead, she popped it into her bag; to give to Leah later.

***

Anne-Marie boarded the tube at Ealing and to her relief, it was one of the newer trains, so blasted out cold air. She smiled, something that she found herself doing more of over the last few days; she'd even given smiles to other people. She looked up to the sky half expecting her mum to be looking down on her; perhaps talking to Leah had parted a couple of dark clouds and now streams of sunshine were beginning to penetrate through into her life. As the tube went through Hammersmith, her phone beeped with a message from an unknown number and without a thought, she clicked on it. *I hope you don't mind, but I wondered if you wanted to have dinner with me some time, I'd love to know more about your film making? All the best, Adrian @ the video shop.* What the fuck is happening today?

Leah met Anne-Marie in the lobby and asked if she wanted a drink?

"Sure, it's so hot out there, I think I need to cool down before spreading heat around your room."

"What can I get you?"

"A lager please."

With drink in hand, Anne-Marie turned to Leah, "Cheers, here's to Georgia," giving a silent toast to her mum too.

"Oh God, don't start me off please."

"Sorry, but I know she'll be proud of you. Right, you know what I'm going to ask, don't you? Did you go to the pub and find the husband?"

Leah took a deep breath. "Yes, I did, and I went to the funeral."

"And were you pleased you did?"

"Yes, and I'm sure Georgia could sense my presence. Thank you for making me see sense; you don't know how much I appreciate it."

Chapter 39

In the Eagle, MJ was getting ready upstairs in Steve's room. Having accepted his offer of a lift, she thought it easier if she got ready there as it would avoid having to totter up the street in heels. She panicked when she heard the event was black tie as the contents of her wardrobe didn't amount to much. She contemplated wearing her bridesmaid's dress but that didn't feel right. She thought about going shopping, but then decided to ask her sister instead if she could lend her something suitable. What was the point in paying all that money for a dress she probably wouldn't wear again? Although being a size smaller than her older sibling, she knew that her sister hoarded clothes and would have a range of sizes in her wardrobe. The next day Jochen dutifully dropped off three different dresses with his brother Niklas, who left the parcel outside MJ's door along with a note from Kate. I hope one of these will be OK and don't forget to send me a photo, see you next week.

MJ tried on all three dresses and found a clear winner; it was the only one that fitted her; the other two left MJ wondering whether she possessed any boobs at all. The blue dress, however, fitted like a glove, which made her think that it may not be one of Kate's in the first place. She messaged her sister and was shocked to learn the blue dress belonged to their mum. A tear formed as she imagined her mum wearing it. The sentiment soon evaporated though when she heard a knock and saw the door edge open a few centimetres and a glass of vodka and coke being pushed through the gap.

"Thought you might like one of these," said Steve.

"Thanks boss."

Fifteen minutes later, MJ gave herself the once over in the mirror and nodded with approval at the result. The figure-hugging royal blue dress made MJ realise that she did have curves after all, as well as a pair of breasts. She took a deep breath and looked around the bedroom, surprisingly she saw no photos of people, just the odd beach, but mainly black and white prints of football stadiums. She then looked back in the mirror and saw material of a similar coloured blue hanging on Steve's clothes rail. On closer inspection, MJ realised that the colour of her dress was an exact match to Steve's Chelsea top. She finished the drink and smiled … let's see who mentions it first.

"Wow, you look great … and wearing my favourite colour too." Steve looked her up and down.

"Haha, thanks! Now get me another drink will you, I'm a nervous wreck. I barely know this guy, and, by all accounts, there's going to be about three hundred people at this do tonight – I just hope they're not all up themselves; Hakim says most of them are pretty cool, although they can be quite cliquey."

"You'll be fine. Won't the others be there too, Andy, Anne-Marie and how about Leah?" said Steve as he glanced over to Graham, who seemed engrossed in the paper and not listening in on their conversation.

"Good point, but with hundreds of people there, I'm not so sure I'll even see them, let alone chat to them."

Alex came out from the kitchen tying his apron behind him. "My god, you scrub up well don't you, bloody hell!"

"Should I take that as a compliment?" MJ asked.

"Abso-bloody-lutely!"

Steve turned the TVs over to the tennis but was still looking at MJ. "What time do you need to be there by?"

"7:30 ish, are you sure you don't mind driving me, traffic's going to be pretty bad, I don't mind taking the tube," said MJ, hoping deep down that Steve would insist on taking her.

"You ain't taking the bloody tube dressed like that, alright. I'm taking you and that's the end of it."

A group of noisy suits walked into the bar and were quick to throw a wolf whistle in MJ's direction. Steve glared at them as only Steve could do.

"Sorry mate," said one of the suits, "you can't blame me though, she looks a million dollars."

Steve grinned. "Right, let's go Cinders."

MJ grabbed her clutch bag and followed after Steve, cursing as she stumbled on her heels. They walked around to the back of the pub.

"Your carriage, ma'am," Steve said, impersonating a chauffeur and opening the passenger door.

MJ laughed and climbed into Vic, the white Vauxhall van. "I cleaned it specially, and I even put up a new Magic Tree freshener for you."

Once they'd gone along the Mall and around Trafalgar Square, they headed to the Embankment and drove east adjacent to the River Thames. As well as appreciating the scenic drive, MJ found Steve captivating, with his humour at its best; she couldn't stop laughing. She felt at complete ease and, despite never being anywhere except the pub with him, it was like they'd known each other for years.

"Right, we're nearly there, so I may need help," Steve said, "Sat Nav's OK but a human is safer in this traffic."

MJ managed to successfully direct Steve to the hotel. As the car pulled over, nerves started to creep back into MJ's stomach.

"Have a good night … and behave yourself."

187

"Of course," said MJ as she wrestled with her seatbelt. Steve turned to help, and their hands met; she looked up at him and saw something different in his face. They were brought out of the moment by a loud knock at the window. MJ turned to the door and saw a face peering in. Hakim. She blushed as she felt Hakim's eyes move from her to Steve and in an instance felt butterflies in her stomach. She turned to the window to mouth thanks to Steve, who returned with a be careful gesture.

"You look beautiful," said Hakim, slipping his arm around MJ's waist, "I'm so glad you come with me; it's going to be beautiful evening, I'm so happy."

He kissed MJ on the neck and squeezed her waist, giving her goose pimples. Lord give me strength, she thought glancing upwards and taking a deep breath as they walked into the hotel.

***

In room 602, Leah stood gazing out of the window over St Katharine Docks, reading through her speech one last time. A handful of expensive looking motorboats bobbed up and down whilst tourists gazed on in awe. In the background, the high-rise buildings of the City rose up, interspersed with numerous cranes indicating the skyline would look even more congested in the coming years. Leah took a deep breath and finished her speech, feeling confident that she'd be able to manage it without the prompt cards. Anne-Marie came out of the bathroom smiling at the cold air being pumped out by the clunky air conditioning system. Catching the tail end of the speech, she intervened.

"And despite not having a degree, the winner is … Anne-Marie McPearson."

Leah turned around to see Anne-Marie pretending to be given the award and bowing to the cheers of the admiring audience. "I don't know at this stage who the winners are, so don't give up hope."

"Aye and pigs might fly. Can you zip up my dress please, my arms don't reach that far? ... Don't go touching me up, though."

"Aw you disappoint me," said Leah pulling up the zip.

"Right, shall we go and face the crowd?"

"Before we do, can I give you this please?" said Anne-Marie handing over a DVD case, "I believe this belongs to you."

Leah nodded and put the DVD in her bag; nothing more was said about it.

Chapter 40

Up on the 12th floor, guests were flooding into the reception hall. MJ took a glass of champagne from the tray and gave an orange juice to Hakim. "The view from here is just amazing, isn't it," said MJ.

"Yes, but I also liked the outlook we had from the Shard last week."

More like four weeks ago, thought MJ, but kept it to herself. Andy popped up behind them, looking fresh.

"How is my favourite barmaid? I hope this young man is treating you well?"

"Of course," said MJ noticing a vacant look on Hakim's face.

"I'm sorry, I need to go to the bathroom."

"Have you been putting vodkas into those?" Andy asked MJ as he watched Hakim head out through one of the double doors, "or was it something I said?"

"No idea, he seems fine and then every now and again it's like his mind drifts away."

"Oh well, I have you all to myself now," said Andy with a twinkle in his eyes. "Can I say that you look stunning tonight."

"Well, I thank you and can I say that you don't scrub up too bad yourself," said MJ admiring Andy's smart tuxedo and stylish new haircut. She spotted Leah in the distance looking elegant in a striking navy jumpsuit and nude heels, her tall frame carrying off the side splits in the wide trouser leg, and her upper body wearing the thin straps to perfection. With Leah walking towards her, MJ raised her head and looked at her face instead, which looked just as immaculate.

"Hey, how are you both?" Leah turned to MJ, "good to see you out of your jeans."

MJ blushed and turned the conversation back onto Leah. "You look amazing, it's not everyone that can carry off a jumpsuit; I'd probably look like Bob the Builder."

Andy piped up, "An attractive builder though! Everyone's looking good tonight, look over there, even Anne-Marie scrubs up well. It's weird, but tonight she's the happiest I've seen her in ages, like a weight has been lifted from her shoulders. Strange given that her mum passed away last week."

Leah nearly spat out her drink, "What do you mean her mum died? She's been round at mine this week and didn't mention a thing?" With that she excused herself and took off. She had nearly reached Anne-Marie when Colin, from GBT, collared her and said he needed to discuss the awards presentation.

Andy looked puzzled, "Since when did those two hang out together?"

"Errr, no idea, you?" asked MJ.

"Your guess is as good as mine. I'm going to go and find Hakim for you; I'll be back in a minute."

"OK," said MJ, feeling miffed that everyone left her on her own to stare out across the River Thames.

"Is that you MJ?" asked Anne-Marie, "Why are you stood here on your own?"

"Hey, how are you doing, you've had a tough week haven't you?" said MJ.

"Aye, but I think I'm over the worst of it now. You too by the sounds of it, didn't you take Leah to the funeral?"

"Yeah, not something I want to do again in a hurry, but it must've been a hundred times worse for her. Listen, when Andy mentioned, just now, that your mum had passed away, Leah didn't seem to know."

191

"I didn't want to burden her, but I'll mention it in due course. That reminds me, I also need to tell her about a conversation I overheard at her local Sainsbury's."

MJ's ears pricked up, "Go on."

"It may be nothing, but one of the girls mentioned she had been interviewed by the police about the accident, you know when Georgia got knocked down, and she said that she hadn't told the police that there were two guys in there the day before discussing which woman they needed to … deal with, said they sounded menacing so worried about the consequences if she mentioned anything. Seemed a bit odd to me. I'll remember to mention it to Leah over the weekend, I don't want to distract her before the awards."

Andy and Hakim came back together just as the announcer called guests through to take their seats for dinner. Hakim looked at MJ, "We're on table 16, in the middle, I checked the plan."

Hakim introduced MJ to everyone else on the table, most of whom worked for Global Tickets or were guests of those who did. She sat next to a guy called Frank, who worked in international sales and had brought his partner Ed along. Next to them sat Anders, Leah's co-director and his wife Marie, their son Tomas (who worked in IT with Hakim) with his girlfriend Elena. On the other side, were Jamie and Alexa from the sales team and Martin, Hakim's direct boss, and his wife Linda. MJ turned to Frank and asked where Leah would be sitting.

"We have another table of people from the office, so she may be there but at a guess, as she's presenting the awards, she'll be on the top table."

Conversation on the table flowed and everyone appeared in high spirits. The tourism industry seemed just as sociable as the pub trade … lots of drinking and lots of talking.

She saw Hakim look up as Robin walked over to the table and knelt down next to him. MJ turned to say hello, but Robin looked straight through her.

Hakim pushed the remains of his main course around the plate like a child who didn't want to eat his greens.

"Hey, wakey-wakey," said MJ waving her hand above his plate. "Anyone in there?"

Hakim returned to planet earth and whispered into MJ's ear, "Come on, let's get out of here."

MJ picked up her clutch bag and followed Hakim's footsteps not knowing what else to do. Nobody on the table seemed concerned and probably presumed it was either a call of nature or nicotine. Once out of the main room, Hakim picked up the pace and encouraged MJ to stay with him. "Where are we going?" asked MJ, sensing something offbeat.

"I'm not feeling too well." Hakim took MJ by the hand and into the lift pressing G for ground. They quickly went out through the main reception and he called a taxi over.

"Where are we going?" asked MJ feeling nervous.

Looking flustered, Hakim seemed confused, "I have to meet someone, but the taxi driver will drop you off at yours."

She decided not to ask any more questions, instead she watched Google Maps on her phone and followed the taxi's journey. When they reached Upper Street, the driver slowed down.

"I'm so sorry MJ, I feel very ill, I think the food did not agree with me. I need to find my cousin, he has the key to the flat," and with that Hakim gave some notes to the driver and hurried away.

The taxi driver looked in his rear-view mirror, "Are you OK love?"

"I've no idea, one minute I'm at a summer party being wined and dined, and the next he bundles me into a taxi and then leaves me in Islington."

"That's foreign blokes for you love, you need to find a good Englishman," smiled the taxi driver with sympathy. MJ smiled back, something about him reminded her of Steve. "Do you know where you're going now?"

"He said to take you back to Victoria but feel free to give me an address. He gave me enough money for a couple of hours, so if you want me to take you back to your party or give you a guided tour of London by night, then I'm all yours."

"Thanks, but I think I just want to go home," said MJ giving the driver her address.

"No worries love, I'll have you back there in no time at all."

"Thanks," said MJ putting the phone back in her bag and turning the volume off by accident. After half an hour, MJ said goodbye to the taxi driver and walked up to the front door, thinking it had to be one of the strangest evenings she'd ever had.

Her brain needed a distraction, but she didn't fancy watching TV, so instead reached for her prized Bose headphones and connected them to Spotify on her iPad. Cranking up the volume, she slipped out of her dress, removed her jewellery, put on her pyjama shorts and vest top and lay down on her bed. The make-up removal process would have to wait until the morning, as she just wanted to be whisked away to some loud Indie sounds and forget the whole evening.

When she woke a few hours later, her right arm fizzed with pins and needles. She removed the headphones and rubbed her eyes, feeling the crunchiness of mascara on her lashes – she should probably give her face a quick wipe or the challenge would be twice as difficult in the morning. She needed some water. With her phone still in the bag, MJ didn't notice it flashing, indicating a message. In fact, during the time it had taken to listen to her playlist, she'd missed nineteen calls and a bunch of text messages. Oblivious, MJ went to the bathroom to clean her face, poured herself a pint of water and snuggled back under the duvet.

Chapter 41

The alarm went off at 8am and woke MJ from a deep sleep. She fiddled around until she found the off button and then tried to work out what day of the week it was. She leant over the bed and grabbed the A4 sheet of paper that Steve still used for staff rotas. Wondering when he'd get with the 21st century, she saw that he'd given her a rare Saturday off. Great, she could have a few more hours of slumber.

At 10:45, MJ woke up again feeling more refreshed and ready to face the day ahead of her. She put the kettle on and took a shower. Dressed in jeans and a t-shirt, she went to the kitchen, debating what to eat. The sun was streaming in through the skylight, penetrating the leather stool, which looked too hot to sit on. After making a U-turn to the bedroom and changing into denim shorts and vest top, MJ thought about giving her sister a call and seeing if she wanted to meet up, but then changed her mind, thinking a few hours sat by the river with a good book would be preferable. She went to get her mobile from her bag and swore when she saw the number of missed calls and text messages.

MJ's initial thought was that something had happened to her dad; but she soon saw that seventeen out of the nineteen missed calls were from the Eagle, and all but one of the text messages were from Steve. OK, let's see what he wants, his mobile has probably got stuck sending a message, either that or he was having a laugh with Alex or Graham in the pub.

r u OK? Sender: Steve Eagle, Received 22:05 yesterday
whats happened? Sender: Steve Eagle, Received 22:07 yesterday

let me no ur OK Sender: Steve Eagle, Received 22:10
yesterday
im worried, pls call Sender: Steve Eagle, Received 22:21
yesterday
pls answer ur fone Sender: Steve Eagle, Received 22:39
yesterday
I can't believe this has happened, r u ok? Sender: Steve
Eagle, Received 22:55
yesterday
pls answer me Sender: Steve Eagle, Received 23:03
yesterday
people r dead, I need 2 no ur OK Sender: Steve Eagle,
Received 23:05
yesterday
every1 is worried, pls call Sender: Steve Eagle, Received
23:17 yesterday
I luv u MJ, I'm praying 4 u Sender: Steve Eagle, Received
23:21 yesterday

WHAT!! I luv u, this must be a joke, what does he mean,
people r dead?

r u there? Sender: Steve Eagle, Received 23:24 yesterday
pls let me no ur alive Sender: Steve Eagle, Received 23:42
yesterday
r u OK? Sender: Steve Eagle, Received 23:48 yesterday
call me Sender: Steve Eagle, Received 00:29 yesterday
text me Sender: Steve Eagle, Received 01:04 today
contact me Sender: Steve Eagle, Received 01:45 today
pleeeeeeassee Sender: Steve Eagle, Received 02:05 today

Confused, and shocked, MJ rang the pub, and Steve
answered.
"Hey boss, how drunk were you last night?"

There were a few seconds of silence before Steve spoke. "Fuck sake, why didn't you call back, what the fuck happened?"

"Hand on my heart, I have no idea what you're talking about."

"I did drop you off at the Tower Hotel last night, right?"

"Right"

"And you did spend the evening there being wined and dined, right?"

"Right"

"So why did you manage to completely avoid a bomb going off?" Steve sounded angry and upset.

"A bomb? Shit, I had no idea, we left early." MJ leaned forward from the sofa and reached for the TV remote from the coffee table. A male reporter with a sweaty forehead stood in front of the hotel, which looked more like a scene from an earthquake.

"Are you listening to me?"

"Sorry, I've got the news on – I can't believe what I'm seeing."

Chapter 42

The doorbell chimed. Leah put her coffee mug on the counter and opened the door. DI Johnson. Leah made a comment about the inspector moving into the spare room and went to the coffee machine. She knew the officer would want a cup of proper coffee as according to her, the machine at the station should be condemned. The DI took a mouthful of coffee, groaned in pleasure and then asked Leah how she was.

"I mean, I know I was there, I know what I saw, smelt, felt and heard but it was like I was seeing it all on TV."

"You do realise that we think you were the bomb's intended target, don't you?"

Leah reached out to the breakfast bar for support, a wave of nausea washing over her. The DI hesitated between grabbing the bin or stool. She guessed correctly and guided Leah to sit down. Leah listened as the DI explained how the investigators think the source of the explosion was a large amplifier left by the bar. An amplifier someone expected to be on stage, metres away from Leah.

"You're lucky to be alive," the DI told her.

Leah looked down at her coffee mug wondering who and why someone would want to ruin her career, murder her girlfriend, and now try and eradicate her from the planet too.

"Am I that unpleasant?" Leah kept her eyes on the liquid, watching it move around her mug in a constant swirling motion.

"Let's just say you shouldn't have joked about your spare room." The DI moved closer and gently lifted up Leah's chin with her hand and looked her in the eye. "Trust me when I say the team are working around the clock to find out who is responsible; in the meantime, you're going to need police protection 24/7."

As Leah struggled to get her head around the seriousness of the situation, she asked if the investigating team had any theories so far but was already resigned to the fact that it was looking like an inside job, a fact that a concerned looking DI confirmed. In a flash, it occurred to Leah that she had no idea who the casualties were. She coughed back the thick bile and mid swallow turned to the DI.

"Do you know who the victims were?

"Yes, the bodies have all been identified now, do you want to know?"

She didn't want to know; it wasn't like finding out who the nominees for an awards ceremony were, she had to know.

DI Johnson took out her notepad and read off the names, Sarah Jefferson, Kristin Schmidt, Carlos Ramos from the hotel, Abby and Stevie B from GBT and then a list of names that Leah, although familiar with, didn't have personal connections to. The last name however caused her stomach to churn, prompting the DI to hand over the bin this time. Leah threw up until her body had nothing left to give. DI Johnson took her notepad and highlighted the name, Anne-Marie McPearson.

"A friend of yours?" asked the DI, getting a glass of water from the tap and checking the presence of the unmarked car.

"You could say that," said Leah bringing her legs up to her stomach and leaning her head back on the sofa. "Shit, what is going on? Why is someone doing this?"

The DI sat down with her serious face on as if ready to talk to a teenager about the birds and the bees. "I want you to start telling me everything about everybody, your friends, your family, your colleagues; someone out there is causing a trail of destruction and wreaking havoc. We need to stop them, but we can only do it with your help. Do you understand? You need to be completely honest with me, tell me everything regardless of how insignificant you think it may be, is that clear? Let's start with Anne-Marie."

Leah proceeded to tell the DI about the history between her and Anne-Marie, a story which after twenty years still felt raw. Leah had no problem recounting the moment she found out that Anne-Marie wanted, not only to tell the world, but also show the world, that her housemate was having a secret affair with an older female student.

"Apparently, her tutor wanted to put it forward for some national university film award as he rated it highly. Anyway, I put the mockers on the whole thing and said that under no circumstances was she to show the film to anyone else or use it for her own benefit. I was just coming to terms with being gay myself without the whole world judging me."

"What did she do?"

"As I asked; and as a result, didn't submit her dissertation, and therefore failed her degree," Leah said, tailing off.

"Wow."

After a night of worrying about Anne-Marie and contemplating letting her show the film after all, Leah recalled a phone call the following day during which Anne-Marie seemed genuinely not bothered about her degree, in fact she seemed bullish and resilient to the fact that she could succeed without it.

"When we both ended up in the same industry twenty years later, I thought we could be friends again, but I received the cold shoulder, she wanted nothing to do with me."

201

"What happened to change that?"

"After Georgia died, she came round and picked me up, told me what to do and how to do it. We talked about what happened in Manchester and she opened up about how she had blamed me and held me accountable for everything that had happened to her, and for her being like she was."

"Which was?"

"Having no confidence, not being able to hold down a relationship, having an eating disorder, lack of self-esteem, drinking too much … I had no idea, otherwise I would've tried to help."

"Why did her attitude change?"

"That I don't know, but I heard that her mum died a day or so before Georgia so perhaps there was a connection?"

"She didn't say anything about her mum, then?"

"No, nothing at all." Leah began realising the enormity of Anne-Marie's actions, not only twenty years ago but also in the last couple of weeks. Now there was no way to say thank you, as her life had been stolen by a bomb that was meant for Leah. "I can't believe what's happening, everything I touch seems to be going up in smoke at the moment."

The DI listened patiently and assured Leah that Operation Carousel, the team behind the investigation, would get to the bottom of it. She encouraged Leah to follow Anne-Marie's advice. "She seemed like a decent person; I mean who would sacrifice their own career for someone else?" That was too much for Leah, who put her face in the cushion she'd been squeezing.

"I'm sorry, I didn't mean to make things worse. One more question and then I'll make myself scarce. Did you ever see the film?"

Leah's eyes expanded and her fingers clicked as she remembered what Anne-Marie gave her the previous night. She got up and went over to her bag, which was still in the same place she'd left it when she'd got back at God knows what time. She pulled out the DVD, holding it like it was going to explode. "Here it is," she said nervously.

"Are you going to watch it?"

"Will you stay with me?"

There was a single nod from the DI.

Leah hesitated, wondering if she could stomach it. "I don't know if it's a good idea," she said kneeling in front of the DVD player.

"You can stop any time you want."

Leah opened the plastic case and prised away the shiny disc, sliding it into the DVD player. At first nothing happened, and Leah thought maybe the joke was still on her and that there was nothing on the disc, but then she saw the familiar façade of the red-bricked townhouse they shared. Her face appeared on the screen, a fresh-faced 20-year-old, with long hair tied back except for a few thick strands which partially covered the right side of her face. Leah lifted her hand up to her bobbed hair and noticed that even now, she liked it to come down and disguise this part of her face. On screen, her face then dissolved into a whirlwind effect and the colour flicked into black and white. Leah sat motionless and watched as the whirlwind morphed back into her black and white body. She was stood on the steps at the back of their campus. A dark-haired woman pulled her close and kissed her; she remembered it was the most unbelievable feeling, which she wanted to pause and stay like forever. Blue ice started rising around them until they were

203

motionless and covered in what looked like a giant ice cube.

The film ended with the silhouette of two women holding hands with streaks of blue icy water running between them; they continued walking towards the sun and the streaks began to change from blue to orange. Bob Dylan's "Tangled up in Blue" played in the background as the credit's page remained on the screen:

Tangled up in Blue

Written and Directed by Anne-Marie McPearson

Inspired by Leah Pope

By this time Leah was completely and utterly drained emotionally. Ignoring the DI,
she hauled herself upstairs and crawled into bed reaching for the Chicago Cubs shirt.

Chapter 43

Andy was given the all-clear and released from hospital on Sunday afternoon. When he got home, he curled up on the sofa and stayed there until Phil returned from a long twelve-hour shift. When Phil walked into the dark flat, he found Andy staring into space. It was pitch black, except for the glaring lights of the TV. Andy looked up. "I don't know how you can deal with things like that."

"Bombs, shootings and stabbings aren't daily occurrences Andy. Have you slept?"

"Can't. Every time I close my eyes, I see pieces of bodies flying over me. Still, at least I'm not seeing that girl's red hair anymore."

Despite his macabre humour, Phil knew that Andy was going to need some serious help to get over what he had witnessed in the last few weeks. He'd make some calls and arrange for Andy to meet with someone. In the meantime, after a cat nap, he would take him out for a walk in the fresh air and perhaps go to a pub for some food. Phil had discovered more bad news for Andy about one of the victims, but now wasn't the time to tell him.

***

MJ arrived at the pub at 11:30 ready for the long, all day Sunday shift. You never could tell what a Sunday around Victoria would be like; one week there would be only a handful of punters all day and then other weeks it could be rammed to the hilt with various groups of overseas tourists, day trippers and football fans. A lot of pubs in the area closed on Sundays, but Steve was more than happy to open on the off chance it was a rammed to the hilt kind of day; he couldn't face losing out on a full day's takings, especially from high-spending tourists.

"Ah, here she is," said Steve to Roxy, as MJ walked through the doors, "The woman that had us all worried out of our minds and thinking the worst. Even you were getting worried about your supply of gravy bones, weren't you girl."

MJ took off her jacket and put it with her bag on the back of the bar door. When she returned, Steve stood by the hatch holding his arms out.

"You owe me a hug," he said. Roxy sat behind Steve with her head tilted to one side and eyes fixed on him. She then gave out a thunderous bark and jumped up at Steve's back.

"Don't get jealous Rox, you'll always be my number one girl." Steve looked at MJ and continued, "So, are you going to tell me what happened, then? Why did lover-boy really leave half-way through the evening and take you with him? Did you put your hand on his cock? Or perhaps he told you he's trans? Or how about he's a terrorist, hates his job and wants to blow everyone up?"

"Not funny Steve, just because he's a young Asian male, it doesn't make him a terrorist."

"Sorry, bad taste I know, but you have no idea what Friday was like in here for us. When I couldn't get hold of you, we all thought you were toast. We all felt we should've warned you away from him, cos if we had of done, you'd still be with us. God, we felt so guilty. But it turns out he actually saved your life and made sure you weren't even near the hotel when the bomb went off. It just seems too much of a coincidence, but one that I'll be eternally grateful for.

"Stop being soppy, it doesn't suit you," said MJ changing the music from The Jam to her Sunday playlist.

"Have you heard from him since Friday?"

"No, but who knows what's going on. Now, as touched as I am, please can we change the subject and go back to sex and football?"

"My pleasure," said Steve putting the front door on the latch and changing the pub sign to OPEN. "Sex and football," he said.

"Yes please, to both," said Graham walking in.

MJ was pleased to be at work, busying herself serving drinks and making small talk with people she didn't know. She also had the familiar faces of Steve, Graham and Alex sat at the bar who, although probably knowing everything, kept quiet. She guessed Steve warned them of her sensitivity.

A few orders for food came in and Alex scuttled off to the kitchen, commenting about people always ordering fish and chips. Steve looked up and gave MJ one of his looks. Oh God, she thought, what now? It was Andy and another guy, not really deserving of a look from Steve she thought. MJ asked Andy if he'd like his usual. He nodded and asked for the same for his friend. Getting Peroni on draft was an inspired decision by Steve; even at £1 a pint more than other premium lagers, it was still the best-selling product in the pub.

"MJ, this is Phil my flatmate, Phil this is MJ."

"Pleased to meet you," they said in unison.

"You're doing food, aren't you?" asked Phil.

"Yep, menus are on the table, but I suggest you don't order fish and chips … the chef has a thing about it today and you know what they say, never upset someone who's going to give you something you'll put in your mouth!"

Phil laughed. "Thanks for the warning, think I'll go for the burger with a side of onion rings. Andy?"

Andy got a sudden lump in his throat. "Don't think I can stomach meat, have you got anything vegetarian?"

"Caesar salad? Veggie lasagne? Feta and sundried tomato tart."

"Let's go with the salad please, with some chips – just no meat, I can't face meat," said Andy before taking his pint over to the window table.

After their food and second pint, Phil and Andy came up and sat at the bar next to the hatch, with Steve and Graham. Andy seemed more relaxed than when he arrived, probably thanks to the 5.1% alcohol in the Peroni. Graham, who usually saw Andy with Anne-Marie, gave the pub a quick scan.

"Where's your Scottish friend? She's good value after a couple of pints."

Andy shrugged his shoulders. "She lives near Ealing so, at a guess, she's there."

"Aye," said Graham.

Phil fidgeted on his stool. "Listen, mate, there's some news on that front I'm afraid. There's no easy way to say this but Anne-Marie was one of the victims from Friday night."

Andy looked at him startled, "Why the fuck didn't you tell me earlier?"

"Listen, I'm sorry mate, I know you two were close."

Silence fell around the bar, until Graham raised his pint, "to Anne-Marie," and then everyone else followed suit, "Anne-Marie."

MJ looked at Phil. "How did you know? I haven't seen anything come out on the news yet about the victims?"

"Sorry, I should explain, I work for the police in the armed response team; I was at the scene on Friday."

Question after question rushed through MJ's inquisitive mind, her thirst for knowledge back with a vengeance, "Do you know who else died?"

Graham looked up and grinned, "With any luck that whore bag who was fucking my wife."

Steve shot him a look, "Shut it or you'll be gone, have some respect will you."

"I'm not sure which whore bag you're talking about," said Phil sitting up straight.

"Leah, the lesbian, Pope, I think her name is."

"No, but by all accounts, the bomb had her name on it."

"You're kidding?" said Andy.

"Sorry, I've said too much but it'll all be in the news tomorrow."

"Somebody really has got it in for that poor woman, haven't they?" said Steve.

"I don't blame them," said Graham as he edged off his stool, "silly bitch is running out of lives."

Andy edged off his stool too, prompting Phil to put a hand on his friend's shoulder.

MJ picked up on the tension and, leaning in close to Steve, asked him if she could take Roxy out for a walk. Roxy wagged her tail, happy for an impromptu trip outside. As MJ walked past Andy, she tapped him on the shoulder and asked if he wanted to join them. He didn't say anything, but he finished off his pint and walked out giving Roxy a fuss.

With things having calmed down, Graham went off to the Gents. Steve looked at Phil.

"He may be rude and foul mouthed, but he's no killer."

"I'll take your word for it, but he shouldn't joke about it in public. Clever move by your barmaid, though."

"Yeah, she's one in a million."

Phil said he thought Andy had been suffering from PTSD following the shooting at the theatre, and that Friday's events could push him over the edge.

Steve promised he'd keep an eye on him and try to prevent Graham from winding him up, although it wouldn't be easy, especially without Anne-Marie around, who, he informed Phil could've been Graham's twin sister the amount she swore and drank. "It's not just Andy who will miss her, my tills will too."

***

To begin with MJ and Andy didn't speak but, with the pub out of sight, they touched on the subject of Friday night. MJ explained how she left early and didn't find out what had happened until the next day, when she saw endless messages from Steve.

"I wish I'd left with you," said Andy remembering back to Friday. He had seen Hakim take MJ's hand and led her out of the ballroom, and thought they were off for a bit of action. The green-eyed monster in him contemplated following, just to see, but decided against it and turned back round to join in the conversation with Anne-Marie and a couple of others from the team. Andy fancied another beer, so had suggested he go to the bar. Anne-Marie told him to stay put as she needed to visit the Ladies, so would pick up the drinks on the way back.

"That was the last time I saw her," said Andy.

MJ sensed that he wanted to talk more, so encouraged him to explain what happened next. He didn't remember too much but the scenes he did were so vivid he often felt he was still there. Leah had just breezed on stage and made some comment about the setting resembling a festival as opposed to an awards ceremony; he remembered laughing and turning to Anne-Marie's empty seat. He assumed she was still at the bar, necking a quick shot and looked towards the double doors to see if he could see her. His eyes fixated on the doors and that's when the trance began. Without warning, silence

210

prevailed, and he was alone, in a cloud bubble with his hearing numbed. The doors came loose and floated towards him, he ducked down in slow motion and watched as the doors flew like a graceful Concorde over him. As the second door hovered passed, it fell like a ton weight, BANG and a cacophony of glasses and plates smashed around him. Like planes queuing up in the skies above Heathrow, Andy stared at the bodies coming towards him one after another, limbs in the wrong places, heads on back to front, vital organs dropping out of them like food parcels falling from the sky. His eyes tracked one of the parcels, which dropped into his cupped hands, a heart, a bright red heart continued to beat in and out. It floated away from his hands and then a torso glided across with a heart shaped gap of flesh missing. The scenario continued, but in the background, he could hear somebody calling his name over and over again.

"The next thing I know I'm in a hospital bed and the nurse is leaning over saying my name."

MJ stopped and turned to Andy, who resembled a jelly. "Hug?"

With one eye on Roxy, who seemed to be staring back with intent, his shaking body turned to MJ. By the time they returned to the pub an hour later, to everyone's relief Graham had gone. Andy headed straight to the toilet and MJ went back behind the bar to carry on from where she left off cleaning the fridge doors.

Phil looked up from his empty pint glass, "I like what you did before."

"Thanks," said MJ. "I could see trouble brewing, so had to do something."

"Well, not everyone would've handled it with such tact. Ever thought of a job with the police? We could do with more brains like yours."

MJ brushed the comment aside and asked him if he wanted a top up.

"I wasn't joking and no, I'm OK thanks; I'm going to head home, but I'll see what Andy is doing first."

MJ went to the other side of the bar to serve a family who had come up to the counter. As she poured a couple of pints of Guinness, MJ watched as Andy came out of the toilets and spoke to Phil. They exchanged a few words before Phil patted Andy on the shoulder and left the pub. MJ smiled and hoped that she'd be able to get to spend some more time chatting to Andy. He was growing on her at an alarming rate, definitely more her type than the elusive Hakim.

Chapter 44

The alarm went off at 9am. MJ reached over and hit the snooze button before falling back on her pillow feeling exhausted. She thought for a minute and then it dawned on her why she was feeling tired. She turned her head and saw him lying next to her looking dead to the world. She examined his bare upper body and smiled approvingly. The sheet covered his lower body and, despite the relative darkness in the room, there was no mistaking some tent building going on down there and MJ's lower regions pulsated; she had a sudden urge to climb on top of him. Although they had both felt up for some action when they reached MJ's flat, after chatting and listening to music, they both fell asleep as soon as they lay down. MJ leaned on her side, bent her elbow and rested her head on her hand contemplating her next move. Andy's eyes opened, he stretched and reached out to stroke her shoulder.

"What's on your mind?" he asked.

MJ decided to bite the bullet and be honest, "Hmm, just deciding what I should do, and I have come up with three options."

"Oh yeah," said Andy shuffling his body closer to MJ's, "and what would they be?"

"OK, option one is to get up and put the kettle on."

Andy moved his hand up and put his fingers through her hair, "sounds OK," he said, "I like my coffee black with one sugar. Option two?"

Andy's chest edged closer and she shivered, becoming more aroused. "Option two … is to turn off the alarm and go back to sleep."

"And option three?"

MJ moved forwards and gave Andy a lingering kiss. They were content to let their bodies lead the way, enjoying their sexual instincts. Andy, for once, was content to be submissive and let MJ take control; she pushed him back with some authority and ran her tongue over his glossy chest. In pleasure, he closed his eyes, but with them shut, images of floating body parts appeared and he opened them quickly back up. Whilst he could easily let MJ do those things with her mouth all day long, he needed to see her face, he needed to look into her eyes and see life. She didn't need any encouragement to lift herself on to him; he held her waist and they locked eyes, watching each other intently. Andy took a photo with his mind and hoped it would be the image he recalled when he next closed his eyes.

Chapter 45

Leah and Helena met outside and shared a prolonged hug. No words were needed. They entered the restaurant and were immediately spotted by Beppe, who rushed over to them.

"Ladies, I haven't seen you in like three weeks, what's happening? You not a like my food anymore?"

"Ah Beppe," said Leah, leaning down to fit under his arm, "it's got nothing to do with your food I can assure you, just lots going on in my life I'm afraid."

"Eh, I'm sorry to hear that but happy it's not my food keeping you away. If you need some Italian lovin' you just say the word, you beautiful lady."

"That's very kind of you."

"You're welcome, although you may have to share me with the other lady in my life," said Beppe turning to the television in the corner.

"Wozniacki?" asked Helena, knowing her tennis players.

"No, no, no, the beautiful Camila Giorgi," said Beppe standing with his hands on his hips, looking at one of the blondes on the screen.

"They both look the same to me," smiled Leah, "I wouldn't kick either of them out of bed."

Helena rolled her eyes before heading off to their usual corner. "Do I take it you are taking small steps in recovery?"

Leah sat and leaned back, "I have to keep my humour Helena, otherwise I'll be up there with Georgia before I know it."

"I'm sorry, I can't imagine what you're going through, but you know I'm here for you don't you."

"Thanks, yes I do, which is why I wanted to meet with you today. The police are convinced it's an inside job. I need us to get our heads together and go through everyone in the office again, OK?"

"Sure, happy to help, what do you need from me?"

"HR files, all of them. Are they all stored electronically? Can we access them via the VPN?"

"Absolutely, where do you want to go to look through them?"

"Do you mind coming back to my place in Chiswick after lunch? Strictly speaking I shouldn't be on my own without a police escort, including here, so I'm going to get a telling off regardless."

"A police escort?" asked Helena, her mouth falling open.

"Yep, looks like Friday's bomb was meant for me."

"Fuck me."

Heads turned and brows were raised, including Beppe's.

"Eh lady, mind your language," Beppe placed two bowls of seafood pasta in front of them.

"Apologies." Nodding in the direction of the TV, Helena asked how Giorgi was doing.

"Not good, lost the first set 2-6."

"Saving herself for Wimbledon maybe?"

"Yes, let's hope so."

Leah waited patiently to have Helena's attention again. "Why didn't you just call me if you're under house arrest?"

"I needed to get out and I'm still not convinced there's a hitman out there, it all seems too amateur; I mean why not just take a gun to my head and get it over and done with?" Leah lifted her hand and put two fingers against her temple.

"Leah, don't joke …"

A loud crash echoed across the restaurant as a waitress tripped over a bag and dropped a trayful of glasses on the floor. Helena jumped out of her seat and just managed to catch her own wine glass before it fell off the table. "For God's sake," she said, "sorry, but any chance we can have these put in a takeaway box and get an Uber back to yours ASAP, I'm a bag of nerves."

"I'm sorry, I didn't mean to scare you, why don't you go outside for a smoke and I'll sort the food out."

Within five minutes, to Beppe's surprise and disappointment, the two women were in the back of an Uber. He looked at the TV, "Just you and me now then, Camila."

In the car, Helena put a call through to her team advising that she wouldn't be back in for the rest of the day. She then turned to Leah with a look of concern. "Are you serious about someone wanting you dead?"

"Yep, you can check with the sergeant sat in the car outside my house or the lovely DI when we get back."

"Jeez Leah," said Helena shuffling around in the car, "how can you be so calm?"

"Same with the humour, it's pointless being scared. If my time's up, my time's up. Of course, I don't want it to be just yet, but the thought of being in Georgia's arms again made me realise I shouldn't be scared of death."

"You believe in God then?"

"I believe in anything that helps me believe in something; make sense?

"No, but I'll go along with it."

The driver indicated to turn left, but Leah told him to pull over and stop on the main road. "We have to sneak in the back way," she said.

"You've lost the plot."

"Busted," said an animated DI Johnson from the back garden. "Are you not taking the threat to your life seriously, Ms Pope?"

"It's Leah, and yes I am but I needed to get out. This is Helena, we're going to go through the HR files together. I need to pop to the bathroom first though, and then into the office to bring down the second screen."

Helena turned to the DI. "Is it true, do you think the person connected with all of these incidents could work for Global Tickets and wants Leah dead?"

"It's a possibility; do you have any theories, seen anything odd over the last few weeks in particular?"

"I don't think Leah's told me everything, but if you ask me, I think the husband needs to be investigated."

"Yep, been there, first person I interviewed and agree there's something off, although since the situation has escalated, there's less evidence pointing towards him."

"What are you two talking about?" said Leah, fixing a second screen to her PC.

"Georgia's husband."

"OK, but for what it's worth, I don't think he's capable of mass murder, which is what this has become," said Leah. "Helena, c'mon, let's crack on with these files, how shall we do this, A to Z or newest to oldest?"

Helena moved one of the dining room chairs across to the computer and sat next to Leah. They chose to work through employees A-Z by surname and look at their CVs and covering letters. As they skim-read the documents, Helena asked if there was anything in particular they were looking for.

"Yes, don't you remember, we went through a phase of asking obscure questions to the candidates?"

"Now you mention it, I do, it was a while ago, though, wasn't it? Didn't a few people object to the questions?"

The DI sat at the breakfast bar listening in on the conversation. "Go on, tell me, what sort of questions did you ask?"

Helena turned to answer. "The main question Leah is referring to is when we asked for a one-page document detailing how candidates would go about ruining a company's reputation."

"Well, that is weird, isn't it?" said the DI.

"Not really, let me show you," said Leah looking for an example, "here you go."

The DI pulled up a chair and nestled herself in between Leah and Helena.

"This person obviously thinks that reviews are key to a company's success and suggests that by having a network of people constantly posting negative reviews, a company's reputation would soon fall into decline. The candidate, you won't be surprised to learn was applying for a job in the Marketing team. Do you see, it's interesting for us to see whether the candidate can see the wider picture and not just focus on their area of expertise." said Leah.

The DI looked baffled. "I'll take your word for it."

An hour and three cups of coffee later, they reached 'K' and brought up the file for Hakim Khan. "OK," said Leah, "let's see what my tea boy had to say." Leah's jaw dropped. "Shit, I wasn't expecting that."

Leah shifted in her chair and looked sideways at Helena before re-reading Hakim's detailed explanation of how to ruin a company's reputation. It mirrored exactly what she and Global Tickets had been subjected to over the last couple of months, everything from the API error to the changing of times on the Director's electronic calendars. DI Johnson sprang up and made a call, "Hakim Khan, 132 Edward Road, send a couple of officers round but have back up nearby and keep me posted." With the same determined tone, she asked, "What's this guy Hakim like?"

"He's smart, has manners, is good at his job and we get on; there is no reason whatsoever for him to want to hurt me," said Leah.

"OK, that may well be the case but after seeing this, we at least need to bring him in for questioning, I'm sure you'll agree."

Leah moved over to the sofa and fell into her default protection position, knees up to her chest, with arms wrapped around them.

"I'll come back later Leah OK, perhaps Helena can stay with you until then? And you still have the officer parked outside if you need anything."

Helena phoned her husband to say she'd be back late, and then went to sit with Leah.

Chapter 46

The DI called Leah just before 9pm to tell her there was no-one at Hakim's address, but there were signs of someone having been there in the last twenty-four hours; they were putting a couple of officers outside on watch. "I'm just driving through Hammersmith now and am toying with the idea of picking up a takeaway because, unlike somebody I could mention, I didn't sneak out for lunch."

"Haha," laughed Leah realising the pasta was still in a box in the fridge and her stomach was grumbling, "sounds good, I'll have whatever you're having."

Picking up on the conversation, Helena stood up and put on her jacket. "If you're having food delivered, do you have any objections if I take both of the pastas please?"

"Sure, sorry, I should've asked if you wanted food too," said Leah, feeling bad.

"Hey, don't worry, I better get off to see what damage my lot have caused today. Shall I wait for the DI to get back or will you be OK?"

"She's in Hammersmith, and don't forget I have my boy in uniform out front."

"OK but lock the door when I go. Keep me posted won't you and remember to call if you need anything. I don't think it's Hakim either, but you have to admit it's a strange coincidence; maybe he'll be able to provide some insight if nothing else."

"Good point, thanks for today."

The two embraced and Helena left for the tube station. Leah gave a wave to the police officer in the car before going back inside and bolting the door. Ten minutes later the DI stood at the front door with two brown bags. The smell made Leah drool.

221

"Curry?"

"Yep, I ordered a selection, didn't know what you liked?"

"I'll eat anything."

The two women sat at the breakfast bar devouring the food.

"You've got a good appetite on you," said the DI watching Leah piling the food up on her plate.

"Well, I forgot to mention that I didn't actually get to eat my lunch because Helena got freaked out about there being a hitman in the restaurant, so we left before even a mouthful of food passed my lips."

"You shouldn't have gone you know."

"I know, but at least we've moved a step forward."

They both moved over to the sofa, Leah tucked her legs under her and cradled a glass of red wine.

"I've read through the paper submitted by Hakim and wanted to ask you more about it," said the DI, treading carefully. "I've got the tech team going through what he mentions and comparing it to what happened in your system, but how about the other things he suggested, about messing with diaries, outlook calendars etc. Did any of those things happen to you?"

"Yes, but at the time I didn't think they were connected."

"Tell me what happened," said the DI.

Leah talked through the last couple of incidents, but this time as she spoke, she became resigned to the fact they didn't happen by accident.

"Pieces are beginning to fit together, I'm afraid to say."

Both were silent for a moment.

"I think I could eat another bowlful," said Leah getting up, "how about you?"

"Yeah, why not." The DI followed Leah to the kitchen and noticed the plastic bag of Georgia's things she dropped off after the accident. She pointed at the phone. "Anything on there?"

Leah turned, dropping a spoonful of dal in the process, "Shit, yes, I forgot to tell you, there was a message in the draft folder, which she composed minutes before she was hit."

"May I look?" asked the DI.

"Sure, let me unlock it," said Leah, "here you go."

I saw detailed plans of the Apollo Theatre in your office ...

"Why didn't you tell me about this when you first read it?"

Leah closed her eyes and put her hands up to her face, frustrated with herself for not mentioning it sooner. "I'm sorry, my head's all over the place."

"Hey, don't beat yourself up. It's pretty incriminating evidence though; I'm going to have to get a team over to the office straight away, I take it that's OK with you?"

"What, now?"

"Yep, better than waiting until people are there in the morning. Can you explain to me exactly where Georgia was looking?"

"Why don't I come with you and show you?" said Leah, keen to make up for her forgetfulness.

"OK, but I need my team there as well. Let me make a call and then we'll head off."

The journey took just under twenty minutes door to door; Leah was impressed how the DI handled the car with speed and agility. She also noticed scars on the top of her left hand in the shape of rough triangles and wondered how she had got them. Two marked vehicles were parked outside the office waiting for Leah. She unlocked the first door and de-activated the alarm before unlocking the second door, which led up the stairs.

"Who else has the codes for the alarm, and how about keys?"

She turned to look at a bearded officer. "Initially, the majority of the team, but after the system problems, we changed the locks and alarm codes, so I guess now perhaps ten to fifteen people."

"Including Hakim Khan?"

Leah looked concerned, "Yes, he often worked late, we have partners in the US."

On hearing this, all four of the uniformed officers drew their guns and signalled for the DI to keep behind them with Leah.

"Shit, you don't think he's here now, do you?"

"It's a possibility, he's not at home, nobody has seen him for days and he has access to this place."

Her heart rate increased. They slid into the office against the wall, like she'd watched in many a cop drama, their guns primed and ready to be fired in their outstretched arms. "Look, I honestly don't think he's here OK."

After a quick sweep on the main floor, they deduced nobody else was there.

"Show me the desks where Georgia was looking," said the DI.

"Here, this is where the IT team sit, including Hakim; it would've been one of these desks."

The DI instructed the team to go through the desk and trays and pay particular attention to any paperwork. She then turned to Leah, "What date did this happen?"

"Hmm, a few weeks ago, it was a Friday as I'd let the team go early ... maybe the last Friday of the month."

"And talk me through why Georgia was here looking through the desks?"

"I know it sounds weird, but the system must've been hacked, and I was led to believe it could be someone internal behind it all. I'd gone over it many times in my head and thought having someone not involved might notice something I'd overlooked."

"And you asked Georgia?"

"Yes, we closed the office and opened the terrace bar. Georgia arrived just before 6pm I think."

"Was the office empty?"

"Yep, just me and Georgia."

"And she didn't find anything of note?"

"No, just some coding documents and papers in Chinese."

Leah gave a wry smile, and is if reading her mind, the DI turned and asked.

"What happened next?"

"Then she joined me in my office for … um … grown up time."

The DI struggled to keep a straight face. "And where's your office?"

Leah pointed straight ahead, "Do you want to take …"

"Ma'am, I think we have something."

They all stood behind the officer, who, with gloves on, laid out six sheets of A4 paper, all containing detailed maps and descriptions of the Apollo Theatre, including fire escapes, toilets, entrances and seating plans.

"Good work. Now let's get them bagged up and taken back to the station to be analysed please. Ms Pope, your girlfriend may have just provided us with a significant piece of evidence."

"Do you still want to see my office?"

"Ah, yes please."

Leah sat on the edge of her desk and watched as the DI scanned the room from left to right and top to bottom, pausing to take in one of the framed photos on the wall, before her gaze turned to Leah. For a moment time stood still, but then the DI's face turned green, prompting Leah to fly off her desk.

"AHHHH, what the fuck! "Get in here now!" the DI yelled loud enough to wake anything in a ten-mile radius.

Leah on instinct looked under her desk but regretted the decision instantly and began to retch. The DI ordered her out of the room and took out her phone.

"We have a deceased male body of Asian origin, multiple stab wounds, looks recent, get forensics over here now."

"Is it him? Is it Hakim?" asked Leah, squatting outside with the curry-covered waste bin by her side.

"Hard to tell, but it could be. Can you remember anything significant about his appearance?"

Leah tried her best to recall anything.

"Does he have a scar on his neck?"

"Not that I recall."

The DI wanted to get Leah back in there to give a positive identity but couldn't risk the crime scene being contaminated by saag aloo, the smell of the regurgitated curry would put her off takeaway for a few weeks.

"Gov, there's a note stapled to the back of his head."

"Good God, stapled?" Leah reached for the basket again, wishing she hadn't gone back for seconds of her takeaway.

The DI signalled for the victim's head to be moved forward in order for the note to be read. It said: If you want a job done properly …

"Any idea Gov?"

"Could be a range of things. Right let's get her out of here," said the DI, requesting an officer drive Leah back home. "I need to stay here." The officer nodded.

Leah turned to the DI, "You will let me know if it's Hakim, won't you?"

Chapter 47

Leah was in a deep sleep, lost in a dream about her and Georgia on a sailing boat in the Pacific Ocean, it was magical. The phone rang and brought her back to reality, back to a life without Georgia. She looked at her clock, 05:47, and then at the caller ID and pressed accept. It was DI Johnson. "Do you ever sleep?"

"Ms Pope, sorry for the timing, but I thought you should know, the body in your office didn't belong to Hakim."

"Who was it then?"

"Hakim's cousin, Nazir Khan."

"What's he got to do with it, and what the hell was that note about?"

"We're working on it, Ms Pope."

"How many times, call me Leah!"

"Sorry Leah, I need to come round, there have been some new developments I need to discuss with you in person. We also need to speak to Ms Atkins, Hakim's girlfriend."

"OK, when will you be here?"

"I'm on your front doorstep now."

"Jesus Christ woman, give me five minutes."

***

MJ had been wide awake for several hours, mulling over the events of the last few days. Waves of confusion were swimming around her brain, thoughts coming in and out, sometimes with a crash, sometimes with a silent sweep. Although the bomb explosion at the hotel had been playing on her mind, the emotions surrounding Hakim, Steve and Andy were more prominent. That mixed with the sensual dream she had last night about Leah had just added to her confusion.

She thought of her sister and how planned out her life had been so far … university … job … house … marriage …

227

baby; straightforward and uncomplicated. After not being told about the baby, Kate said she'd make it up to her sister and today had invited her along to the hospital for the twenty-week scan. MJ was looking forward to spending time with her sister which, with any luck, would prove a welcome distraction from her own thoughts.

Out of the shower, MJ got dressed and settled down on the sofa with some tea and toast. She turned on the TV and, as expected, the BBC were still concentrating on the bomb at the hotel. They showed images of the ballroom and bar area following the explosion, hard to believe that she'd been there with everyone else, all dressed up and drinking champagne. Photos of the victims started to be shown, with the presenters taking it in turns to say a few words about them. The shot of Anne-Marie appeared and hit her in the stomach. Although she'd heard the news from Phil, seeing a photo of Anne-Marie, with what looked like the Eagle's bar in the background, made things even more scarring. Surely, nobody could believe that Hakim had anything to do with this? There's no reason on earth why he'd want to hurt Leah or damage the industry, let alone kill innocent people. The presenter turned to interview an older-looking lady who'd been a guest at the event. She began describing how the sound of the blast had been so great that she had been left with minimal hearing. She continued to describe the charred bodies she saw with bulging blooded eyes protruding from their faces and the limbs she saw hanging from a chair with the associated torso having been tossed on the floor and trampled on by others, all desperate to escape the devastation. MJ hoped that there weren't many children listening and becoming traumatised before heading off for a day at school.

The police have advised that they have a number of leads but are appealing for anyone who was at the Tower Hotel earlier that day and saw anything suspicious to contact the police as soon as possible on the number below.

***

Andy was watching the same news channel and thought back to Friday afternoon when he arrived at the Tower Hotel early to see Anne-Marie and Leah having a drink together in the bar. Odd, he thought, but not suspicious as such. Maybe Leah was pretending to Anne-Marie that everything between them was OK when, in reality, she wanted her dead. He then thought he was being far too dramatic and why would Leah want to kill people at her own event? It still troubled him, though, that Anne-Marie could be full of hate for Leah one week and then having a drink with her the next. And what was it Leah had said at the drinks reception, that's right she's been round at mine this week, yet didn't know that her mum had died? Something just didn't ring true, but he guessed he'd never know the truth now with Anne-Marie gone for good.

Chapter 48

The train pulled into Wokingham Station bang on time. MJ spotted Kate's black BMW arriving and waved. She climbed into the passenger seat and gave her sister a hug. As she tried to move away, however, Kate wouldn't let go and her chest was shuddering. She was crying. MJ immediately thought the worst, that something had happened to the baby. She encouraged her sister's chest away from her own. "Is it the baby?"

Kate nodded and MJ's heart sank.

"No, no, sorry the baby's fine."

MJ was confused but remained quiet and waited for her sister to be ready to tell her.

"It happened at my hen party, one minute I was dancing with Suzy and Freya, the next I'm outside getting some fresh air and then he's inside me."

The hairs on MJ's skin started to raise, "Sorry I'm not with you, did someone take you somewhere, did they hurt you?"

Kate shook her head. "No, nothing like that, he walked outside with me, we went to what I presume was his office and well, I wanted him just as much as he wanted me. MJ, the baby is his, what am I going to do?"

MJ was gobsmacked. Kate was shaking and had gone pale. "Hey hey, c'mon, we'll sort something out, but in the meantime, you need to calm down and pull yourself together; you have this little one to think about now remember. Whatever's happened has happened and it's not the baby's fault. Now let's swap places, I'm not letting you drive."

MJ sat in the soft leather driver's seat and put her hands on the steering wheel before pausing.

"It's automatic and there's satnav, you'll be fine," said Kate.

They left the station car park with MJ following the irritating lady's instructions. Turn left and then go straight on. Take the next right and you have reached your destination.

Inside the hospital, tranquillity presided; Kate led MJ to the ultrasound department and headed over to register with the receptionist. Kate finished off her water bottle in much the same manner as MJ had seen Anne-Marie drink Peroni. "Apparently the scan works better if my bladder's full."

"Hello Mrs Hoffman, you're here for your anomaly scan, aren't you?"

Kate looked confused, but another receptionist reassured her by saying, "your 20-week scan?"

"Yes, that's right."

They didn't have to wait long before the doctor called them through.

"Is it OK if my sister comes too?"

"Of course," said the doctor, who had a reassuring smile. "Hello Kate, I'm the sonographer, let me take you through what is going to happen at today's scan. In a minute, I'll ask you to lie down on the table and lift your top so I can reach your tummy; you'll need to pull your leggings down as well. I will then put some jelly on this probe before running it across your abdomen. Your baby should then appear on the monitor and I will check that everything's OK and as it should be at this stage. It's the same as your 12-week scan except the baby is more developed. Do you have any questions?"

Kate shook her head and climbed onto the table, folding down her leggings and lifting up her shirt. She then had some paper towel placed around the rim of her leggings,

231

which were pulled down a little further by the sonographer. MJ looked around the darkened room at the various gadgets and machines. Her eyes focused on the TV monitor, which flickered for a few moments, before the image of a wriggling baby appeared on the screen.

"There's your baby … looking very active."

MJ felt a tear brewing but blinked it away before glancing over to her sister, who had more than one tear in her eyes. MJ gave her a tissue and held her hand, "He looks a lively little thing, he can't keep still."

"You see, there, the arms and … keep still … the legs, let's just move this around." The probe continued to explore Kate's belly. "The brain, the heart, the bladder … everything looks perfect, you have a very healthy baby."

An hour later, the sisters were sat in a country pub. They ordered a couple of jacket potatoes, one plain with a sprinkling of cheese and the other with chilli con carne and considerably more cheese, bringing a smile to MJ's face. They had important things to discuss, though.

"What shall I do?" Kate asked?

"That's a good question. First things first, who is the father? Did you get a name?"

"David, Drew, Stu … I don't know."

"Local, tourist, old, young?"

"Local I think, but maybe not, I think Freya said they were police officers."

"Well at least this little one should have some discipline," said MJ, attempting some humour. "OK, tell me more about him, what did he sound like, what did he look like?"

"Why all the questions?"

"Because my advice will depend on your answers."

"He was normal build, short hair …"

"Skin colour?"

"MJ, it was dark, so hard to tell, I don't think he was black though; he wasn't big enough." said Kate with a hint of a smile.

Well, that's something, thought MJ, not knowing whether to laugh or cry. "So, a regular bloke you reckon, would you recognise him again?"

"I don't think so." Her voice became higher as she smashed a forkful of potato on her plate. "He did make a joke about being a boy-next-door type and, now I think back, he seemed younger than me, but I could be wrong."

"What do you think you should do?" asked MJ.

"I've asked myself that question ever since I took the pregnancy test. If I tell Jochen, then our marriage is over, full stop; he's so excited about the baby, it would break his heart if he found out it wasn't his."

"If it was me, I wouldn't say anything, not yet anyway. If you knew who the father was, then that would be different, but you don't so – even if you wanted to tell him – you couldn't, so the kid would end up with no father anyway, shit, what a mess."

"Tell me about it," said Kate closing her eyes for a moment. "Enough about me, what's been happening with you?"

MJ brought her sister up to speed with the bomb at the hotel and Hakim but left out her sleeping with Andy.

"He sounds weird, and you've heard nothing from him since last Friday?"

"Nope, nothing. I've sent him a couple of WhatsApp messages which I know he's opened, but I've received nothing back."

***

On the train home, mental exhaustion filled MJ's whole body. She wanted nothing more than to crawl in to bed and sleep for twelve hours solid, if only she hadn't agreed to babysit for Niklas and Sarah. Still, on a positive note, perhaps the company of a 3- and 5-year-old might be the distraction she needed. She remembered she needed to turn her phone back on, having turned it off when Kate had the scan. Fingers crossed there wouldn't be any more messages from Steve saying he loved her, the thought though gave her butterflies. There were just a couple of messages, neither from Hakim though. The first was from Steve saying Graham had been taken in for questioning again and the second from Leah, which MJ clicked on with bated breath.

Hey, the DI needs to see you, can we come round later please?

What's that about, she thought, perhaps they'd found Hakim. She messaged back. *Soz, have been with my sister, come round after 8pm*

Leah must've been online as she replied straight back. *Great, text me the address, thanks*

Niklas and Sarah didn't mind MJ having guests around if the boys were asleep, which fingers crossed, they would be by then. MJ took an all too brief nap and woke up just as the train pulled into Waterloo. Back home, she took a hot shower and put on her joggers and rugby shirt but, when she remembered who was coming around, changed into some smart chinos and a crisp white shirt.

Chapter 49

The DI and Leah walked up to the shiny black front door, which had a door knocker in the shape of an aeroplane in the middle of it.

"Nice pad," said the DI, "what did you say she did workwise?"

The door opened immediately, and MJ led them up a few wide steps into a huge open-plan kitchen-dining room and offered them a drink.

"Coffee please," said Leah.

"I'm good thanks," said the DI looking around the striking room.

"So, have you found Hakim?"

"No, we haven't, although we did recover a body yesterday in Ms Pope's office."

"A body? As in a dead body? Who?" asked MJ firmly gripping the kettle.

"We believe it's Hakim's cousin," the DI said.

"Nazir?"

"Did you know him?"

"Not really. I met him once at the pub when he came round to fix the TV, and then Hakim mentioned him a lot, sounded more like a brother to him; he's going to be gutted."

"Ms Atkins …"

"Call me MJ, please!"

Leah shook her head, "She struggles with first names."

The DI ignored her, "MJ, please can you confirm the last time you saw Hakim Khan?"

"On Friday. We went to the Awards Dinner together at the Tower Hotel. He said he wasn't feeling well after the main course and asked me to leave with him. We got a black cab to Islington and then the same cab brought me back here."

DI Johnson looked up. "Sorry, go back a step, you went with him in a taxi to Islington and then the driver brought you back to Victoria?"

"Yeah, that's right, I didn't know what he'd said to the driver to begin with, so thought that perhaps he'd invite me into his."

"Did he talk to you at all on the journey? How did he seem?"

"He said he felt ill, which looking back, he also said during the reception drinks when he walked off, Andy went after him."

"Andy? Surname please?"

"Sorry, I don't know."

Leah interrupted, "He works ... worked with Anne-Marie, you know the lady who was killed, I think his surname is Blackwell."

The DI made a note to get one of the team to talk to him. "OK, let's go back to the taxi ride, how did Hakim seem? Was he agitated? Did he sleep? Where did the taxi drop him off?"

One question at a time thought MJ, trying to process the interrogation. "Quiet, he just looked out of the window, didn't message anyone from what I could see, and he wasn't sick as such," she recalled. "I had Google Maps open and could see that we stopped in a road just off Upper Street."

"Can I have a look at your phone please?"

"Sure," said MJ unlocking it for the DI.

"There, it's still on your phone, that's great. One minute please." The DI excused herself and, holding MJ's phone in one hand, made a call from her phone on the other.

"Can you send a car round to the Turkish cafes along

Upper Street please, question the staff about Friday and show them Hakim's photo?"

MJ and Leah both heard an assertive Yes Ma'am on the other end of the phone.

"There is something else I need to tell you, not about Hakim though, it's something that Anne-Marie said to me at the event on Friday," MJ said.

The DI looked up from her notebook and Leah sat up straight.

"She wanted to tell you, Leah, but only when the time was right. She told me that, at the Sainsburys near you, she overheard a conversation from two of the women who worked there. They said there'd been two guys in there the day before the accident talking about which woman they needed to deal with. They didn't say anything because the guys looked menacing and neither woman wanted to risk anything happening to them."

The DI stood up and was about to use her phone again but sensed there was more to come. "OK Miss Marple, I want to hear everything you know, sounds like you've got a lot in that head of yours."

"That's what working in a pub does for you." MJ smiled, a little nervously.

Leah, still trying to process what Anne-Marie had overheard, remained quiet wondering what else MJ knew.

"Look, there's nothing in particular, it's all probably something and nothing. Over the last few weeks in the pub, there's been a lot of talk about Leah and what's been going on. One night, Graham, Anne-Marie and Robin were all in the pub having an argument about who hated her the most, so yeah, I heard stuff, but I guess the drink had something to do with it. There's a photo of them together on our Instagram account, do you want to see it?"

"Yes please," said the DI.

Leah joined the DI at the table and they looked at the phone, enlarging the photo and tactfully ignoring the three suggestive text messages in a row from Andy which scrolled across the top of the screen.

The DI looked puzzled. "OK, let's rewind. I know who Graham is, and I know who Anne-Marie is, but who's this person here, Robin, where does he fit in?"

"Robin Franklin?" said Leah looking surprised. "Why would he hate me? OK, I was up against him for the role, but things were always friendly – even during the debates, we always got on and agreed on most things though."

"Yep, but by all accounts," MJ informed them, "he's had the hots for you for years and you always turned down his advances." She wondered whether she should've used different terminology.

"Is this true?" the DI asked.

"Well, he's asked me out for dinner a few times, but that's it," said Leah. She started racking her brains about when and where he'd asked her out, the last time being a couple of months ago in Berlin.

As if mind reading, MJ continued, "And he told Steve, that in Berlin ..."

"Hold on, who's Steve?"

"Pub landlord," said Leah willing MJ to continue with her story.

"He told Steve that he saw you in your hotel room ... with ... um ... your head between another woman's legs."

"Is this correct?" asked the DI.

"Me declining his offer of dinner, or having my head between somebody's legs?"

MJ tried not to laugh.

"Did you see him at your hotel, Leah?" asked the DI.

238

"He walked me back to my hotel and then said he needed to use the bathroom. I didn't give it a second thought and just went up to my room to see Georgia. I can't believe he came snooping after me.

DI Johnson continued writing in her notebook and without looking up asked, "Name of the hotel and date please?"

"Westin, beginning of March, a Tuesday."

They all looked up as a small figure dressed in Paw Patrol pyjamas appeared in the doorway. "Can't find monkey," said the little voice walking over to MJ.

The DI stood up and put her notebook into her bag. "I'm going to the pub to talk to Steve, I'll call you later, can you stay here with MJ please?" She turned towards Leah and whispered, "Is that her kid?"

Leah shrugged her shoulders and turned to look at MJ. "Shall we go upstairs and see if we can find monkey? He knows he shouldn't play hide and seek at night, doesn't he?" With Oskar's arms and legs wrapped around her, MJ walked up the stairs, her face nestled into his, breathing in the innocent smell of child.

After a few minutes, Leah started to get a bit spooked sitting in the vast space on her own in silence, so walked up the stairs, following the sound of MJ's soft voice. She peered in the door, which had a Paw Patrol sign on it indicating Oskar's room. The boy curled up with monkey, in much the same way as Leah had been with the Cubs Shirt, and sucked on his thumb; his eyes looked heavy. MJ turned the last page of a book and finished with the infamous phrase and they all lived happily ever after. She kissed him on the forehead and then proceeded to kiss and say goodnight to the monkey too. She backed slowly away from the bed and then turned, surprised to see Leah in the doorway.

239

"Sorry if I startled you, I was enjoying the story," said Leah in a whisper.

"That's OK, but please tell me you didn't see me kiss the monkey."

"You're a natural MJ, how old is he?"

"Three, and his brother's five, they can be a handful at times, but they have a lot of love to give, so I never mind babysitting."

The penny dropped with Leah, "Ah, it makes sense now, so they're not yours then?"

"Good God, no! They're my sister's nephews; I babysit a couple of times a week and in exchange I get a discounted rent on the bedsit on the top floor. It's a win-win."

Chapter 50

The DI met with one of her team outside the Eagle and brought him up to speed with the rapidly developing situation. They went in and asked to see Steve. MJ had already sent a hurried text letting him know of the impending visit, so he had time to send Graham on his merry way. There were only a few other people in the pub, so he asked Alex to stay on the bar with Polly as he showed the officers to a booth.

Steve took them through everything he knew, including how Robin had told him Leah had ruined his career and broken his heart. As the police officer listened and jotted down notes, Steve looked up to see Andy walk in the bar. "Hey Steve," he said scanning the pub, "any sign of MJ? She's ignoring my messages."

The DI looked up, "if it's the same MJ I've just been with then she's at home with her kid."

Steve and Andy did a double take at each other. "MJ doesn't have a kid?" said Andy.

"True, but she does babysit the two boys from downstairs," said Steve.

"Are you the Andy who knew Anne-Marie?" the DI asked.

"I worked with her and, yeah, we were friends. Have you found the scumbag who killed her yet?"

"Please sit down, you may be able to help us."

"Sure," said Andy getting his phone out. "If you've just been with MJ, I suppose she told you about the photo sent from Boy1?"

The DI bit her tongue and tapped her fingers on the table. "No, she didn't, so please go ahead," she said, "enlighten me."

"Well, on the night that Leah got the role, someone sent Robin a photo of her celebrating at her office. Georgia, stood next to her in the photo, and we thought …"

"Sorry, who's "we"?"

"Me and MJ," Andy said, before continuing, "we thought it odd that Robin received the photo."

"Did Robin show the photo to you?"

"No, he showed it to me, and I told MJ," said Steve.

"Who then told me," said Andy. "So, a few weeks later, when we were all in here, I told Robin I needed to make a call and didn't have my phone, so I asked if I could borrow his and he obliged. Anyway, I scrolled through the WhatsApp photos and found the one in question and noted it was from 'Boy1'."

"And did you get the number for Boy1?"

"Just the last 4 digits 1990, that's the year I was born."

"Please can you confirm Robin's surname?"

"Franklin."

"Thanks, you've both been a great help. Please give your details to my colleague in case we need anything else from you. In the meantime, please be vigilant and, if you see or hear anything else suspicious, please call me immediately," said the DI passing her card across the table.

In the car, the DI made the first call. "Get me everything you can on a Robin Franklin please, including phone records from 4th April – pay particular attention to a number ending in 1990. Find out who the number belongs to. Also get onto the Westin Hotel in Berlin and see if they still have their CCTV footage from 4th March. It's unlikely, but then again, they're German, so hopefully their efficiency will reward us. I'm going to keep the target, Ms Pope, with Ms Atkins overnight as the location is unknown to both suspects as far as we know. We're onto these fuckers."

"Yes ma'am."

Then she made the second call. "Ms Pope, I'm going to have to ask you to stay with Ms Atkins until it's safe for you to return to your home, is that OK?"

Leah had already put the DI on loudspeaker, so MJ put a thumb up indicating it was OK for Leah to stay. "Ms Atkins says it's fine for Ms Pope to stay at her property, thank you Detective Inspector Johnson," Leah said, mocking the DI's formality, before looking at MJ, "Looks like you and me are going to be roomies for the night."

MJ turned her back to Leah and gave an inward jump for joy, which quickly turned to panic as she wondered what state her flat was in. Were the sheets clean? Had she left dirty underwear on the floor? Had she rinsed the bath after shaving her legs?

***

Niklas and Sarah arrived home at 11pm. MJ introduced Leah to them as a friend from the pub and thought it best to leave it at that.

"Did you see the police car outside? For a moment, I thought something had happened to you or the boys."

"No, everything's fine. I didn't hear a peep from Jakob, but Oskar came down once as he'd lost monkey. He went back to sleep straight away though. Did you have a good night?"

"Lovely thanks, although with a bellyful of food as well as a baby, I need to go and lie down," Sarah said holding her tummy.

"We'll leave you in peace then, goodnight." MJ led Leah out of the front door into the porch and then into the adjacent door and up three flights of stairs into the eaves of the property. She unlocked the door and did a quick

243

scan around to see if anything dodgy had been left. All clear, she thought.

"Cosy," said Leah looking around the well-designed layout. "Just the one bed?"

"Um, ye ... yes," said MJ berating herself for coming across so nervously. "There's a sofa bed as well though, that's where guests usually stay."

"Perfect," said Leah.

"Unless you'd like to ... stay with me?" said MJ, not daring to look at Leah's face as she awaited her response.

"That's a very tempting offer, but I'll be fine on the sofa bed thanks. Oh, and a message from the DI, she suggests you reply to Andy, seems like he's got it bad for you and wants a repeat of Sunday night."

Chapter 51

To her surprise, MJ woke up with someone next to her in bed for the second time that week. She looked over at Leah curled up beside her in the England rugby top that she'd lent her but couldn't recall when or how she got there. Should she get out of bed, should she say something to her, should she move the strands of blonde hair away from her soft face? Was she developing feelings for Leah that went beyond admiration? MJ held her in high regard, for sure, and admired her resilience – nothing acted as a deterrent against this woman's determination to get on with life.

***

Little did MJ know that the activity taking place in Leah's mind was the polar opposite of her exterior. Her head was a mess and her heart completely broken; she'd climbed into MJ's bed that night for safety, comfort and to feel life next to her. As she lay on the sofa bed, she heard noises, smelt smells, saw things she couldn't face. Next to MJ she took comfort in another human's breathing, a chest going up and down, a mouth letting out smooth rasps of air, reassurance that she was indeed alive and not living in a hellish nightmare. Leah kept hearing Anne-Marie's voice and words of encouragement in her head, Be strong for Georgia. She knew it was true, so made a pledge to herself that whatever her head told her, she would portray strength, confidence and humour on the outside.

***

The decision about what to do was soon made as Leah turned over and gave her a sleepy look. "You didn't mind, did you, it looked a lot more comfortable."

245

"Of course not." I just wish I'd have known about it, thought MJ to herself. Confusion began to develop in MJ's head, the last twenty-four hours really screwing with her brain. The confusion evident when she tried to put the orange juice in the cafetiere and coffee in the glasses. How did she feel about Leah? Pushing the thought to one side, she carried on getting the drinks ready and putting the sofa bed back to the sofa position. As she debated whether the sheets needed a wash or could be put straight back in the storage compartment of the large footstool, she heard footsteps coming upstairs and a knock on the door.

"I'm leaving you some pastries outside, I got far too many this morning and the boys are typically having a cereal day."

Sarah, what a star thought MJ opening the door, calling thank you downstairs and taking the tray of goodies inside to the coffee table.

After a shower, Leah put on her clothes from the previous night, leaving the rugby top neatly folded at the bottom of the made bed. She walked over to MJ with her nose in the air inhaling the fresh coffee. She looked at the impressive array of food and drink in front of her and smiled. "I could get used to this," she said grabbing a mini pain au chocolate and making herself at home on the sofa.

MJ joined her just as Leah's phone rang. "It's the DI," she muffled to MJ, savouring the chocolate in the pastry. "Hey, what's up?"

"It's a long story, we're giving a live press conference on the BBC at 10. Most of the details will be covered, but I'll pop round straight afterwards and fill in the gaps; there are a few details we don't want the press knowing yet."

When the credits started running indicating the end of Homes under the Hammer, a voice interrupted the tune and advised that a live press conference would follow in light of the recent events in London. The interview room was a hub of activity with journalists wearing headphones and holding microphones, as well as a variety of phones, tablets and laptops. In front of them, sat at a covered trestle table were a couple of uniformed officers, a senior-looking man and a relaxed looking DI Johnson. Additional police officers and official looking personnel were standing next to the table in front of the door. The DI drank some water from the glass in front of her, coughed to clear her throat, and waited for her cue to address the nation.

Leah and MJ sat together on the sofa and waited with bated breath.

"Do you think she's attractive?" asked Leah.

Surprised by the casual question, MJ studied the DI's rusty tanned face, home to sporadic clusters of freckles. Her hair, a random style of its own, neither long nor a bob, not blonde but not brown either, and it couldn't be described as curly or straight. The more MJ studied her, the more unique she considered her appearance. "She's got something about her," said MJ just as the DI introduced herself and Operation Carousel.

"I can confirm that we believe the shooting at the Apollo Theatre on Wednesday 12th June is related to the bomb attack at the Tower Hotel on Friday 21st June. There are also several more incidents that we believe may be connected. These are, as we speak, being investigated further by my team. However, I can advise that on Monday evening, we discovered the body of Nazir Khan in the office of the ticketing company, Global Tickets. We have identified two individuals who we would like to

247

question, Mr Hakim Khan, cousin of the deceased and Mr Robin Franklin. We ask the public to be vigilant and not to approach either of the said men, but to contact the number that's being shown on your screen now."

Leah shook her head, "I can't believe it's come to this, a member of my team and an industry colleague." She opened her mouth to make further comment but stopped when she realised there would be questions from the gossip-thirsty journalists. The first asked the police if they were treating the events as terror-related. The Chief Superintendent, who Leah assumed was the DI's boss, answered straight away. He advised that, although it's one line of enquiry, other motives are, at this stage looking more likely.

Next came a question asking if there was a link between the theatre shooting and the fatal road accident which took place on the same day. Leah's body tensed and her hand reached for MJ; the question hit straight in the heart and she hoped that neither her name nor that of Georgia's would be mentioned.

"Yes, this is one of the incidents we believe is connected," said the DI refocussing and pointing to a lady with sunglasses on for the next question.

"Do you think the attacker is targeting tourists?"

The DI looked to her boss who gave a succinct answer.

"Again, it's a line of enquiry we are pursuing."

The last question came from a geeky-looking man, who looked barely old enough to vote let alone have a job as a journalist. "Do you think the incidents are being carried out by a professional?"

The Chief answered, "We are considering two different theories at present. On the one hand, we believe there must be some degree of professionalism but there is also evidence pointing towards an amateur. The team led by

DI Johnson are working day and night on the case, investigating every theory. Thank you everyone."

As soon as the press conference finished, DI Johnson re-joined her team for a briefing. "Mr Khan left the hotel around 10pm in a black cab with Ms Atkins. They were on a date, albeit with hundreds of other people and, despite showing some odd behaviour last Friday, Ms Atkins says he showed no sign of any hatred or anguish towards anyone, including Ms Pope. Ms Atkins did however come forward with other circumstantial evidence which is being looked into. I don't think she's in danger but it's worth keeping in close contact."

MJ and Leah sat motionless on the sofa. MJ looked at the array of food in front of her and fought back nausea. Photos of Hakim and Robin appeared on the screen, followed by Nazir. MJ spoke first. "Why would either of them want to hurt anyone and ruin their industry: it just doesn't make any sense."

"I've got a horrible feeling that this could all be my fault, all this hurt and killing down to me."

The doorbell went and MJ looked at Leah before freezing. Leah made a phone call. "It's the DI," she said, "you can let her in."

MJ pressed the buzzer and opened the door, calling downstairs for her to come up to the top floor. She continued to watch as the DI sprang up the stairs, taking them two at a time.

"Cosy," said the DI as she walked into the bedsit not a bit out of breath but just with a drop of rain at the end of her nose.

"That's just what I said," said Leah making sure her exterior remained strong and confident. "Coffee?"

"Yes, please."

Leah looked at home, making coffee in MJ's compact kitchen, whilst the DI walked around surveying the area, paying particular attention to the bed; MJ expected her to pull on a pair of blue gloves at any minute. She sat down on the large footstool and beckoned Leah and MJ over to the sofa. With the TV still chirping away, DI Johnson assumed they'd seen the press conference, but thought she'd check anyway.

"Yes, we did."

"Do you have any questions, or shall I tell you both the things that weren't mentioned?" The DI continued not waiting to hear if they had any questions. "As you're both very much involved with this case, you have a right to know the following, but it can't go any further. Do you understand? MJ, that means in particular no mention of it in the pub OK. As I've found out only too well in the last couple of days, pubs are breeding grounds for both truth and slander."

MJ nodded, as did Leah.

"Our investigations have shown that Robin Franklin owned the property occupied by Hakim Khan and his cousin, the deceased Nazir Khan. In addition, we know that he received the photo of Leah celebrating her new role from Hakim, aka 'Boy1'. We found further details about the Apollo Theatre on Hakim's PC. The evidence is incriminating, whichever way you look at it. As you are aware, Leah, the paper Hakim produced when he applied for his role at Global Tickets contained his exact actions subsequently carried out. We have statements from colleagues saying he was in your office whilst you attended a meeting at the Houses of Parliament and our tech team have confirmed that his login was used to access your calendar and change meeting details."

Whilst Leah knew most of this, MJ sat with her mouth open and eyes bulging. "Are you saying that Hakim shot people at the theatre, drove into Georgia and planted the bomb at the hotel?"

"It's looking like it could have been him or his cousin, or both."

"And what's the link to Robin, that I don't understand?" asked Leah.

"This is the more worrying part, which I want you to stay calm for. After Robin's wife died in 2012, he moved to Hamburg and worked for a publishing company. He also volunteered at a local refugee centre, which is where we believe he got to know the then teenager Hakim Khan. We are still trying to establish all of the details hence it wasn't announced to the public just now, but it appears as though Hakim's family may have links to terrorism. We have people working on the case in Hamburg as we speak, including the anti-terrorism police."

Nobody said anything; DI Johnson's eyes went from Leah to MJ looking for a reaction or emotion, but silence persisted. There was a knock on the door and all three women jumped up in surprise, as if the starter's gun had just been fired.

"Emmerjay, can I come in? Monkey wants to see you?"

"Tell monkey I'll come down in a bit. Maybe he'd like to set up a tea party?"

"OK, see you later alligator."

The intervention by the 3-year-old lightened the mood and brought back a smile to Leah's face, which MJ found infectious.

"He's so cute. If I was you, I'd be having permanent tea parties with him," said Leah.

"Me too," said the DI, "beats police work any day. Talking of which, I better get on, we've got some more interviews

251

to conduct. Leah, I've arranged for the patrol car outside to drive you back to Chiswick. We still have a car outside your house and officers are in the area, so you shouldn't worry but you should stay indoors. MJ, you're OK to go out, but please remain vigilant and remember what I said about keeping what I've told you to yourself. Here's my direct number, if you need me at all, please just call, OK." The DI watched intently as Leah walked into the bedroom and picked something up from the bedside table.

"Enjoy your tea party and thank you for last night. You have my number too, so please keep in touch," said Leah.

"Thanks, I will do and please look after yourself." MJ walked down the stairs with them and went into the adjacent front door for her picnic.

Chapter 52

As the police officer turned the unmarked black Toyota Corolla into Vernon Drive, Leah noticed a shiny Volvo in the driveway. The officer received a call to say the vehicle didn't pose a threat and told Leah it was nothing to worry about. She got out of the Corolla, put her jacket over her head to shield herself from the rain, and walked towards the Volvo. The driver and passenger doors opened at the same time.

"Mum? Dad?" Leah said, surprised to find them there.

"Leah dear, just because we're old it doesn't mean that we don't watch TV or listen to the wireless, and you must remember that Dad reads the paper every morning. Did you honestly think we wouldn't recognise your name and face everywhere?" said Leah's mum shaking her head.

"Come in, come in," said Leah ignoring the statement. "Let me get the kettle on. How long have you been sat on my drive for?"

"Not long dear, but your father does need to use the bathroom as soon as possible; we got through our flasks of coffee in record time and this rain isn't helping matters."

"Don't you have keys?" Leah asked.

"Yes, but we didn't want to intrude."

Leah couldn't believe her parents sometimes. "The toilet is just round there, Dad."

Leah's mum helped carry the drinks over to the living room and sat next to her daughter on the sofa, whilst dad sat on the armchair. He got out his paper and started reading. Typical, Leah thought, he hasn't seen me since Christmas, and he reads the paper. Leah's mum puffed out her cheeks and waved her finger.

"Dad is looking for something dear, we have a question we'd like to ask you."

He found the page featuring the photo of Leah with the team outside on the office terrace and pointed to Georgia. "Is she your ... how do you say it, Lou?"

"Partner, we want to know if she is your partner?"

Leah took a deep breath and looked up, thinking of Anne-Marie. "Yes mum, but she was killed in a road accident."

"There, I told you about the accident, didn't I Lou."

Leah's mum moved closer and coaxed her daughter's head towards hers and, for the first time in years, they savoured a mother-daughter hug, something that Leah had longed for, a feeling magnified since Georgia's death. Her father continued to look straight ahead at nothing in particular, but Leah could tell by the intense frown he was wearing that he was worried.

"Is someone trying to hurt you?" he asked.

"Yes, the police think so."

"Is that why your, er, your partner was killed?"

Leah couldn't tell which bit her dad was most upset about, her having a partner or someone wanting to hurt her, so decided to bite the bullet and ask, "Are you disappointed in me?"

Her mum replied, "Oh Leah dear, how could you think that? You're our eldest daughter, of course we're not disappointed. We just want you to be happy, do you understand. It's not up to us who you fall in love with; oh Leah, we should've been here for you, I can't believe you've been going through all of this on your own."

"Well, at least you're here now," said Leah.

Chapter 53

After a couple of hours' tea party play with Oskar, Jakob and monkey, MJ escaped back upstairs, but not before Sarah gave her a big hug and thanked her. She tried taking the stairs two at a time, as DI Johnson had, but only made the first flight before her breathing became strained. That's why you work in a pub and she's a police detective, she said to herself. The thought of the pub made her crave some familiarity, not to mention a stiff drink. Although it was her day off, she knew Steve wouldn't mind her propping up the bar.

Before long, she was opening the door to the Eagle, a comforting wave of alcoholic breath hit her and a stampede of voices all vying for their opinions to be heard. Busy was an understatement. Without giving it a second thought, she went behind the bar. "Yes please," she said to a waiting customer, "what can I get you?" Whilst on a Fosters-pouring marathon, she gave the pub a quick scan and guessed that it shouldn't take more than twenty minutes or so to serve those waiting, get the tables cleared and glasses washed.

Two hours later, MJ put the last tray of clean glasses away and took up her position with the regulars on the other side of the bar, enjoying a large glass of wine. "Where did everyone come from?" she asked.

"No idea, but my tills said they enjoyed that last couple of hours," said Steve, smiling from ear to ear.

"I bet they did, does that mean you're going to buy me a drink?"

"Of course!"

"Looks like you helped the police yesterday," said MJ, "did you see the press conference this morning?"

"Yep, looks like your boy is involved after all."

"Which one?" said Alex with a wink, remembering having caught her and Andy getting down to it in the corridor before they left on Sunday night. He then answered his own question. "The Turkish bomber."

"Don't call him that," said MJ, taking her frustration out on a beer mat.

"Sorry, but you've got to admit that the evidence is stacking up on him?"

"Yes, but perhaps he was forced into it?"

The other regulars were oblivious to the conversation and were more interested in their own discussion about some upcoming football game, so MJ continued. "What I don't understand, is how Leah can be so assured about everything. I mean, I know she broke down after the funeral, but apart from that she's so confident and strong. And that's even after seeing Naz's dead body in her office on Monday."

Steve's eyes bulged, "What?!"

"Shit, sorry, forget I said anything," said MJ, reprimanding herself for doing what the DI told her not to do. "I just find it impressive how she goes about her life, even managing some humour."

Steve didn't press her on the dead body statement. "Brains work in different ways, just because she looks strong, she may be a complete mess under that assuredness, you just don't know."

"Maybe," said MJ, "but it's still admirable."

"From what I see, you're just as tough as her; don't let what you think of others get in the way of looking after yourself and, above all, act on your impulses and trust your judgement. Now, before I have to start turfing everyone out, I am trusting my own judgment and I'm going to walk you home OK, you look as though you need a good sleep."

256

"Thanks Steve," said MJ getting up. "Shall I get Roxy?"

"Yep, although when she sees the rain, she might not be so excited."

"Watch out for the Turkish bomber," said Alex, irritating both Steve and MJ.

Outside the pub, Steve opened the large red and white Sky Sports umbrella and held it over MJ as she held Roxy's lead. As expected, the dog wasn't enamoured with the weather but, with her tail down, she kept alongside MJ looking up at her every few minutes. As they reached MJ's home, Roxy caught onto a scent and began pulling on the lead.

"What is it girl?" said Steve. Edging towards the metal railings outside of the property, Roxy's paw started tugging at something.

"Urgh, a kebab," said MJ, "I hate it when people just throw their left-over food over the railings when there's a bin just up the road. Hey Roxy, stay away, the last thing Steve wants is to deal with you after you've eaten chilli sauce-covered lamb. Here girl, what are these?" The distraction with gravy bones worked.

"Right, you get yourself inside and to bed OK, you're working tomorrow and it's quiz night, so I need you on form."

"OK boss, understood loud and clear," said MJ with a smile.

Steve gave her a quick hug and kiss on the head before pulling Roxy away and heading back to the pub. MJ made a mental note to bring down a plastic bag and gloves in the morning to deal with the take-away deposit. She felt better after talking to Steve and having a couple of glasses of wine. Her sister had sent her a few messages, so she decided that she'd get ready for bed and then give her a call. Rolling the duvet back and climbing into bed with the phone, she looked at the space that Leah occupied the previous night and Andy a couple of days before that. She plumped up both German-style square fluffy pillows, put them behind her and got comfortable for the call.

Chapter 54

Bzzzzzzzzzzz Bzzzzzzzzzzzzz, went the door buzzer. Shit, who can that be, thought MJ rolling out of bed. She pictured the three solid doors between herself and the person on the other side of the buzzer and picked up the receiver. "Yes, hello?!" Silence. "Hello?"

"It's Hakim, can I see you please?"

MJ's hands were shaking. "Are you OK?" Why did she asked such a stupid question, of course he wasn't OK. MJ knew she should call the DI there and then, but a little voice inside her head stopped her. Instead, she pulled on a pair of jeans, an oversized Gap hoodie before slipping her feet into her sliders. She walked down the stairs, her heart beating faster with every step. Pausing at the door, she pushed her hair behind her ears before opening the inside door followed by the main front door. She saw the tall frame of Hakim and, after a quick scan around, didn't think he had company. "What on earth has happened to you? Are you OK? Come on in."

Despite all the suspicions that had built up around him, MJ couldn't help feeling concerned and escorted a shy and awkward looking Hakim upstairs. Once inside her brightly lit flat, MJ took a closer look at him and realised he was not only wet but also filthy. Breathing through her mouth, she put her hand under his elbow and walked him into the bathroom. Questions could wait she thought; he needs to get himself cleaned up first. A few minutes later, she heard the shower start followed by several low whimpers and long moans.

A maternal instinct kicked in, and she went to the kitchen and started making a hearty noodle dish. With the water simmering, MJ went to her wardrobe and dug out a pair of old tracksuit bottoms, which she thought might fit Hakim, along with her biggest shirt, the England rugby top that still smelt of Leah from the previous night.

"I've put some clothes outside the door for you," MJ called through the bathroom door.

"Thanks," came a muffled response from the shower.

MJ went back to the kitchen and began chopping a few vegetables whilst her mind worked overtime; why come to me? why now? She gazed over the breakfast bar and noticed the trail of muddy, wet footprints went from the front door to the sofa, and probably down the stairs too. Sarah was a stickler for cleanliness, and MJ knew she would be asking questions about this tomorrow; she just hoped it wouldn't bring on a premature labour.

Hakim emerged from the bathroom and looked like a normal human being again. MJ encouraged him to sit on a stool at the breakfast bar whilst she carried on cooking. He got out his phone, which resembled his appearance when he arrived. He gave the screen a thorough rub on the rugby shirt, much to MJ's annoyance, before opening the photos and swiping left for a few seconds.

"Look," he said passing the phone to MJ, "look what he did to Naz."

MJ took the phone and focused on the photo. She screwed up her face and turned away from the screen in disgust. "Who did this?"

Hakim took the phone back and switched it off. "I couldn't kill her, I couldn't do it. She gave me a chance, she respected me. But I had to show willing, I needed to do something but so many people got killed, so many innocent people, I didn't mean to, what am I going to do?"

MJ's jaw dropped as she looked at Hakim, his hands trembling and head held low. She got down from her stool and held out her arms. He didn't need much encouragement and in an instant his body sank into the comfort of MJ's embrace. He held onto her, his grasp not relenting. Despite her arms struggling under his dead weight, she was content to stay still until she clocked the boiling water spilling out of the pan. She moved his arms back to the table and turned down the heat to a simmer. Neither of them spoke as MJ watched him finish off three bowls of food. He looked at the empty bowl and MJ thought he may lick it clean. For a moment he looked as though he didn't have a care in the world, but the minute he finished eating, anguish returned to his face.

"Who couldn't you kill?" MJ knew the answer but wanted to hear it from him. She leaned forward and looked Hakim in the eyes.

He recalled how Robin had become obsessed with Leah over the last few months. Whilst he felt threatened by her at first, he was confident that he would get the tourism role and at the same time he'd convinced himself that she liked him in a physical way too, so asked her out. "It hurt his ego when she turned him down," Hakim said, "and then when she got the role, that's when he lost it. He became angry, destructive and abusive."

"But I don't understand why you are involved with Robin, what's your connection with him?"

Hakim sighed and started stroking the back of his head. "It's a very long story but do you remember when we were out together, I told you about how I spent my teenage years in Hamburg? Well, Robin was there too. As well as his regular job, he also worked in the same refugee centre as my mother did and he became like a father figure to me."

"What about your real father?"

"Please don't be angry that I didn't tell you before, but it's not something I'm proud of."

MJ nodded for him to continue.

"He's in prison for terrorist offences, along with my uncle. My brother should've been there too, but the police got to him first and shot him dead. When Robin said he wanted to return to the UK, my mother begged him to take me and Naz with him, get us jobs and somewhere to live in London, get us away from everything. I think they were more than just friends, but we never knew for sure. Anyway, he agreed and that's how come we're here. We owe so much to him, I said I'd do anything to repay him, to say thank you, but I didn't think it would be this. I should've said no to begin with and just faced the consequences."

Hakim carried on talking and MJ carried on listening until the early hours of the morning, until they were both wiped out.

"Why don't you stay here tonight, get some sleep," she suggested. He didn't need asking twice and he was asleep in minutes. MJ couldn't sleep though, and paced around the living room throughout the night, messaging Leah, but nothing came back. She knew she should call the DI but couldn't risk her simply taking Hakim away. Leah would know what to do for the best, she'd be more reasonable. There must be some way out for Hakim.

Towards the morning, still before dawn, she heard Hakim yell out and turned to see him as pale as a ghost, dripping with sweat and his eyes wide with rage. Hakim handed his phone to MJ. Her stomach did a flip. There was a photo of Hakim with his arm around a proud looking woman, which MJ knew must be his mother. Underneath were the words – She's Next.

Chapter 55

Hakim shot up and made a beeline for the door. "I have to warn her."

"Where are you going?" MJ asked, trying to bar his way.

"Germany, to protect her."

"But your name and face are all over the news, you'll never get to the airport let alone board a plane."

"It's OK, we have a disguise and fake passports, look." Hakim showed the passport to MJ which pictured him with full beard and long hair against the name Emre Osman. "I have to go, I fly to Frankfurt and then take the train to Hamburg, it's better I think."

"Wait, does Robin have a fake passport too? What name does he use?"

"George Bennett." He pushed past her and took off before MJ could say take care ... or ask for her rugby shirt back.

Trust your judgement and act on your impulses, isn't that what Steve told her? MJ checked her watch and noted the time; she had an idea. She tiptoed down the stairs so as not to wake the others in the main house, but she knew that there would be one person awake at this time. She waited just outside of the front door and, within five minutes, she saw a figure jogging along the street. Regular as clockwork, Niklas always took an early morning run. As he reached the front railings, he looked up in surprise.

"I've never seen you up this early, or are you just getting home?" he asked chuckling. His smile soon faded when he saw the look on MJ's face.

"Can I ask you to do something really important for me please, but at the same time not ask why I want the information?"

"Sounds ominous, tell me and I'll decide whether it's something I'm able to do," Niklas replied. "Close the door and let's take a walk."

Fifteen minutes later they were back, and MJ ran upstairs with the information she wanted. She called Andy. "Pack an overnight bag, bring your passport and meet me at Victoria Coach Station in an hour."

"What the fuck?"

"Oh, and can you send me a photo of your passport please, the page with your details on?"

***

MJ waited at the coach station and wondered whether Andy would actually show up. Nerves were creeping into her body including a swishing motion in her stomach. Someone's case fell over sending her up in the air like a jack in the box. She continued to pace on the spot until Andy sneaked up and covered her eyes with his hands. Without realising who it was, MJ thrust her elbow back into his stomach. She turned, and, seeing who it was, cursed,

"What the fuck, Andy? What do you think you're doing?"

Andy raised his hands and apologised. "Why are you so jumpy, is it anything to do with this?" He showed her the front page of the Metro. "Did you know about this?" he asked. A photo of a smiling Robin and stern Hakim were placed next to each other under the bold headline, Police search for dangerous duo.

"Where do I start?" said MJ.

The two boarded the busy National Express AIRail coach to Heathrow and chose a couple of seats near the back. Andy then listened in bewilderment as MJ retold the story of how Robin's obsession for Leah had taken over his life and led to him blackmailing Hakim and Nazir into carrying out, at first minor misdemeanours, before sabotaging the booking system and then stepping things up a level. The final act was meant to result in Leah being blown to smithereens off the stage at the Summer Awards, but due to the bomb being placed in the wrong amplifier, her life remained intact and, instead, the lives of many more people were taken – including that of Anne-Marie.

***

At Terminal 5, once through security, Andy led MJ straight to Wetherspoons. He'd endured her stomach talking to him for the entire coach journey so decided she needed to eat, and they both needed a drink. He couldn't fathom what MJ's plan was but, as he was stupid enough to turn up at the Coach Station, he may as well continue with her on whatever crazy mission she was on. Even though he hadn't seen her since they spent the night together on Sunday, he felt a real closeness to MJ and hoped that their relationship could develop further. He was experiencing feelings he'd never had before, a kind of protectiveness towards her, alongside a need for her affection and appreciation.

The food and alcohol seemed to help MJ as not only did her stomach stop grumbling, but she appeared brimming with sheer determination to get to Robin and stop him from hurting Hakim's mum.

Andy looked at the departures board and asked MJ what their flight number was. "C'mon, looks like we're on time for boarding. Gate A19," said Andy. He took her hand and they headed off across what felt like the whole length of the terminal, passing designer shop after empty designer shop. They were all there, Gucci, Prada, Burberry etc. Andy wondered whether anyone ever purchased anything; surely it would be better use of space to have some affordable shops in their place.

265

At gate A19, they sat opposite a man with a briefcase, who was glancing to his left and right without moving his head, his body rigid. With the briefcase on his lap, he flicked up the metal clasp and lifted the lid, again moving his eyes first to the left and then to the right.

Andy watched on with curiosity. The man looked in his late 40s and, apart from a few strands of hair, his head was as smooth as an egg. He wore pokey round glasses, which hung off his pointy snout.

"You know MJ," Andy said, nodding towards the man, "not all terrorists are Asian, some are middle-aged bald men who keep guns in their briefcases."

Not sure whether to laugh or start hyperventilating, she stared at the bald man as he started to rustle around in his case; was that a clicking noise?

"There, that's the ammo being placed in the gun," Andy whispered.

"Would you just stop it!"

The man then did another look left and then right, before lowering his head into the case. MJ gripped hold of Andy's arm. They both froze as the man lifted out a missile-shaped object and raised it. His mouth rose open like a cave and in went the baguette, the filling oozing out down his chin. The pair burst out laughing, a huge release of nervous energy, and couldn't stop giggling. It lifted the tension and they were still smiling when they took their seats on the plane.

***

When the air stewardess announced that boarding was complete, Andy moved into the middle seat next to MJ who, like an excitable child, had rushed to take the window seat. They watched the safety video with amusement but didn't talk until the wheels clunked back into position and the plane's angle wasn't so severe.

As they soared in the air, the gravity of what faced them dawned on MJ and she became lost in her own world, trying to come to terms with what she was doing. Andy took her hand and asked what the plan was. That was the fifty-million-dollar question, and one she didn't have the answer to. They knew that Robin's plan was to go after Hakim's mum. They also knew, thanks to Niklas and his contacts, that Robin's alias, George Bennett, was booked onto the Lufthansa flight arriving at 16:45 that same afternoon. They'd chosen to fly with BA from Terminal 5 to avoid the possibility of seeing Robin at the airport. Their flight was due to land at 15:55 which, in theory, would leave enough time to find the Arrivals Hall and wait for Robin.

"Do you have an address for Hakim's mum or is your plan to stop Robin at the airport? What happens if he shoots or stabs us?"

"He'll have just got off a plane, so unless he attacks us with his briefcase, we'll be safe. Besides, airports always have security guards and cameras everywhere, so he won't try anything." MJ wasn't particularly convinced by her previous statement, bearing in mind he may have been responsible for killing Nazir in cold blood, but she wanted to believe he wouldn't hurt her.

"And then we talk to him, appeal to his caring nature and hope for the best."

"You should apply for a job with the police you know," said Andy with a tone of sarcasm.

"Have you got a better idea?" She knew the plan wasn't that of a mastermind but, not having preventing murder as an attribute on her CV, she thought it would do to begin with and would at least buy Hakim some time.

The seatbelt sign lit up, followed by a chorus of window blinds being pushed up and seats clicking back to the

267

upright position. MJ felt another surge of nerves run through her body and wondered why she'd boarded the plane in the first place. Could they simply just talk to someone linked to multiple deaths and prevent him from taking another life?

"We're here now, so let's just stick to the plan, OK?" said Andy.

MJ nodded and thought to herself, be like Leah, be strong, be confident.

Chapter 56

Steve received the message from MJ and alarm bells rang instantly. The text itself didn't look right, let alone the content. Something was up he was sure of it. He needed to think on his feet; first things first, he decided to check she wasn't at home. He shouted through to the kitchen and asked Alex to hold the fort, to shut the kitchen if necessary. Leaving Roxy upstairs, he grabbed his jacket and then reached above the door, moving his steady hand between the gap. He removed the knife and put it in his inside jacket pocket, recalling the Scout motto 'Be Prepared'. En route, he called MJ's mobile, but it went straight to answer machine. He was about to close his phone case when he noticed the business card that the detective had given him on Tuesday. He contemplated whether to ring the number or not.

He arrived at the front of the house and noticed that the discarded kebab was still in the front garden, which set off more alarm bells; maybe she was home but in danger. If anyone had touched her … he would kill them. He rang her bell several times but there was no answer. He then rang the downstairs bell and Sarah opened the door.

He didn't beat around the bush, explaining that he thought MJ was in some sort of trouble; he said he needed to take a look in her flat immediately. Sarah hesitated, but could see that Steve was genuinely worried so handed him a set of keys indicating which one was for the flat door.

"Shall I come up with you?" asked Sarah.

Steve looked down at her protruding stomach and said it was best she didn't, but to listen out and have her phone at the ready. He cleared his throat and walked up the three seemingly never-ending flights of stairs. With each step, he went over the possible scenarios that could greet him. Would Hakim be holding her hostage? Would she be lying in a pool of blood? Perhaps she'd been drugged. Or perhaps she wouldn't be there at all. He unlocked the door and grasped the handle, as if he expected it to scald him. Once inside, he crept around the flat, listening out for signs of life … or death, but everything was still. He checked the bathroom and noted a pile of wet and dirty men's clothes. He'd seen enough cop shows to have a basic understanding of police procedure and didn't touch them, as they would be bagged for evidence. After another scan under the bed, in the wardrobe and around the furniture, he relaxed and was confident the place was empty. He heard Sarah calling upstairs asking if everything was OK. By the time he opened the door, she was stood outside, so he suggested she come in and sit down; it was safe.

"What's this all about, there have been comings and goings non-stop over the last few days, is MJ OK?"

"I hope so, did you hear anyone here last night?" asked Steve.

"Yes, someone arrived quite late; MJ came down and let them in and then I heard two lots of footsteps going back up. Because of this one," she said patting her belly, "I'm not sleeping too well at the moment. It surprised me just how busy this staircase has become at night."

"Any idea who it was, I mean did you hear a man or woman's voice, was there shouting or laughter? Anything?"

"Sorry, I didn't hear much conversation-wise. I did hear the shower go on late though, which is unusual."

That would account for the pile of clothes in the bathroom, thought Steve.

"What's been going on, should we be worried?" asked Sarah.

"She's just got herself caught up in something, that's all, but MJ has got her head screwed on, so I'm sure she'll be fine. You may have a visit from the police, though." Steve thanked her for giving him access and said he was going to head back to the pub. He handed the keys back and waited as Sarah double locked the door.

As she turned, a shocked look came across her face, "What on earth? I didn't notice all these filthy footprints when I walked up. Whatever trouble she's in, she'll be cleaning these or paying for a cleaner to do it for her when she gets back."

Steve rushed back to the pub, sat down at the table near the front window and did what he should've done straight away, he dialled the mobile number for DI Madeline Johnson.

Chapter 57

No sooner had the plane touched down, than passengers were reaching for their phones like their lives depended on it. MJ was about to do the same but decided against it, she didn't want to get distracted from the task ahead of her. When the doors opened and the queue started to thin out, Andy edged out into the aisle and made room for MJ to join him.

"Are you ready?" he asked.

"As I'll ever be."

"Let's go then, we have a job to do, we have a life to save."

"That sounds so corny."

They left the plane and walked up the ramp into Terminal 1. Andy checked on his phone and saw that Lufthansa flights went to Terminal 2 and that the 16:45 arrival from Heathrow was scheduled to land on time. Once in Terminal 2 they worked out which gate the London flight was due to arrive at and found a café-bar located opposite, giving them a perfect view of arriving passengers. The nervous wait began.

***

DI Johnson thanked Steve for his call, and within five minutes, there were two police cars parked outside MJ's house and officers inside taking samples from the muddy prints and bagging up the clothes.

"I'm 99 per cent sure, Ma'am, that the suspect was here last night."

"Thanks, Sarge." What the fuck was she doing talking to him, let alone having him in her flat – he's a suspected mass killer. The DI scratched her forehead and then put a call in to the team requesting the surrounding CCTV be checked. She then dialled Leah's number.

"Hey, what's up?"

"Miss Pope, sorry Leah, there's been a worrying development."

Leah listened as the DI told her about MJ's late-night visitor. "Where are they now?" Leah asked.

"That's a good question, you haven't heard from her, have you?"

"Well, funny you should ask, when I checked my phone this morning, I had several texts and missed calls from her asking if I could talk. I tried to call her back, but the phone went straight to answer machine."

"Unbelievable! Is nobody taking this seriously? We've got a deranged man, a member of a known terrorist family …" her phoned beeped, "sorry, I've got to take this call."

"Ma'am, they've picked Mr Khan up at Frankfurt Airport, boarding a train to Hamburg."

"Great news, any sign of Mr Franklin or Ms Atkins?"

"No, Ma'am."

"Keep looking; check passenger lists for all flights to Germany today and tomorrow."

She loved this part of an investigation, a rapid influx of calls and I think we have something, ma'ams. It reminded her of doing jigsaw puzzles as a child, jigsaws that her foster parents would bring home from car boot sales and church fetes, meaning that more often than not, the pieces would come in a bag and not a box resulting in her having no idea what the picture would be. Once the corner and edge pieces were identified, it would then take weeks to establish the picture, with pieces being put in and then taken out again. When momentum took hold though, there would be no stopping her and with every new piece of puzzle fitted, the next one would follow, and a clear picture would be established. She would rush to finish it and the climax of putting in that last piece would give her a long-lasting buzz. For DI Johnson, solving a crime was the same and she could feel the momentum building, sensing that they would soon have the final piece of this jigsaw; unless people withheld vital information that was, and stopped her from finding the last piece of the puzzle, something the other kids had found satisfying. They would take pieces of puzzle and hide them in various bedrooms knowing that whoever's room the pieces were found in would get attacked by the feisty girl. She knew how to look after herself even then. One of her team put a sheet of paper in front of her detailing the flights arriving in Hamburg that day, along with passenger lists. She scanned through the names. There was no sign of Robin Franklin, but, on the third page, a couple of names popped out Ms Mary Jane Atkins and Mr Andrew James Blackwell. She picked up the phone to Leah again.

"You know those calls from MJ last night? They were probably to tell you she and that lad were going to Hamburg. Please can you send her a message and ask that she calls me ASAP, she may be in serious danger."

One of the officers called her. There, on the screen, was a photo of a smiling woman cuddling a youthful looking Hakim; underneath were the words she's next. The officer confirmed that the message was sent to Hakim by Mr Franklin at 05:30.

"Sarge, can you contact the team in Germany please and find out if Hakim knew about MJ going to Hamburg?" Another member of the team handed over a phone advising it was Niklas Hoffman, MJ's landlord. The room watched as the DI took the call and scribbled something down on her notepad. "Thank you, Mr Hoffman, you've been most helpful."

The DI got the teams' attention and told them to inform all concerned that Robin Franklin has an alias, George Bennett, and is on flight LH245 due into Hamburg Airport at 16:45.

"Good work team, let's hope our German counterparts can finish the job off with no more bloodshed."

Chapter 58

Oblivious to the mounting police activity in both London and Hamburg, MJ and Andy waited for what seemed like hours for the passengers to exit flight LH265. Andy stared into space and MJ made funny faces at an animated little girl sat opposite. The woman, who she presumed was the girl's mother, sat partially obscured by a post, but MJ detected a head of long black hair. The girl had a rounded face and a pair of cute pig tails tied in red ribbon. Her hair, MJ noted was a lot fairer than that of her mother's. With a sense of ease only a child has, the girl reached into a bag and took out a colourful padded book and walked over with it.

MJ and Andy were so engrossed with the little girl's charm and animated reading, they didn't realise that the passengers were already filtering out of the gangway and dispersing into the terminal, including Robin, who, having been sat in business class, was one of the first ones to exit.

Andy looked across and did a frantic jump off his stool. "Quick, I think he's off already."

MJ looked up; she couldn't believe she'd taken her eyes off the ball. She looked over to where the child's mother was, but both woman and bags had disappeared. "Andy, she's left her kid."

Andy grabbed his rucksack and began to walk away from the table. "Just leave her, we have to find Robin."

"I can't just leave her!" MJ protested.

"Yes, you can, she's not your responsibility – leave her."

MJ looked down at the child whose eyes looked familiar. She seemed scared at the raised voices; their exchange had also caught the attention of other customers. Think,

think, think, she said to herself before lifting up the child and carrying her out of the café-bar, hurrying after Andy, who was already a good fifty metres or so in front of them. They followed a swarm of people heading towards exit and flight connections, with MJ trying to keep Andy in view, which wasn't easy as he wasn't the tallest of men. "HALT HALT!" came a shout from somewhere around them.

There was more commotion ahead. MJ stopped in her tracks and was forced to go backwards but, with another crowd forming behind them, a crush looked imminent. The little girl tightened her grip, MJ needed to get her out of the crowd. To her relief, behind them, security guards were now managing the flow of people. MJ called out to Andy, but it fell on deaf ears, the cacophony around her had reached an excruciating level. Armed police ran past, their arms outstretched, firearms poised. MJ pushed the girl's head into her chest, trying to shield her from the scary scenes playing out around them. They moved to a quiet spot in a corridor by the toilets and MJ took out her phone, it was only a few seconds but felt like minutes until the Apple came and went from the screen. Ignoring the string of messages and missed calls, she took out the DI's card and dialled her number. All the time, MJ was absorbed by the girl's face, which was now watching her with intent. A shiver went down MJ's spine as it dawned on her where she'd seen the piercing green eyes before.

* * *

DI Johnson's counterparts in Germany established a live video feed with the team so they were privy to every step of the evolving situation. With Hamburg Airport now on lockdown, the team from Operation Carousel formed a tight bubble around the DI's desk, their eyes glued to the screens in anticipation. A few hearts skipped a beat when the phone in front of the screen started to ring, the vibrations sending it scuttling across the desk. It wasn't a number she recognised, but without hesitation the DI clicked on accept and then on speaker. "DI Johnson."

"I'm sorry, I'm in Hamburg, I'm at the airport, I have a child, I've lost Andy, I don't know what to do."

She mouthed It's Miss Atkins to her colleagues, one of whom mouthed back, Whose child? "It's fine, stay where you are and stay calm, I'm going to send a couple of officers over to you." The DI got the attention of her German-speaking officer. "MJ, I want you to call me back using the video call OK, we need to find out where you're located."

Thanks to modern technology, within a few minutes two female officers were sat with MJ in the corridor behind the toilets.

***

Andy, meanwhile, headed off in pursuit of Robin and found himself in the hub of the commotion. He'd just spotted Robin and had nearly caught up with him, when the dark-haired woman he'd been walking behind, reached into her bag. In one smooth swoop her arm brought out a bottle and smashed it into the centre of Robin's face causing him to collapse in an instant. She continued her assault and jumped on top of him, pummelling him with the broken bottle, puncturing his body until it resembled a mini fountain of red water. Blood was everywhere and screams rang out. Andy lay motionless on the ground, too, covered in blood and shards of glass.

A message was sent to London saying that both Robin and Andy had been killed, causing a lump to form in the DI's throat. There was nothing worse as a detective than the perpetrator turning up dead, it was like finishing the jigsaw with a piece missing; you'd never get to see the whole picture. She wanted to know the Why's, When's and How's. Now she'd never know, and nor would Leah. And to make matters worse, the life of another innocent victim had been taken.

The news filtered through to the two officers with MJ, but, unaware of her connection to the victims, they didn't pass it on. MJ was scared, she had no idea what was going on and continued to hold the girl close and gently stroke her face, as much to comfort herself as the child. Despite several attempts by the police officers to prise the girl away, she remained firmly attached to MJ.

The DI was about to put a call through to MJ and speak with her directly, when she received an unexpected update about Andy. He was alive and unhurt. After the first strike to Robin's face, which sent blood and glass flying everywhere, Andy's brain must've sent a message to his body to just shut down, it couldn't handle any more death, causing him to collapse. Being so close to the victim, he got covered in blood and glass himself, so people naturally assumed he too had died.

Chapter 59

Several months later ...

"Bloody hell, I didn't think she'd ever leave," said Steve. He walked over to the main door, locked it and put a sign in the window Closed for a Private Party. He called for everyone to come downstairs and get to work. Alex had been busy prepping food in the small kitchen upstairs so as MJ wouldn't clock him, and he couldn't wait to get back to the pub kitchen with its decent-sized oven and fryers. Roxy couldn't understand what was going on – the smell of sausages was driving her crazy, as well as the balloons floating around the flat, which for some reason she wasn't allowed to chase.

Steve messaged Andy and asked him to keep MJ out of the pub until at least 7pm, so everybody had time to get there. The two of them had managed to contact MJ's friends and family and invite them to her birthday karaoke bash. Even Sarah, who had given birth to a baby girl a couple of months ago, said she would try and make it for an hour. Either way, she'd make sure that MJ's birthday cake was brought round to the pub. Steve was amazed that, even with three kids under five, she was able to whip up a birthday cake. He just hoped it tasted as good as it looked from the photo she'd sent him.

With Graham having taken his new lady-friend on holiday, Steve had sent an invitation to Leah. He knew that she and MJ met up several times over the summer and thought it would be a nice gesture. She messaged him straight back and said she'd be delighted to come. Then a second message arrived asking if she could bring her new girlfriend with her. Steve was glad that both Graham and Leah seemed to be moving on after Georgia, small steps granted, but new relationships, however serious, were part of the healing process.

***

MJ stroked Andy's shoulder. "Are you sure you don't mind going back to the pub for karaoke?"

"You're the birthday girl," said Andy.

"Yes, I am," smiled MJ, "and didn't you promise me an extra birthday treat when we got back?"

Andy took out the bottle of massage oil and instructed MJ to strip off and lie on the bed. During his counselling sessions for PTSD, it had been suggested that having a massage would relieve some of the stress and knots that had developed in his body, as well as being relaxing for the mind. After the first session, he got talking to the masseuse and, just a week later, he'd enrolled on a course. Although only a few months into it, he discovered a hidden talent and found it just as therapeutic giving massages as receiving them.

After squeezing the aromatic oil onto his hands, he rubbed them together to ensure he didn't give MJ a cold fright. He straddled her naked body and slowly started massaging her back, gently running both hands upwards either side of her spine. As soon as he started, his mind began to wander, he'd often get flashbacks from the shooting or bombing, but he had learnt to process the thoughts and not let them ferment inside him. More recently though, he would think of the woman lying under him and how lucky he was to be with her. As the thoughts grew, so did the bulge in his trousers. He struggled through massaging MJ's back and shoulders, trying not to let it distract him, but when he moved down to her thighs, the temptation proved too much and he asked MJ if she was ready for her special massage.

***

With the music in the bathroom turned up high, MJ was oblivious to the knock on the front door, so didn't hesitate in walking out of the bathroom with the towel loosely wrapped around her. She was unaware that Jakob and Oskar had come in, they didn't give two hoots how she was dressed, or not, and excitedly ran over to give her a birthday hug. Struggling to keep her towel on, she suggested they go and play with Andy for ten minutes whilst she got dressed; she could then hug them properly without her wet hair soaking into them. Thank god they didn't come in ten minutes earlier, she thought.

With the music turned down low, she got dressed and then sat on the end of her bed listening to Andy play with the boys. He was a total natural. During the few weeks leading up to the birth of Jakob and Oskar's baby sister, MJ and Andy had taken the boys out a lot to give Sarah time to relax and get some sleep. She was extremely grateful, but if MJ was honest, she loved having them, especially when Andy was there. They must've looked like a real family as often strangers would make comments about the boys being a spitting image of their dad or having their mother's eyes, and it wasn't worth correcting people. Jakob, however, would sometimes cause some alarm when he came out with, they're not my parents, before he'd follow it with a hug and tell them that Andy and MJ were the best grown up friends ever.

Every time MJ saw a girl of a certain age, however, her mind wandered painfully back to Hamburg Airport and the clutches of the scared little girl who didn't want to let go of her. Whether it was instinct or fate, she'd never know, but as soon as her eyes looked deep into the little girl's, she knew she had to protect her. Her features touched a nerve; they were exactly the same as her father's, the same man whose body had been punctured multiple times by a contemptuous woman who felt her family had been betrayed by the one person she had entrusted them with. Hakim managed to get a message to his mother just in the nick of time, advising of Robin's intent, so she hatched a plan of her own. Nobody disrespected her family. MJ couldn't help wonder that perhaps if Robin knew about his daughter, his demise into the dark side could have been prevented, maybe it would have given him hope. She would never know. And now, with Hakim in prison in the UK, and their mother in a detention centre awaiting trial in Germany, the little girl, Hakim's half-sister, had no family to look after her and was placed into foster care. At night MJ had recurring dreams of the little girl living with her.

***

Due to her family's love of karaoke, MJ suggested that Steve introduce it on the first Thursday of the month. Whilst the quiz was popular, she thought it better to keep things fresh and introduce new events. This would be the third karaoke session and, as a birthday gift, Steve said she could have the night off from behind the bar. Rather than opting to go somewhere else, MJ thought it would be fun to be on the other side of the bar in the pub she loved for once and get involved with the karaoke properly. She knew Andy was no shrinking violet, and didn't mind getting up on stage, so hoped he'd be happy to spend her birthday at the Eagle, although it would be a bonus if he could take her out for dinner at the weekend too.

When they reached the pub, she noticed the Closed for a Private Party sign but went in regardless. A chorus of Happy Birthday rang around the pub, followed by an encore of party poppers. Steve appeared next to her, as if by magic, and handed over a glass of prosecco, which she took and slugged down a couple of large mouthfuls. The karaoke DJ then beckoned MJ to the makeshift stage and handed her the microphone.

"What's it to be then, birthday girl?"

MJ whispered to the DJ and he nodded in approval. The minute the guitar rift began, everyone knew the popular Guns N' Roses song. By the time the first chorus started, everyone was on their feet singing along to "Sweet Child o' Mine", and by the second chorus, Steve joined her on the stage for some animated air guitar, to which everyone cheered and clapped.

MJ grinned and imagined her heart smiling too. As she stood on stage and got everyone to put their hands in the air and clap, she looked around the pub and smiled back at the happy faces. She left the stage to huge applause, as Alex planted a large kiss on her cheek. He then took the microphone and didn't disappoint with his rendition of an Erasure song.

MJ went over to see Kate, who looked like she was going to burst at any minute. "Hey mum-to-be, how are you feeling?"

"Fat," she answered, looking slightly fed up.

"I wasn't expecting everyone to be here, this is amazing. Can I ask, was it Steve who arranged everything?"

"It was your friend Andy actually, who I still haven't met; I take it he's here?" she said pointedly.

"Of course, I'll go find him and introduce you." MJ turned to see him going up to the makeshift stage. "It may have to wait, that's him up there, I'll get him to come over after he's entertained us. In the meantime, let's go to the bar and I'll get us a drink."

MJ helped her sister up, and they stood at the bar chatting as Andy got into the role of Ricky Martin by stripping off his top. MJ gave him a wolf whistle, as did several others, much to his delight. Kate was pleased to see her sister happy and in love; she turned and took a good look at the man on stage, who had boyish looks and a firm torso. Something wasn't sitting right with her but she couldn't put her finger on it. Jochen joined them at the bar.

"Hey, you know what the doctor said, you shouldn't spend too much time on your feet over the next couple of weeks and should rest as much as possible," he scolded her gently, kissing her on the forehead. It was clear how in love he was with his wife, how much he cared for her especially as she was carrying his child, or so he thought. As Jochen escorted Kate back to the table, MJ was joined at the bar by Leah and her new girlfriend – DI Madeline Johnson, or just Maddy as Leah now referred to her. The three of them embraced and Leah handed over a birthday gift. MJ thanked them, and turned to Leah, "so, tell me, is the DI still calling you Ms Pope?"

DI Madeline Johnson lifted her finger and pointed at MJ, "very funny Ms Atkins," she said sarcastically, "when I sign you up as my sidekick, you'll be doing the same."

Leah took Maddy by the hand and led her to the stage; MJ couldn't wait to see what they'd be singing. "It's Raining Men", of course – how ironic, she laughed to herself. She glanced over to see Kate staring at Andy. Oh shit, that's what I was going to do, she thought to herself, walking over to him.

"Hey Andy," she said, "come and meet my sister; I got told off for not introducing you two earlier."

Andy wrapped his arms around MJ's waist and nuzzled her neck. "Of course."

Kate stayed seated as Andy offered his hand.

"Pleased to finally meet you." Kate's face slowly began to change colour as her hands mounted her stomach. "Ooh, that was one big kick!"

Jochen leant over and put his hand next to Kate's. "Oh wow, I see what you mean, do you think it's enjoying the music?"

Kate looked up at Andy again, as another wave of heat gradually flushed her face. The DJ called Andy's name over the microphone.

"Gotta go, my adoring public need me," he said.

Maddy asked MJ if her sister was OK as she looked a bit red.

"Yeah, I think the baby's been kicking her pretty hard, that's all. Great song by the way, very apt."

They watched as Andy took to the stage again. MJ hadn't realised just how much he liked being in the limelight; they'd have to do a duet before the end of the evening. The music began and he started singing his favourite song, "American Pie". MJ stood up and headed to the stage to sing along with him.

Kate was in a trance, looking towards the stage, she was having flashbacks to her hen night, to being on the dancefloor, to being by the river, to falling over the photocopier, to having him inside her – it was him! Oh god, she had to tell MJ. She stood up and was about to walk over when a gush of liquid ran down the inside of her trousers. She stopped dead and looked down as a small puddle was forming at her feet.

Andy continued to sing his heart out, oblivious to the fact that Kate was about to give birth to his child.

About the author

Heather Egerton is the author of the new novel, *Last Orders.*

In her professional career, Heather works in international tourism sales, which (in a normal year) would mean endless hours spent in airports, trains, and bars – a time for her imagination to run riot.

Heather first put pen to paper in 2010. The manuscript was left on a shelf gathering dust until it was picked up again during the spring of 2020.

Last Orders is her debut work and is the first instalment in a series of suspense novels.

Born and raised in Gloucestershire, Heather spent many years living in and around London until moving to the South Coast in 2019. When she is not working, Heather can usually be found in a pub, on a tennis court, or at the Emirates Stadium, but don't hold that against her!

Printed in Great Britain
by Amazon

18401827R00164